PRAI

"Brilliant . . . Offers new things to the world of YA and there is much to look forward to in the next books."
    ~In'Dtale Magazine

"The perfect gift for someone who likes Kiera Cass."
    ~NewInBooks.com

"Best dystopian fiction I have read since *Red Queen*!"
    ~Sheri, Reviewer

"Gripping, from beginning to end . . . a tale as action-packed as *Divergent* yet as introspective as *The Giver*. . . . Sure to be an instant classic in the genre."
    ~R.J. Craddock, author of *The Children of Cain* series

"WOW! I loved this story. From start to finish it was fast-paced with interesting characters."
    ~Tina, Reviewer

"Better than Scott Westerfeld's *Uglies*."
    ~Karen, Reviewer

"Amazing! It captivated me from page one and kept me wanting more, even at the end . . . It has romance, but it's not just another love story, it really digs deep . . . I would recommend this to anyone, literally anyone."
    ~Kat, Reviewer

NUMBERS
IGNITE

ALSO BY
REBECCA RODE

Numbers Game
Chan's Story: A Numbers Game Short

How to Have Peace When
You're Falling to Pieces

To every girl
who has ever had to start again;
and to my husband
for whom I would cross the desert
a thousand times over.

NUMBERS IGNITE

#1 BESTSELLING AUTHOR
REBECCA RODE

ISBN: 978-0996153249
Diamond Patch Press
www.AuthorRebeccaRode.com

1

TREENA

I stood on the threshold of an abandoned stucco building and reached out, fingering a flake of orange-pink paint on the splintering wood. My senses had played tricks on me over the past few days as I stumbled through this awful desert wasteland. Choppers overhead that never appeared, the smell of pine trees where there were none, giant puddles of elusive water, and cities that vanished when I drew close.

A sharp pain registered in my finger, and I pulled it away to examine it. A splinter had pierced the skin. I pulled out the piece of wood and stared at the tiny wound, watching it fill with blood. Definitely real.

A town in the middle of the desert. The people of Old America were a special kind of crazy.

I tried sucking on the sore finger, but my tongue was too dry and swollen. Water. That was my first priority in this creepy place. Any water left outside would have evaporated long ago under the hot desert sun, but maybe there was something in one of these buildings. There had to be. The mountains—and Vance—were at least another week away. If I didn't find water or food soon, I wouldn't last through tomorrow. I couldn't wait to find the thieves who had befriended me and then stolen my supplies while I slept, including the nutrition pills they hated so much.

They'd be sorry. Assuming I could survive until then.

I stepped inside the musty house. A section of the roof had fallen in decades ago. Broken roof tiles and debris filled the small space, which opened up to the darkening sky above. A light wood table knelt on two legs in the far corner, revealing the only clear area in the entire structure. Tables meant cooking areas. It was as good a lead as any.

I picked my way through the debris, stumbling and sliding, until I reached the table. It was covered in roof tile pieces and mouse droppings, but there was no sign of food containers or water packets. Kneeling carefully, I peered underneath.

Bones.

I yelped and scrambled away too quickly and fell backward onto some debris. The ancient pile of roof materials, undisturbed after decades of rest, groaned in protest under my weight. I jumped up, ignoring the sudden dizziness that seized me. Within seconds I had leaped through the door. I plastered myself against the wall and panted.

It wasn't like I was surprised that someone had died here. Every citizen knew what happened back in 2024, the destruction leaving gutted towns and darkened cities dotting the country. We'd studied it in ridiculous detail, including the political factions that had split Old America in half. Historical clips depicted people rioting, looting, shooting each other in the streets. A president assassinated, then the next and the next, until finally nobody would step up. The wreckage of government buildings and monuments and then entire cities as law enforcement was disbanded.

Worse, their weapons had emitted toxins that bounced around in the atmosphere, latching onto water molecules and burning them up before they could hit the ground. That was the beginning of the end. Water became currency. Those who hadn't been killed in war hid in the wreckage of their homes, watching their crops and livestock die off, and then their family members. I'd known all that since Level One school.

The thing was, NORA was supposed to be far from all that—and yet death was right here in front of me, just days from the border. The human remains under the table were proof. The decayed body flashed through my head again, as hard as I tried to stop it, and I knew I wouldn't be able to forget the sight as long as I lived.

The skeleton of a child.

I leaned against the outside of the building, closing my eyes against the bright sunlight. When my heart finally slowed, I shaded my eyes and squinted at the huge expanse of land between me and the mountains. So far away. Even if by some miracle I made it, how would I know where to find them? Vance and his settlement could be anywhere. It could take days of wandering before I found them.

You can go back.

I shoved that thought away. It wasn't an option. And, frankly, I was done with this town as well. No more grave robbing for me.

The blue sky was fading into pink as I reached the edge of town. It felt as if an entire world, endless and dead, lay between me and Vance. The thought of spending another night on the hard desert floor, shivering in the chilly night air and jerking awake at every sound, made me grit my teeth in dread.

Voices.

I froze, then relaxed. I'd heard voices in my head for the past two days, and they never turned out to be real. It was just the creepiness of the ghost town getting to me. Or maybe the dizziness of my dehydrated mind.

The voices grew louder. The words sounded scrambled, strange. It took me a moment to realize they weren't speaking English. And they were arguing. Footsteps crunched on the road.

Instinct took over then. I leaped behind the nearest structure, a tiny building that had probably once been a shed. An entire wall was gone, and the roof had fallen in and buried various pieces of equipment, but there was enough left to hide me. I sat back on my haunches, not daring to look around the corner, every muscle taut as I listened. The arguing had intensified, although I still couldn't understand what was being said. As the men passed, I gathered my courage and looked around the corner. Two dark figures made their way along the road, backs toward me.

A headache throbbed behind my eyes. It would've been better had my brain made this all up. There were still people here. Scavenging was definitely out of the question now.

But maybe if I begged for just a little water . . .

No. I couldn't risk being recognized.

When the voices died off, I slowly stood. The sun had begun to touch the horizon, painting the usual brown a colorful blue and purple. If I hadn't already lived out here for eight days, it would be a beautiful sight.

You can go back.

It would be easy enough. NORA sent out scouting planes once a week. I could head back toward their usual route to the east and be home in days.

No.

As exhausted as my mind was, as weak as my body felt, I knew that would never be an option. My ex-boyfriend, Dresden, had stolen the throne from me. My stepfather, Konnor, had gladly handed it over. If Dresden got his hands on me, he'd either throw me in prison for life or parade me around like a prize, using me like he'd used me since the beginning. That wasn't even the worst part. Sooner or later I'd have to look into the accusing eyes of those who had lost loved ones. They'd died for nothing. They were dead and I was still here, and that was the worst part of all.

With one last glance at the empty road, I headed back the way I'd come. It would be safer to go around the town than through it. If its previous inhabitants had left anything of value, those men had probably found it already. Time to put some distance between me and the skeletons of the past.

I made my way down the slope, picking my way carefully through the sagebrush. It hadn't taken long to learn that lesson. My pant legs had torn long ago, and my calves looked like they'd been whipped, all crisscrossed with dried blood. Now if only I could make it down before dark fell—

Fire shot through my ankle.

With a shriek I stumbled backward and fell, lifting my foot to wipe the fire away. A soft *click-click*, a rattling, sounded from my left as a long animal slithered off. Pulling my ankle closer, I could see two tiny dark circles in the skin.

A snake. I'd never seen one, but that was all it could be—Oh, fates. The pain was growing by the second. My ankle had already begun to swell.

Snakes were poisonous. No, that wasn't the word. If only I had water to wash the wound out. But what good would that do? The poison was in my bloodstream, not on the skin. I wrestled with my brain, wanting to scream in frustration. How was I supposed to treat something like this when I was too weak and tired to think straight? My body began to shake, a violent, uncontrollable shiver.

Those men. There it was, a hint of reason in the murkiness of my mind. I turned and looked upward at the shed I'd just left. If I screamed loud enough, maybe I'd be heard. "Help! Somebody!"

My voice echoed, then died off. I tried a few more times, then listened for a long moment. The men didn't return. Or if they had, they couldn't find me down here.

I positioned my foot and tried to stand, then screamed in agony. How was it possible for such a small bite to hurt like this?

My injured leg couldn't hold weight. I knelt on the sandy ground and tried pulling myself along by the elbows. The world tilted and spun. When had I last eaten? I couldn't remember.

My elbows buckled. I collapsed to the desert floor with a strangled gasp and rolled over to face the blood red moon. "Help," I called out again. Nothing.

It was ironic. The empress had tried to have me killed several times in the past weeks, and I'd survived the desert heat for days with no food or water—only to succumb to a pair of sharp fangs. Tali would find it funny, I was sure. She'd lived just like the bomb that had taken her life, torridly and explosively. She'd managed to die twice. Not many people could say that.

My leg was stiff and swollen now. Even moving it would be excruciating, much less trying to walk on it. The molten fire had already begun to move up the veins in my leg.

I lay on my back, facing the navy-blue sky and letting the heat from the desert floor burn through my clothes. Purple clouds floated lazily by. Puffy, rainless.

It was a shame that I'd never gotten the chance to feel snow on my skin. The mountains had snow in winter. Vance had described it to me once. I wondered if the moon looked red from the mountains as well. The sad thing was, he'd probably be happy to find out I was gone. He had come back for me, admitted his feelings and opened his heart, and I'd rejected him. I deserved this.

A thought swirled in my head and began to scream through the haze. *Don't you dare give up.* It sounded a lot like Tali.

"Are you happy now?" I yelled at the moon, hoping the fates were listening. My voice sounded like a croak. I tried to lick my lips, but my tongue felt like sandpaper on my sunburned mouth. Not that it mattered now. "I've already lost everything. Guess that wasn't enough for you."

I heard rustling in the gravel, and the hot, dry wind seemed to pick up a little.

"I didn't even want the throne," I muttered. "Never asked for it, you know. I just want—" Pause. It was hard to say what I wanted now. My dreams were a series of images, fleeting wishes no more real than puddles of water in the desert. Peace. A new life, far from NORA. One last day with Vance. A chance to tell him I felt the same way.

My body sunk deeper into the hard ground. My feverish accusations had taken all that I had left. Consciousness flickered like a broken transmission. Snake. Strangers speaking in gibberish. Dresden's blue eyes flashing in anger. The stone Vance left behind inviting me to join him. My mother choosing to run. Always running.

Can't go back.

"Somebody help," I whispered.

The last thing I saw was a shadow above my head. A man. I tried to focus, to see if it was Dresden or Vance, but then the darkness claimed me.

2

VANCE

I stood at the ridge, awed by the sight below. Dumbfounded was a better word. Even Anton, my former best friend-turned-captor, paused next to me and gave a low whistle. I'd seen plenty of settlements as the son of a clan leader, usually hidden in low valleys or nestled protectively on high peaks. But I'd never seen a camouflage screen this large before. These settlers had mastered the art of hiding.

From higher up, the mountain peak had looked like every other, carpeted with lush green trees. But as we drew nearer, the view had shimmered unsteadily. Now I saw the mountain for what it really was—the walls of a funnel-shaped valley.

And there was a city nestled inside.

Structures were cut into the valley walls, and a long road wound from top to bottom. No, not one road.

There were three different trails, all switchbacks. Probably so the settlers wouldn't have to circle the entire valley a dozen times to reach their destinations. The buildings were clumped together, mostly along the eastern wall, leaving the western side for hundreds of terraces full of green plants. Water the same gray as the sky filled the very bottom. A slightly higher muddy line revealed where the water had once been. It was down to nearly half that. They were having water issues here as well.

"Brilliant," Anton breathed. Like me, Anton hadn't bothered to shave on our journey, and his beard grew in ridiculous tufts around his chin. I still couldn't figure out why he'd been assigned to lead me and a bunch of men twice our age. "How did they do that? It looks like a regular mountain from above."

"Laser technology," a voice said.

Anton jumped in surprise as we turned toward the trailhead. A clean-shaven bald man with Asian features stood with his hands at his sides. I hadn't heard him approach. He inclined his head. "Welcome to Blackfell, the last official refugee camp in America. I am Ju-Long."

Anton stepped forward. "I'm Anton, and this is the prisoner, Vance." Newell, the man to my right, cleared his throat. Anton caught his meaning and added, "My men also seek asylum."

Ju-Long gave a slight bow. "You are all welcome, so long as you follow our laws."

"Is this one of the original postwar settlements?" I asked.

Ju-Long's eyes flicked immediately to the scar on my forehead. I'd had the implant removed before turning myself in weeks before. "The prisoner will have many questions," he said, "most of which I am not permitted to answer. But, yes, it is."

"What about heat-seeking tech? A camouflage screen wouldn't stop sensors from finding signs of life here."

"Shut up, Vance," Anton said. "None of that matters to you."

Ju-Long still watched me, expressionless. "You worry for the safety of your people."

I shook my head. "I worry for everyone. If NORA decides to follow us—"

"—they will meet the same fate as every other attacker," Ju-Long cut in. "You mention Old American technology. We have a few surprises of our own." He pointed at something near the top of the ridge. I squinted. There was a structure there with a needle of some kind pointing upward.

"Antiaircraft gun?" I asked. I'd never seen one before, but it made sense. A quick search of the ridge revealed three more, all stationed like quarters of a clock.

"Brought in all the way from the Eastern Continental Alliance," he said. "We don't rely on the rusty old American weaponry. Too many people rely on us for protection. We cannot allow for error."

"The ECA," I repeated. I'd never even heard the term before. "That's where you're from?"

His gaze turned inward, and a slight smile graced his mouth. "We keep our people safe here. That is all you need to know. As for you, it took much debating among the assembly to allow you entrance, but our governor insisted that you have a fair trial."

I froze. "I'm here to answer to my clan. Not your governor."

"As your people are now citizens of Blackfell, you will be held accountable for our laws. The assembly will decide your fate."

"We don't need your assembly to intercede."

His lips thinned as his polite smile tightened. "This was the condition Rutner agreed to when your people were taken in."

Rutner. My father's trusted friend and counselor. He had negotiated with me on our clan's behalf weeks before. Our arrangement had been simple: my clan's help getting Treena on the throne in exchange for their freedom—and a trial for my crimes. Like a fool, I'd agreed, intending to be miles away before they came for me. That had been before Mills shot off a missile and destroyed the capital city square, trying to take out the entire NORA government. Only Treena and a few stragglers had survived.

I still remembered how she looked the day I left the hospital—her eyelashes long and dark against her cheeks, her skin mottled with bruises and cuts, her lips full and soft. It was hard to accept that she wasn't mine. Treena had gone back to her boyfriend, Bike Boy. Her choice.

I shook myself back to the present. Of course Rutner had been the one to find this place. But it wasn't like him to hand our clan over so easily and quickly. They could be cannibals for all we knew. I shook my head. "I don't really care what Rutner arranged. This is a private matter."

A dangerous glint appeared in the man's black eyes. "I'm afraid it is not up for negotiation—"

"Uh, you know what?" Anton interrupted, drawing up to his full height. "We've been traveling for weeks. We're very eager to deliver the prisoner, so if you could please show us the way, that would be great."

Ju-Long met my glare with one of his own. "Follow me."

The head of the trail was marked with a symbol carved into a smooth gray rock. It was rough, and few people would have recognized it, but I knew exactly what it was. I'd seen several of them on our journey.

Two squiggly lines with a square in the center—an iron belt. A sign that Iron Belt Hawking's clan was gathering again, and a beacon showing the way.

Anton's thugs practically ran over me in their eagerness to get down the trail. I couldn't blame the men for their impatience. Their families were probably already here. Hands grasped my shoulders and pushed me along as I picked my way slowly down the dusty dirt path. It wasn't as steep as I would have expected and definitely wasn't as worn as it should be with thousands of settlers living below. Maybe these people never left the valley.

"The prison is near the lake, Hawking," Ju-Long said. "It is a long walk, but I believe you will find your quarters quite comfortable." I gave him a sideways look. Despite the uneven, sloped trail, he walked purposefully and with a confident grace.

"How many NORA refugees have you received?" Anton asked.

"Eight hundred are reported to have left NORA's borders," Ju-Long replied evenly, "but less than six hundred have arrived. It is my understanding that nearly all your clan is here."

What was left of it, anyway. The Hawking clan was as dead as my father. We were just refugees now, searching for a home. It seemed Rutner had found us one, strange as it was.

Soon we came to a set of stone steps that cut into the winding trail and led straight down about a hundred yards. The stairway was barely wide enough for two people.

Anton stood aside and motioned for me to go first. I smirked at the realization that he still didn't trust me. One well-placed kick, and he'd go flying. It was tempting.

When we reached the bottom, the staring began.

At first the settlers watched us pass with curiosity. They avoided Ju-Long's gaze, looking away with discomfort when he passed. Most of the settlers wore colorful, patterned shirts and trousers, men and women alike. A few noticed the chains on my wrists and whispered amongst themselves. Nobody looked familiar. If my people were here, they were hiding themselves well.

It wasn't until we were nearly to the gray lake at the very bottom of the funnel that I found them.

Hundreds of shacks constructed mostly from muddy wood and tattered cloth dotted the edges of the water. Skinny human figures with faded, muddy NORA uniforms sat nearby. It didn't take them long to recognize me.

"The Hawking boy," someone called out. "He's actually here!"

"Hey, Fauna, look who just arrived," the nearest man drawled. My head jerked up. I'd know that voice anywhere. Carter Holladay, a good friend of my father's. Holladay approached, making Anton take two steps backward to avoid getting stepped on.

"Didn't think you'd show, boy," he said, stabbing me in the chest with a fat finger. "You've no idea how happy I am that you're here."

Anton eyed me. "Vance is pretty happy too. He's been telling me how excited he is to pay his debt to the Hawking clan."

"And it's a big 'un," Holladay said. One sleeve of his uniform was torn completely off, and the other was nearly there. "You arrested my wife. Still haven't seen her. Could be dead 'cause of you, and I'd never know it."

I didn't answer. Our little group had traveled ten days before arriving at the settlement site last night only to find a chopper sitting in the clearing instead of construction. Three dozen refugees camped nearby, waiting for their turn to be transported. The pilot had recognized my face and bumped me ahead of everyone else in line. Apparently the governor had wanted me here as soon as possible. I hadn't seen Holladay's wife among the refugees, though. Not that I was about to tell him that.

Anton led me away as more settlers came out of their huts and the jeering began. "Thought you could get away, did you?" "Justice always wins, my friend!"

"Enjoy your last days because I'm putting a knife in you myself!" "Just wait until Mills is done with you."

I tried to turn, to see who had mentioned Mills, but the guards shoved me forward. Mills had absolutely nothing to do with this. Next time I saw him I'd wring his lying neck. Slowly, painfully. The man had gathered support for an uprising, planned a protest, put Treena at the head of it, and then waited until they were all at the palace before trying to blow them all up. He deserved to die a thousand times over.

Holladay simply watched us go. Anton's thugs broke off from us one by one as they found their loved ones. Soon it was just me, Anton, and Ju-Long left. We turned toward the water and plodded through a foot of black-brown mud toward a square box of a building made from stacked concrete stones and no windows. It sat nearly at the water's edge. What had looked like a freshwater lake from above was actually a murky pond. Cattle grazed nearby—a fact I could have discerned just from the smell. Ju-Long looked unaffected, but Anton plugged his nose with two skinny fingers.

So this was Rutner's promised land.

Ju-Long's version of "comfortable" was a far cry from my own. The prison was small and dark. Four tiny cells covered each corner, each barely large enough for a man to lie diagonally in, and a drain filled the remaining floor space in the center. The cells were empty. In fact, this building looked like it hadn't been used in a very long time—except by the clouds of mosquitos. A thin film of black grime covered every surface.

"Our governor will be here shortly," Ju-Long said. He gestured to the cell in the far corner. "Enter."

A tiny part of me wanted to fight my way free. Anton's men were gone. I could easily take Anton and Ju-Long on. But the thought of traipsing up that trail again made me bone weary. Besides, I had come so far to find my family. If they were in this hellhole somewhere, we'd bust out together or not at all.

I walked in and kicked the bedroll in the corner. Dust exploded from its surface. It smelled as if it hadn't been washed since Old America fell.

Ju-Long pulled the door closed. With all these old-fashioned metal bars around, I expected him to pull out a huge iron key to fit the rusty bars. Instead, he activated something with a device from his pocket. A beep signaled and the door clicked twice. The lock looked brand-new.

Ju-Long gave a slight bow and left me and Anton alone.

"Take my cuffs off now," I told him, holding my hands toward the bars. He'd only removed the chains a couple of times, usually for a few minutes so I could treat the skin where it had been rubbed raw inside my wrists—and even then they'd pointed their guns at me the whole time.

"Nah," Anton said. "Apparently the big guy's on his way. Better not take any chances. I'll let you get settled in." With a smirk, he left.

———◆◆———

I was almost asleep when Ju-Long returned. He brought a bright solar lantern that seemed like overkill for such a small room, the only indication that it was night. He eyed me with the usual suspicion and said, "Behave yourself."

Finally. I could meet this so-called governor and demand to see my family again. If they were living in the mud like the rest of my clan, I'd have some words for him.

Ju-Long stepped back, allowing the visitor to pass. His lantern cast a long shadow on the governor's face as he approached my cell. "You have no idea how happy I am that you've arrived."

Horror spread throughout my limbs and cemented me to the ground. I knew that voice. I'd sworn to kill this man as soon as I found him, and here he was—standing with his hands clasped behind his back, smiling.

Mills.

Governor of Blackfell.

3

VANCE

I sprang to my feet. "How dare you show up here."

"Show up?" He blinked in mock surprise. "Dear boy, I live here. I've kept the peace for over a decade now. Do you know how hard it is to keep a city like this a secret?"

"Call me 'dear boy' again, and I'll kick you through the mountain and out the other side."

Mills just gave a grim smile. His hair was thinner than it had appeared on the screen, and gray stubble lined his chin. "I know your solution to everything is violence, Vance. We are a peaceful people. If you hope to survive longer than a day or two, you will curb that reaction immediately."

My solution? Rage pulsed through my body. "You blew up hundreds of innocent people!"

He gave a deep, exhausted-sounding sigh. "I thought you were smarter than this. Ju-Long, will you give us a moment?"

His assistant stood firmly rooted in place. "You'll be safe, sir?"

"Safe enough from this boy, yes."

Ju-Long opened his mouth to protest, then walked out, still shaking his head.

The patient smile on Mills's face disappeared. "You throw accusations at me like that again, especially with others present, and you won't even reach your trial."

"Accusations?" I couldn't believe this. "My entire clan knows what you did. You can't lie yourself out of this one."

"The missile was an unfortunate incident," Mills said. "We're looking for the instigator now. In the meantime I suggest you start thinking about your own hide. Your trial is next week. Between now and then your first priority should be convincing the people that you are their friend. Your life depends on it."

I squeezed the bars, wishing Anton had released my hands so I could strangle Mills. Maybe Anton knew me better than I thought. "Don't pretend you care what happens to me. I just happened to be out of range, or you would've killed me, too."

"I'd stop bringing that subject up if I were you."

"Why, because your people will find out the truth?"

"They already know the truth. Everyone knows you are the one who blew up the palace, Hawking."

I rocked backward. "*What?*"

A glint of satisfaction appeared in his eyes and he started to pace, his hands still clasped behind his back. Too relaxed. "Our investigators have discovered that it was someone inside NORA's borders who arranged the attack. Someone without a techband who had the skills to maneuver freely at night without being detected. Someone who held a huge grudge against the empress and her council and wanted to be seen as a savior of sorts, perhaps to change his fate." He stopped and faced me again. "Witnesses say you appeared just after the missile hit and began organizing rescue efforts. Where were you before that, Vance?"

I stared, unable to form the words I desperately wanted to say. Maybe it was for the best—my mother wouldn't have approved of them anyway.

"That's what I thought," he said. "They were already prepared to execute you for turning against them. Now that the depth of your betrayal is known, it's your family's fate you are writing with your accusations and denials. Accept your guilt, and you can save them—and perhaps die with the slightest shred of dignity."

4

TREENA

I was running through a city, terrified of something behind me. Not a person, but something nobody could stop, like liquid fire coming from the sky. It made a high-pitched whine as it approached, and I threw my arms up to stop it, knowing well that it wouldn't help. The blast hit, its power blowing through buildings like they were made of paper. The debris went right through me as if I was invisible.

The people around me, however, were not. A collective scream of terror went up but was silenced as roads, buildings, and people were blown to pieces. Liquid fire. I kept running; toward what, I couldn't say, but I knew I couldn't stop.

When I got to what was left of a huge building, I dug through the debris until I found two bodies. One was a girl my age, beautiful and broken. The orange numbers on her forehead flickered as if her life force itself was fading. As I knelt, her distant eyes focused on me accusingly. "You killed me."

The other body was a woman too, though older, and her blonde hair was streaked with dark red. She sneered, exposing blood-stained teeth. "You think you've won, but I'm the victor here."

When I turned away, hundreds of bodies lay around, broken, some burning. The eyes watched me with a strange detachment.

"You've killed us all," they chanted as one.

I woke up shaking. My eyes opened to a dirt ceiling bathed in a golden glow. Had the ghosts buried me alive? No, the dirt was several meters above my head and scraped smooth. My fingers grabbed at the surface beneath my back. A blanket?

When I tried to sit up, pain slammed through my ankle. I gasped with the force of it, like a knife had been rammed into the bone. I lay back down, breathing hard.

"I wondered if you'd ever wake up," a boy muttered.

I turned toward the voice. It *was* a boy. He looked brown from head to toe—brown hair, light brown skin, dirt-colored clothing. He sat in a chair that looked as if it had been carved and woven from desert brush. He looked about fourteen or fifteen, just slightly younger than me. Panic began to set in, adding to the pain. Did he know who I was? NORA could be on their way right now. I didn't dare even move my leg, much less walk on it.

The boy smiled. "Hey, calm down. I'm not going to hurt you."

"Who are you?" My tongue was still swollen and dry, and I sounded like a stranger. I took in the bed, the curve of the ceiling, the pieces of dirt floating softly down.

"Coltrane. I saved your life."

I stared at him, trying to decipher his words. "I've never seen you before."

"That's because you passed out after the snake bit your leg. Carried you on my back all the way here."

Snake. The memory rushed back. I tried pushing myself up on my elbows, slower this time, and looked down at the ankle that peeked out of the blanket. It was swollen beyond recognition. It looked like a huge fat man's leg, all blue and purple. No wonder it hurt so bad.

"Coltrane," a woman's voice said from outside in a warning tone. "Don't mislead the girl."

He sighed. "Fine. Mom helped me carry you once we reached the tunnels, so technically I didn't carry you *all* the way here. She's a physician, and she says you'll be fine."

"Once you stop your yammering and get her some food and water," the woman said, pushing aside a cloth that hung from the doorway and stepping inside. Her dress was a deep, brownish red, although her skin was the same light brown color as her son's. Her long black hair hung to her waist in a single braid.

"Yes, ma'am." Coltrane immediately stood.

She stepped aside to let him pass, then approached the bed. I caught a glimpse of silver roots in her dark hair. She smiled, but it never reached her eyes. "I'm Lillibeth. I have to apologize for my son. He doesn't get much practice talking to girls."

The inner panic went down a notch. These people thought they were helping a simple desert wanderer. I lay back down again, then winced when my ankle moved slightly. "The snakebite?"

She sighed. "You were lucky. You'll keep your leg, although I'm sure there was some tissue damage. We won't know the extent of it for a while. The swelling should go down in a few days. I'll keep you on healing stimulants and see how we do. Has your painkiller worn off?"

I started to nod, then winced again.

"I'll give you another injection after you've eaten."

Coltrane emerged, holding a plate with a lump of something soft and yellow. It jiggled when he handed it to me across the bed.

I took the plate, unsure how to proceed. "Thanks."

"What in the dying stars were you doing out there all by yourself?" Coltrane asked. "No gear, no food, and that ridiculous number on your head."

"Hold your questions, Coltrane," the woman said quickly, taking the plate from my shaking hands. She scooped a metal tool into it and held it to my mouth. "It doesn't matter now. This will have you feeling much better."

I stared at the food for several seconds. "Um, that's okay. I'll do it." I took the tool from her hand. Nice or not, this woman would not be feeding me like an infant. I took a tiny taste. It was overwhelming, like an explosion of flavor in my mouth. It took everything I had to swallow.

"A little strong?" Lillibeth asked. I could swear she hid a smile. "Well, I know just what you need. I'll be right back."

After she left, Coltrane took her chair and leaned toward me, hands clasped together. "I know where you come from. I've heard about that big competition they have in the cities. Yours is the highest number I've ever seen. What's your name?"

I set the plate aside, suddenly feeling nauseated. No matter their intentions, these people couldn't know who I was. "Um, you can call me Amy."

He sat back with a satisfied smile. "There, now. Was that so hard?"

"Coltrane," Lillibeth said, walking back in. She nodded toward the doorway. They engaged in silent battle for a moment, but Lillibeth's stern expression won out. With one last glance, Coltrane slunk out and dropped the curtain behind him.

As Lillibeth twisted the lid off a tube she held in her hand, it made a familiar click. I squinted at the bottle. She shook it and a pill fell into her palm. A nutrition pill. I'd know them anywhere.

"Just one for now," she said, handing me the pill and a glass of water. "You can take another in a couple of hours if your stomach adjusts. Figure it's what your body's used to, anyway."

I didn't ask her how she'd gotten it. The water was silty and metallic, but it was the most wonderful thing I'd ever tasted. I drank every drop before handing her the glass. "Thank you."

Lillibeth set the glass down and slid the tube of pills into her pocket. The container was full. There had to be an entire week's worth of pills in there. That single container could get me the rest of the way to Vance.

The woman retrieved a syringe from her pocket, then twisted open a small tube. "While I inject your medication, I don't suppose you want to tell me who you really are?"

Panic welled up again. It must have shown on my face because she chuckled and shook her head, filling the syringe and then replacing the lid. "Well, that answers that. Nobody is forcing you to talk. I just want to make sure you aren't a danger to our community. Our generosity extends only as far as our self-preservation allows, especially with NORA so close." I felt a prick as she plunged the needle into my thigh. Within seconds the fire in my ankle receded.

I felt my shoulders relax. "That's amazing. I barely feel anything."

"Our medications are far superior to those in NORA," she said, withdrawing the needle. "Your government refuses to allow outside technology. They're significantly behind the rest of the world."

As the pain faded, I let myself sink into the blanket again. What had I told Coltrane again? "I'm Amy."

"And where are you headed, Amy? It doesn't look like you have any supplies."

"My stuff was stolen."

She waited for me to continue, but when I didn't, she nodded again. "Very well. We've had a couple of NORA refugees stop by on their way to the mountains. I'm going to assume you're among the group recently released and headed back to their clans?"

"Of course." It was mostly true, but I felt guilty for implying even that much. I put my palm against the hard dirt wall beside me. It was smooth, and a faint powder coated my fingers when I pulled them away. "What is this place?"

Lillibeth took a deep breath, held it for a moment, and let it out. "You're safe. That's all you need to know right now. Our community accepts all wanderers, including the injured and worn of spirit, no matter their past, as they will you. Assuming you're peaceable, of course." A glint of anger appeared in her eyes, and then it was gone.

You've killed us all. The voices from my nightmares echoed in my mind, and I pushed it away. "No question of that."

"If you're going to stay here, however, you'll need to agree to the pact." She pasted a sweet smile on her face. "Now, hold still so I can check your bandages." She bent over my leg and pulled the corner up.

"What is the pact?" I prompted, wincing at the pressure on my swollen ankle.

Satisfied, she lowered the bandage. "You must agree to leave your past at the door. Peace is our first and only law. Weapons are outlawed. Those who resort to violence to solve their problems are disciplined and released into the wild to live like the animals they have become."

I must have looked horrified because she met my stare with one of her own. I swallowed and tried to control my expression. "Even children?"

"The laws apply after puberty. For most of us, that occurs by age fifteen."

"Interesting." I wondered what Vance would have thought of this law. I could almost see the amused grin on his face.

"You don't agree with our laws," Lillibeth noted. "That's a result of your background. But if you want to remain here while your leg heals, those are the conditions. Is there any reason why you can't fulfill them?"

I stared at her, wondering what experiences this woman had had to make her think NORA citizens were violent. She was certainly insistent. "I can agree to that," I said. "I promise to follow your pact of peace."

She nodded, satisfied. "We have thrived for nearly five decades underground. Unfortunately, as you can imagine, not much grows down here. We have to trade for most of what we need. Which brings me to an uncomfortable subject."

Underground. How deep I couldn't tell. The air stirred around me, which had to mean a ventilation system somewhere. The technology they must have had to carve out an underground home and keep it secret for decades was overwhelming.

Then I realized that Lillibeth was watching me expectantly. I squirmed. "I'm listening."

"You used the last of our rattlesnake antivenom," she said. "Extremely expensive. We get it from a goat farmer a hundred kilometers east, and he doesn't come out for two more months. If someone else gets bitten before then, we'll be in big trouble." Lillibeth pulled a piece of paper and started scribbling something on it.

"Oh. Sorry," I said, unsure what to say.

She looked up from her notes and gave a wry smile. "Well, it's not like you meant for it to happen. All I'm saying is that everyone contributes here. As you've dipped into the community's resources, you'll need to stay long enough to pay the debt. Since it will take awhile for your leg to heal anyway, surely that won't be a problem."

My body sagged, and I leaned back against the pillow. Great. First the snakebite, and now this. "How long are we talking? Days? Weeks?"

She hesitated. "Antivenom is very expensive. If your contribution is highly skilled, you could possibly pay it off by the time your leg heals. It's hard to say when that will be. The healing stimulants I've injected are working well so far, but, like I said, there was probably tissue damage. We won't know the extent of it for a few days."

"So it could be weeks, at least."

"It's hard to say at this point." She shoved the paper deep into her pocket and stood. "Why the concern? You were wandering in the desert, you'll recall. Surely you're grateful to have a home."

I took a beat too long to answer. "I am. Thank you."

"You're most welcome. Go ahead and rest. I'll keep Coltrane from bothering you as long as I can." She flashed a practiced smile and left. The curtain divider fell closed behind her.

I tried to sleep, but the moment I relaxed and allowed my mind to slip into unconsciousness, the voices awaited me. Their accusations grabbed at me like clawed fingers and sharp knives. After the third time, I forced my eyes open and stared at the smooth dirt ceiling, my body rigid.

These people absolutely could *not* find out who I was or what I had done. If they were kind, they'd throw me and my injured leg to the buzzards. If not, they'd turn me over to NORA. My hand instinctively dug into my pockets to grab my stone, but it wasn't there. Alarmed, I felt all around the bed and in the blankets, thinking maybe it had fallen out. Nothing. The last reminder I had of home, and now it was gone.

At one point Lillibeth slipped in again and grabbed the bag that seemed to be the source of the room's light. She paused in the doorway for a long time. I feigned sleep, trying to keep my breathing deep and regular.

Finally, she left. The room plunged into darkness, and then I was left alone in the blackness with only my thoughts for company.

5

VANCE

The next morning my first visitor walked up to the jail entrance. I sat forward, listening intently as the voices floated in from outside.

"You're not supposed to be here," the guard said.

"Of course I am," a feminine voice said. It sounded vaguely familiar. "Mills sent me."

"I've received no such orders."

"Now, come on. I appreciate the concern for my safety, but the prisoner is behind bars. Or can he transfer evil with a single look?"

"Young lady, if Mills sent you, you'd have written authorization. Come back when you have it."

There was a pause. I thought for a moment that the girl had left, but she spoke again, softer. "What is that you're drinking there? Because it sure doesn't look like water, Alan."

Silence.

"I thought you'd given that stuff up. I think I recall your wife saying so when I ran into her at the grain mill the other day."

There was grumbling I couldn't understand, and then the guard said, "Make it quick."

"You're a dear."

The door opened, and in walked the last person I'd ever expected to see. I sat up straighter as she approached. "Edyn?"

"Vance." She stopped in front of my cell, one hand on her hip, head tilted to the side. "You haven't changed much, except for that awful beard. Still getting into trouble, I see."

"No other way to live." I tried to look unaffected. The last time I'd seen this girl, she had been eating dinner at my family's table the night of the attack on my clan two years ago. Her father, Rutner, had been my father's assistant and friend. She'd been a little awkward back then, with stringy hair and a love for pranks. Now her blonde hair—the perfect NORA shade, ironically— fell in soft waves over her shoulders. She wore a red shirt and trousers that were tight in all the right places.

She watched my gaze sweep over her and gave a wide smile. "So you see me now. You never noticed me before."

I cleared my throat. "Noticed what?"

"It's not important." She tossed a water pouch into my cell, then pulled up a chair and sat so close I could touch her. She crossed her legs daintily and clasped her hands together. "Might want to drink that before they find out. They won't waste water on a prisoner."

I sat and clicked open the pouch, grateful that the guards had finally removed my cuffs. A whiff revealed nothing about the contents. I stuck a finger in and sniffed, then wet my lips with it. It was definitely water, and not the disgusting NORA kind, either.

"As untrusting as ever, I see," Edyn said, swatting away a mosquito. "We only have eight days before your trial, and most of the settlers think you're a traitor. We'll have to change that."

I took a long swig, then wiped my mouth with my sleeve. Blasted Mills. He hadn't been lying about the settlers' loyalties. Not only that, but he'd also had two weeks to spread rumors about my involvement in the attack before I even arrived. My ragged clothes and stubble as they paraded me down here probably hadn't helped either. "We?"

"Of course. You and me."

"And you would help me because . . . ?"

She rolled her eyes, suddenly looking a lot more like the girl I'd known before. "Because I'm your lawyer, stupid."

"You, a lawyer?"

"I'm the one who should be asking the questions, Vance. But, to satisfy your curiosity, yes. I've studied under Caralyn Kelly for the past two years. She's too old and sick to help you, though, so don't bother asking. Mills is the only other lawyer here, and he's representing the prosecution, so you get me."

"Hold on, hold on." I held up a hand and tossed the empty water packet aside. "You've been studying the last two years?" If she had received her NORA assignment at age sixteen, she could have only studied law for a year. There was no sign of a Rating implant in her forehead, but it could have been removed and healed by now.

A little color swept into her cheeks, but to her credit, she met my gaze levelly. "I didn't get captured."

I sat back. "Impossible."

"Quite possible. While everyone else was gathering, I climbed onto the roof and hid. I saw everything."

With that, the horrible memories of that night came rushing back. Rutner, her father, had started evacuating everyone. When they reached the tree line, the NORA soldiers had attacked. I arrived as the first bodies fell. I didn't know then that the NORA soldiers intended to stun everyone and bring them down the mountain. All I saw were people falling left and right to their silent weapons and the fire spreading behind us. Some of the stunned settlers never made it out. Their bodies were enveloped before the NORA soldiers could get to them.

Yelling to my people to run, barely feeling the rocky ground under my bare feet and fighting for everyone I loved, I had taken out soldier after soldier. I hadn't known that NORA officials were watching.

They didn't shoot me. I had thought I was the only one.

"Even if NORA soldiers missed you somehow," I told her, "the fire spread too fast. Once it destroyed the settlement, it spread to the trees. It took NORA two days to contain it. There's no way you could've gotten out of there alive."

Edyn's gaze wavered. "I found the body of a NORA soldier and stole her clothing. Nobody noticed when I walked away."

She had walked away. *During* the fighting. I set my jaw, my anger fighting to the surface. "We needed everyone we could get."

"I went for help." She laughed bitterly. "Seems stupid now, I know, but I really believed I could talk the Romero clan into coming to the rescue. I walked all night and got there the next evening, but they had fled. Must have known about the attack somehow and relocated."

I shook my head. "You just sat there. Hid and watched your own clan fall, one by one. Watched your own *family* get gunned down."

Edyn jumped to her feet and began to pace, running a hand through her hair. She always did that when she was frustrated. "I watched you fight."

"And that makes it okay?" I snapped.

She stopped pacing and looked at me, pleading. "I was fifteen, Vance. What was I going to do? People were being gunned down in every direction. But I didn't dare look away from you. For some reason I thought that if you could stand against them, everyone would be fine. I watched you ducking behind things, stealing rifles from bodies and shooting, then ducking again. And then that last stand. You fought just like your father."

I tried to hold on to my anger, to keep it from slipping through my fingers, but it began to dissolve. She was right. Edyn had no weapons, no training. Few of our settlers had. They had depended on my father and the circle to protect them. I couldn't blame her for that.

"I've relived that nightmare for two years, Vance. Nearly every night. I see you out there, fighting for us like it was the last thing you'd ever do. Like you expected to be killed any second and didn't even care." She folded her arms and stared me down with a strange intensity. "But there's something I don't understand. After all that, they didn't even shoot you. Everyone else ended up on the ground, but not you. Why?"

Suddenly weary, I sat back against the bars. "That's irrelevant at this point."

"If I'm going to represent you, I need to know why our clan hates you so much."

"You already know the answer to that."

She sat again and curled her legs beneath her. "I want to hear it from you."

I didn't answer for a long time. She just cocked her head and watched me as if she had all the time in the world. The prison that had seemed so empty before now felt too small. Edyn wasn't going away until she had what she wanted. And, frankly, I had nothing better to do.

So I told her. The Demander and the deal he'd backed out on, the empress and her extermination order, Treena and her climb to the throne. I left out the more pleasant moments with Treena and the fact that I'd brought her unconscious body to the hospital. The memory of her peaceful expression, eyes closed in sleep, was as vivid as if it had happened this morning.

Her physician had tried to usher me out several times, but something wouldn't let me leave until I said good-bye.

And then her Rating had changed. One moment it was red; then, in a blink, it was green. In half a second she'd gone from the bottom of her society to the very top.

I knew then that it was a hopeless cause. She'd gotten what she wanted. I was a fool to stay. It was time I shoved my feelings aside and moved on.

"So that girl," Edyn said slowly when I finished. "Treena. You helped her take the throne so our clan could escape under her direction?"

"Yep."

"And that's the only reason."

"Of course."

Edyn cocked her head at my tone. "There were no personal feelings involved there at all."

"I'm not sure what you're getting at."

Disappointment filled her features. "We don't have much to work with, then. It's not like there's any doubt you switched sides. Mills will have tons of witnesses to that effect. And you negotiated with my dad as a representative of NORA, trying to get us to help you and Treena."

"Them," I corrected. "Don't say *us*. You weren't there."

Her lips pursed, but she didn't argue. "We'll have to hide the fact that you tried to run instead of letting yourself be arrested and tried for your crimes."

"What I intended to do isn't the point. I showed up for arrest like we always planned."

"True. You're here now, and that's admirable. Idiotic, actually. But one thing isn't clear. Why? What made you come back to the palace when the bomb hit?"

"I overheard two guards talking about Mills and a bomb that was supposed to hit the square. Our entire clan was headed that way, so I thought I could intercept them before it was too late." *And I wanted to save Treena's life,* I added to myself.

Edyn's eyes flew open wide. "Mills? They mentioned him?"

"You heard me. Mills arranged the attack. And now he's trying to pin it on me. It won't work, though. Too many people know the truth."

She got slowly to her feet, shaking her head. "Mills never left here. If he arranged for a missile attack, he had contact with someone on the outside."

"He spoke with me twice via the feed," I pointed out. It had never occurred to me that the reason he didn't have a Rating was because he lived outside the borders. I should have questioned that.

Edyn gave me a long look. "If you say so. Well, I have a lot of work to do. You managed to screw up a lot of lives along with yours."

"Misery loves company. Can you find my mom and tell her I'm here? She hasn't stopped by yet."

The last time I'd seen my mom was on a tiny screen. Our conversation had been rushed, mostly an explanation of my deal with Mills and how he was going to smuggle them out. She'd sat huddled in an apartment building with gray walls, whispering, her tired eyes darting about the room as we spoke. She never did look me right in the eye. It was like having a conversation with a stranger.

Edyn hesitated. "I'll tell her." Then she turned to leave but paused. "Do you ever think—no, that's a dumb question."

"What?" I asked.

Her gaze looked haunted. "Do you ever wonder what would have happened if NORA hadn't come? If you'd taken your father's place?"

I snickered. "Not really. I would've made a horrible leader."

"That's not what I mean."

I leaned back and stretched casually. I knew exactly what she meant. She was referring to the arrangement our parents had tried to set up, the one we'd both resisted. "It doesn't matter anymore."

"Yeah. I know it doesn't. I just wondered." She pushed the door open.

"Edyn," I called after her.

"Yeah."

"Thanks for your help. It's good to know there's someone on my side."

She shrugged. "I'm probably the only person right now, but you're welcome."

6

TREENA

The hours crept by, then one day, then two. Coltrane took it upon himself to entertain me with stories. For a fifteen-year-old, he had a lot of them, and he rarely paused for breath. I half listened, picking out the interesting tidbits about this settlement. There were several hundred members, all of whom lived underground, and it took forty minutes to walk from one end to the other. Apparently there were far more boys than girls, a strange phenomenon Coltrane dismissed with a shrug.

Lillibeth and Coltrane left twice a day to eat at the cafeteria and bring me back my meal, which always included potatoes in some form—mashed, sliced, baked, seared. If I dared use all of Lillibeth's nutrition pills, I would have asked for those instead. Somewhere in NORA, a young girl had been taken from her father and fostered out, all because of a potato. She had offered me her precious food, and I'd returned her kindness by having her arrested.

And now I had to eat them at every meal. It seemed the fates wanted to keep my wrongdoings squarely in the center of my mind.

If I could go back and help her, I would, I reasoned as I forced down the horrid, mushy food on day two. That girl had probably found a foster family to stay with. She'd have a home and food, which was more than I could say for myself once I left this place.

By evening, when Coltrane finished telling me about the time a rabbit got into the ventilation shaft, Lillibeth came in to check my leg. It had begun to hurt again. After she injected the painkiller, I gave a long sigh of relief. She cleaned up and closed the medicine cabinet and gave her usual practiced smile. "I think your ankle has healed enough that you can travel a bit. Let's have you take a short walk. Coltrane, would you mind grabbing the crutches?"

"You bet." He bolted out of the room.

"Wait," I said. "You mean outside?"

"Of course not," she said quickly. "Just out of our dwelling and into the tunnel, down to the corner and back. Let's see how the tissue is responding to the medication."

"But—what if people see me?"

She gave me a long look. "Why is it a problem if they see you?"

"I'd rather not go out there," I said, thinking quickly. "I . . . got the impression that NORA didn't want to release us. Maybe if they knew I was here, they'd want to bring me back there."

Lillibeth actually rolled her eyes. "Nonsense. Even if that were true, none of us has contact with NORA. They don't even know we're here. If they did, they'd exterminate us. Believe me, we want secrecy as much as you do. Now, let me help you stand."

Her tone left no room for argument. It wasn't like I could hide in here for weeks, especially if Lillibeth was expecting me to work off my debt. I'd just have to be very careful. Besides, after so long in bed, maybe a walk was just what I needed. I swung my legs carefully off the bed and sat up.

Coltrane emerged with the crutches and adjusted the length, and then we were off.

"Just be smart," Lillibeth told us as we left. Coltrane nodded as if he knew exactly what that meant.

Outside the hanging cloth was a long tunnel wide enough for three people shoulder to shoulder. The ceiling curved upward in what was now a familiar arch. A tall person would have to walk down the center to avoid scraping it. Now and then a flat vent poked through the dirt wall, whistling as it blew clean air into the tunnel.

"We'll go to the end of our quadrant and back. Just let me know if you get tired before we reach the corner."

"Quadrant?" My hobbling slowed as I brushed my fingers along the wall and then examined them. Reddish-brown dust. The walls were smooth like plastic, with not a crack in sight. Definitely not hand-carved. What machine could do that to dirt?

"There are four quadrants and four exits," he said, barely noticing that I had fallen behind. "We basically take up the entire valley above us. Remember that old town you were hiding in? It's about a quarter mile northwest and fifty feet above us right now. We actually salvaged some of their underground water and sewer systems for our own use."

I wiped my fingers on my uniform pants—which desperately needed to be washed soon—and hobbled after Coltrane. "Aren't you afraid this will all collapse on your head?"

"Nah. The founders were scientists. Apparently one of them got the idea from studying ant farms or something. We have approved dimensions for tunnels and dwellings, spaced just so, and the ceilings have a very precise arch. In fifty years, we've only lost two dwellings to earthquakes, and that's only because they were in an unstable corner of the west quadrant. It's not perfect, though. We tried to cut a fifth section up in the hills a few years ago, but the soil was too rocky and it broke the excavator. Luckily my dad got it fixed again before he left."

"Where did he go?"

Coltrane shrugged, although his smile faltered. "Nobody knows. He took a bunch of friends on a hunting expedition and never returned. My mom refuses to talk about him."

Then how do you know he's alive? I didn't dare voice the question. He was obviously proud of his father, and I had no right to take that away.

A group of five women turned the corner ahead, chattering to each other, one holding an infant in her arms and a pack in the other. Their hair ranged from dirty blonde to black to a fierce, flaming red. Their gazes fell to my forehead and the women frowned, their conversation dying out immediately. Dread sank my feet into the floor. I could barely hobble, much less run away. There was nothing to do but face these women and act like I had nothing to hide.

"Good evening, Mrs. Van Cott," Coltrane said brightly. "Hello, Mrs. Graff. Have you met our guest? This is Amy, a refugee from NORA."

The women stopped as one. The redhead adjusted the infant in her arms and cocked her head, staring me down. "You're the girl Lillibeth's been harboring?"

"Nice to meet you," I said.

We stood there, the ladies eyeing my forehead with a mixture of disdain and confusion, and me feeling like an animal on display. That was probably how they saw me. I could see the question they wanted to ask. With such a high Rating, why would I leave NORA?

"Well," Coltrane said slowly, "we should get going. Good to see you all."

The women began whispering the moment we left. I felt their eyes on my back as I hobbled down the tunnel. The corner was so far away. All I wanted to do was turn and sprint back to the dwelling and hide under a blanket. Did they know who I was? If these people had helped NORA refugees before, they could have heard stories. Lillibeth had said I was safe here. I wasn't so sure.

"You know," Coltrane said thoughtfully, "it may be best if we loan you some clothes. It's hard to see past that uniform. And you may want to consider having your implant removed. My mom could cut it out for you in a manner of minutes."

I cringed at the thought. I'd intended to have it removed when I reached the settlement. Had Vance and the other settlers had removed theirs by now? Probably. "I'll think about it."

Coltrane was quiet for a moment. The only sound was the steady *thump-plop* rhythm of my crutches and my feet hitting the ground.

"It probably seems ironic to you, our distrust of outsiders," Coltrane said quietly. "The pact says we have to accept everyone, regardless of their past. But when we take in citizens from our biggest enemy, it's hard not to see them as potential spies. It would be so easy for them to go back and tell NORA we're here. I think that's my mom's biggest worry—that someone will do that and bring the military upon us."

"Why do you think they care?" I asked, even though I knew the answer.

"We've been hiding right under their noses for half a century, just days from the border. They'll immediately assume the worst. NORA is so paranoid that they take out settlements that are weeks away. If they knew about us, we'd be toast."

The empress had ordered those attacks. Dresden was in charge now. He'd promised to stop kidnapping settlers for integration. I opened my mouth to tell Coltrane as much, but then I shut it again. After Dresden's political maneuvering and how he'd used me, I couldn't tell Coltrane that he was safe with any degree of confidence. Besides, Dresden's first act as emperor had been to declare war on outlanders. These people definitely qualified.

"You know it's true," he said. "You've lived there. You know what they're like. I mean, not you, but the people in charge. The winners of your game."

Time to change the subject. "Your mom is the leader of this community, isn't she?" I asked.

"When my dad didn't come back, they appointed her harbinger in his place. She didn't want to do it. I think she just wants to be a physician, but people say she does a good job."

"I can tell she really cares about the people here." It made me like her more, this physician-turned-leader who had never even wanted to lead. If Dresden and Konnor hadn't stolen the throne from me, I'd be in that position now.

"I know you don't want to talk about your time in NORA," Coltrane said, lowering his voice even though the tunnel was empty. "But there's something I've been meaning to tell you. The night you got hurt, I was doing maintenance on the sentinel. It's this security system of cameras near the exits, veiled so NORA choppers can't see them. Anyway, my mom thinks I saw you stumbling around and went up to help, but that's not what happened. The truth is, I was already up there. I'd gone up to investigate something the sentinel picked up."

"What was it?" I asked.

"Some kind of aircraft. It wasn't your typical NORA chopper. Those are slow and loud and clunky. This was black and sleek and really fast. The weird thing is, it was dead silent. It whooshed past the sentinel and circled the city, then landed on the other side. I waited until dusk to investigate, hoping it would be dark enough to cover me. That's when I heard you shouting."

A black and soundless aircraft. I hadn't seen anything like that in NORA, even at the military base. A secret government project, maybe? "So you pulled me inside rather than checking it out."

He didn't speak for a moment. Finally he said, "If you had anything to do with that aircraft, you'd tell me, right?"

We had reached the corner. I felt like I'd just climbed a mountain. My uniform was damp with sweat, and my arms ached from the crutches. My entire lower leg was on fire, and I still had to cover the distance to get back to Coltrane's dwelling. But he watched me, his usual lightness gone. I could tell that a lot depended on my answer.

"I've never seen an aircraft like that," I told him. "I walked here myself, every step, and I refuse to go back. It was just a coincidence."

He looked unconvinced, but he nodded. "So you want nothing to do with NORA anymore."

I turned and faced the tunnel, which seemed to extend for kilometers. My mom's face came into my mind, and then Dresden's. Then Tali's mom and brothers. The girl with the potato. The friends and family members of those who had died for me, trusted in me to make their lives better. I shoved them all away and focused on the present. "I'm done with NORA forever."

7

TREENA

The next morning, Lillibeth insisted I was doing well enough to walk to the cafeteria for breakfast. Coltrane had an errand to run on the way and begged me to come along. Minutes later I found myself standing in front of a strange dwelling. A divider hung in the archway, similar to Coltrane's except bright, with floral squares of orange, red, and gold.

"How's that leg feeling?" Coltrane asked, still holding the bin he'd carried all the way here.

He didn't sound winded at all. I, on the other hand, sounded like I'd just run a race. I panted for a moment. If Lillibeth hadn't just injected painkiller, I'd probably be writhing on the ground. "Fine. Who lives here again?"

"You'll see."

"I wish you'd quit saying that."

"Hey, let a guy have his secrets." Coltrane set his box down and gave four firm, distinct claps of his hands.

For a long moment, there was no sound from inside, then an older woman with long silver hair brushed the blanket aside. "Yes?"

"I have your order, Ruby," Coltrane said. "And I brought somebody to meet you."

A wide smile crossed her face. "Ah. Perfect timing."

"How are you feeling today?"

"My bones aren't mad at me today, so that's a plus." She pulled the curtain back the rest of the way and held it for us. "Well? You coming in for a treat?"

"Are you baking?" Coltrane sounded like an eager child. "Oh, we're definitely coming in." He picked up his box and ducked inside. I opened my mouth to protest, but then I took a deep breath. An amazing aroma wafted out the doorway, suddenly making me very mindful of my empty stomach. My body hobbled in of its own accord.

The dwelling was similar to Coltrane's—three rooms with doorways sectioned off with cloths. The walls and ceilings had the same curved lines, all smooth. One of these days I wanted to check out this excavator of theirs. It sounded interesting.

"Glad you could stop by," Ruby said, letting the curtain fall behind me.

"You have a cooking area in your dwelling?" I asked.

She chuckled. "I call it a kitchen, and yes. This body is getting too old to tromp down to the cafeteria for every meal, and I'm a picky eater anyway. One of the perks of serving as an elder. Didn't take too much doing to get it approved."

"What did you make?" I asked.

"Cake," she said with a kind smile. "I'm pretty sure you've never had it."

"How do you know?"

She pointed to my forehead. Of course. It was hard to remember I still wore NORA's badge of shame under my skin. I'd changed into some of Lillibeth's clothing this morning after a bath. The brown shirt hung a little baggy in the shoulders, and the trousers pooled at the ankles, but it was better than the disgusting uniform I'd worn for the past week. I felt like a different person today.

"Nutrition pills may keep your body alive," she said, "but cake for breakfast? Now *that* makes life worth living."

Coltrane sucked in a breath. "Cake? I haven't had cake in forever. Amy, it's like a really sweet bread. You'll love it."

Ruby made her way to a black box set into the wall and pulled the door open. Using a rag, she pulled out a pan and set it on top. Its contents looked like bread, only wider and darker. "This isn't just any cake. This is a chocolate cake. I used up the last of my sugar to make it, and I had half a cup of chocolate powder left. Did your mom trade for more sugar, dear Coltrane?"

"I caught a glimpse of some at the bottom, under the flowers," he said. Then, as if realizing what he'd just said, his face colored. "Not that I was looking through your stuff, of course. I don't—"

"Of course you do," Ruby said, "but it's all right. I couldn't have planned this better. I was hoping I wouldn't have to eat my birthday cake alone. Go have a seat, and I'll bring you a piece." She poked the cake with a fork, then nodded.

Coltrane headed for the woven chairs near the door, but I made my way to the bin he'd carried in. With a glance at Ruby, who was distracted, I peeled back the lid and peeked inside. A floral aroma wafted upward. He wasn't kidding about the flowers, then.

"What are you doing?" Coltrane hissed.

I shrugged and pulled it higher, peeking inside. Two small bags of white powder filled the bottom. A bunch of vines with dozens of wilting orange flowers rested on top. I picked up one of the stems, holding it carefully so I wouldn't damage the flowers. Definitely not plastic.

"I thought you might be interested in those," Ruby said, carrying two plates. "Desert Globemallow, in case you were wondering. My favorite flower."

"What are they for?" I asked, taking a chair. Ruby's chairs were similar to Coltrane's woven ones but padded with soft pillows.

"Lillibeth sends a few whenever she can. These must be the last of the season. I'd never see them if it weren't for her. I'm not allowed onto the surface until November. We get one visit a year, you see, and that's usually at night. Not the best for flower hunting, even if it was the right season."

She handed me a plate with a square piece of light brown cake covered in something white and creamy. I reached to grab a chunk, but she shook her head slightly and handed me a fork. Then she held out the other plate for Coltrane, who thanked her.

After a couple of unsuccessful attempts at breaking a piece off without crumbling it, I set the fork down and broke off a piece with my fingers. Ruby hid a smile.

I put the piece into my mouth and felt my eyes widen. It was *amazing*. So many flavors, all so different. It was easily the best thing I'd ever tasted. The top layer was sweeter than the bottom, which was slightly salty, but the two flavors blended beautifully. I swallowed and grabbed another handful. The gooey whiteness of the topping coated my fingers, but I didn't care.

"I've always wondered about that," Coltrane said. "I mean, Mrs. Brough has an order in for roses. Those make sense. They're hard to find and valuable, and she makes perfume out of them. But Globemallow is pretty much useless, and they grow right above us." He lifted the fork to his mouth for another bite.

"These flowers may be worthless to everyone else," Ruby said, "but they hold infinite meaning for me. There's something special about a bright desert flower. It takes the land nothing else wants and thrives in places where it shouldn't. Where the land is dead and dry, that's where desert flowers thrive—and they throw off some brilliant colors while they do it. It's almost as if they defy science by their very existence."

The last piece went into my mouth. I stared eagerly at the crumbs covering my plate. I considered licking it clean but settled for running my fingers along the crumbs and putting them into my mouth. As I did, I caught Ruby's gaze. Her eyes crinkled at the corners as she chuckled.

"Sorry," I said. "It's just so good."

"It's like a new planet, isn't it?" Ruby asked. "New tastes and textures and colors and people. It can be overwhelming. You're faring far better than I did."

I nearly let the plate slip off my lap before catching it again. "You're from NORA?"

Her smile faded a bit and she looked at the floor. "I remember how strange people looked without numbers then. We're trained to look at the number first and *then* the person. Because their score tells us everything we need to know, right?" She stabbed her cake with a fork almost violently. "But here, you have to actually get to know people. Even so, I think I mentally assigned Ratings to everyone I met for the first year after I escaped."

"And then you met my parents," Coltrane said.

She finished chewing and swallowed. "They were young, but yes. I knew your grandparents as well."

"So you're one of the founders?" I asked. "But why aren't you leading the community?"

"The founders formed a circle of elders, and they voted on the leader. Ruby is the last founder left in the circle." He looked at Ruby, then at the ground. "Most of them went out to look for my dad and never came back. They had to replace them."

"But enough about that," Ruby said. "I heard how you came to be here, Amy. A snakebite, so near the exit, and just when Coltrane happened to be watching. It seems almost too good to be true."

Coltrane stiffened, and I stared at Ruby in surprise. How much did this woman know?

Ruby chuckled again and put her empty plate down on the floor. "Don't worry, I won't ask about the circumstances. But it is rather convenient. I'd say the fates are definitely involved here."

I sat back. "Yeah, the fates have it in for me. First my supplies got stolen, and then a snake attacked my leg."

"And then Coltrane saved you," Ruby pointed out, "and you ended up here. Nothing happens by chance, dear. There's a reason behind everything the fates do. If your journey was interrupted, maybe you were on the wrong journey."

I raised an eyebrow. "Um, I think the snake was a clumsy moment. Now I'm stuck here until my leg gets better. And I have a debt to pay."

"Ah," Ruby said. "So you need to find a contribution."

I made a face. Coltrane grinned. "I think she's sick of hearing that word."

"Call it what you like," Ruby said, "but you'll want to find a skill to help the community as soon as possible. Here, a contribution is the doorway between childhood and adulthood. Coltrane will be presenting his project for approval very soon, as I recall. How long have you been working on it again, dear?"

"Four years. Can I have another piece for the road?"

"Take the whole pan. Your mother will want some, and I have a feeling Amy hasn't had her fill yet."

I stood, then winced as the blood came rushing back into my ankle. "I don't need a rite of passage. I just need to pay off my debt quickly."

"A contribution is the fastest way to do that," Coltrane said as he headed to the kitchen. "Although I don't know why you'd want to rush off. It's not like you had anything going for you out there."

Ruby must have seen my frown because she stood and reached for my plate, which I handed over. "Thanks for joining me on my birthday, dear. I hope you feel comfortable stopping by anytime. I'm always available to talk." She stopped. "Well, whenever the elders aren't convening, anyway."

"Thanks for the cake, Ruby," Coltrane said, clasping the pan with both hands. "I'll bring this back tomorrow." He turned toward the door.

"Oh," Ruby said. She bent over the box and retrieved a vine of flowers, then handed them to me. "Why don't you hold on to these? It would be a shame to keep them all to myself."

"Thank you," I said, cupping the orange flowers in my hands. They felt soft and prickly at the same time. "The cake was amazing. I hope you have a great birthday."

"I hope you enjoy your stay here, whether it be long or short." She leaned closer and lowered her voice. "This place is one of second chances. I believe that everyone, no matter what they've lived through, deserves that much."

8

VANCE

The next day, Ju-Long walked in with three guards. They had similar features except that the guards had straight black hair where Ju-Long's head was smooth and bald. He swiped his device against the door and it clicked open. "It is time."

I set down the bowl of tasteless gruel and stood, eyeing the door. "But the trial is next week."

"The assembly wants a preliminary hearing. Your crimes will be presented to the people, and you'll have the opportunity to declare your guilt in exchange for a lesser sentence."

I snorted. "For my actual crimes or the ones Mills made up?"

"You've been accused of many things, none of which look favorable to you. Now hold your hands out."

"I didn't blow up anybody, and I'm not going. Let Mills hold his hearing without me." I stepped back into a veiled fighting stance, keeping my hands down.

Ju-Long's dark eyes narrowed. "You will come quietly, or in bonds." He motioned to a guard, who approached with a pair of chained cuffs. As he lifted the cuffs, my palm smashed through his nose. The guard recoiled with a yelp, blood dripping onto his uniform. The next guard ran at me, but I tripped him, sending him face-first into the ground. I leaped over him and barreled through the doorway, shoving the third guard aside as I headed for the exit.

But suddenly Ju-Long was there, standing right in my way. I threw a punch. Faster than should have been possible, he stepped aside and redirected my fist, doubling me over and sending me tumbling to the ground. I jumped to my feet and charged, more wary this time. Ju-Long faked a kick, deflected my next punch, and raced into action. I barely saw him move. He spun and threw his arms around my head, then tightened them into a chokehold against my throat.

I was too stunned to react for a moment. I tried to step behind him to get leverage, but his grip tightened even more. Someone jumped in and fastened the cold steel cuffs on my wrists. A little more pressure and my windpipe would collapse. I began to flail wildly, kicking and elbowing anything in sight, then attempted to bash

Ju-Long in the face with my head, but his grip was too strong. The room went out of focus, the objects around me losing their color.

"There are more of us than you realize," Ju-Long's voice said near my ear. "And you are alone. Your stubbornness will only make things worse for you, Hawking. I think you'll find that cooperation is best for your sake as well as everyone involved. Yes?"

I let my body go slack. The moment I did, Ju-Long released my throat and I gasped in precious air. He raised himself to his feet as I lay there gulping, my body trembling from effort and lack of oxygen. The guards who had escorted him watched me with unreadable faces except for the one whose nose I'd broken. He held it with a bloody hand, and his gaze was murderous. But it was Ju-Long's face I focused on. His usual blank expression was now twisted into a self-satisfied smile. If I could have lifted my hands, I would've punched the guy.

He seemed to know it. "Since that's over with," Ju-Long said, patting me on the shoulder, "we will make our way promptly to the preliminary hearing. I do hate to make people wait."

9

TREENA

Four days later, standing in the cafeteria kitchen, I was ready to throw something. Preferably something heavy and breakable. Unfortunately, all that surrounded me were brown bags of various ingredients and hard concrete countertops that I couldn't move in a million years. And one frustrated chef with a heavy beard tucked into a hairnet. Tufts of rough hair escaped here and there from their prison, and I made a mental note to check my food for beard hairs from now on.

"You mix the dry ingredients together first, *then* add the wet," he said. He sighed. "Well, I suppose it'll have to turn out. We don't have enough water rations to start again. Five cups of water wasted."

"I'm sorry," I told him for the fourth time that morning, dropping the spoon and stepping away from the bowl. He'd given me a paper with instructions, a worn piece with ink writing. It may as well have been written in another language—flour, baking soda, baking powder, salt, sugar, water, vegetable oil. I knew that oil was a lubricant of some kind. But this stuff was a deep yellow. And how many types of white powder did one food need?

"Never you mind," he said, taking the spoon in defeat. "Should've known you'd have no experience with such things."

"Cooking may not be her thing," Coltrane said from behind me, "but you gotta admit, the girl can eat."

I whirled and stalked toward him. "That's it. You'd better run." Coltrane threw his hands in the air in surrender, backing toward the door.

"You'll find your contribution yet, child," the chef said. "Best be on your way, both of you. I've work to do." He picked up the mixing bowl and dipped the spoon in, eyeing the brown goop like it was an alien species.

I followed Coltrane into the tunnel and stood aside for the people walking by. I barely noticed their stares anymore. "Thanks for your help in there. I hope you were entertained."

"Oh, I wasn't about to miss that. Best show I've seen in weeks."

I punched him on the shoulder. "You keep talking about this contribution of yours, but so far you just follow me around. What are you, a professional stalker?"

"I'm an inventor." He grinned. "I only stalk pretty girls in my spare time."

I paused. "Coltrane—"

He jumped in. "But seriously, we need to find something you're good at before you take the entire settlement down. Now that you can walk around freely, we're all in trouble."

"You'd better watch it."

He grinned, revealing surprisingly white teeth. "Well, we tried the laundry thing . . . "

"Nobody told me the water needed to be sanitized first," I said.

Coltrane pursed his lips as if trying not to laugh. "And doing inventory didn't go so well, either."

"I'll figure it out eventually," I said without conviction. So I didn't know the difference between lettuce and carrots. That didn't make me a horrible person. My ankle throbbed more painfully by the minute. Maybe it was time to rest and try again tomorrow.

"I have an idea," Coltrane said. "I haven't given you a tour of the southern quadrant yet. There's something I want you to see."

"Let me guess," I said. "More brown tunnels and arched ceilings, with a vent here and there."

"That, and something else. It's exactly what you need. Trust me."

———•••———

Coltrane's baglight started dying by the third corner, so he pulled another bag out of his pocket, dropped it, and crushed it with his foot. The passage instantly lit up with a golden glow.

"Can I hold it this time?" I asked.

"Sure," he said, handing it to me. "Interesting, huh? My aunt invented them. Before that, we used solar gravel, but my mom was worried it was too easily seen."

The bag was less heavy than I'd expected. I squinted at the light. It contained hundreds of tiny glowing pellets. They manufactured them down here, I remembered Coltrane saying. It was the reason traders came this way. They were lightweight, easy to recharge, and produced no heat. I still couldn't believe how cool the clear bag was. "What's the liquid inside these pellets?"

Coltrane smiled wryly. "Can't tell. Not because of who you are, but hardly anyone down here knows the secret. It's safer that way."

"Because the secret would leak and jeopardize your economy or because you don't want them to know the liquid is dangerous?"

A slow smile crept across his face. "Both."

If only they'd let me take a baglight when I left. Vance would be fascinated, I was sure. "As long as it doesn't give me two heads, you can keep your secret. I love all the tech down here. Some of it even rivals what NORA has. Your inventors would be set for life there." I stopped. "If they wanted to live there, of course."

"Don't know why they would. Why anyone would, really." His hand brushed mine as we walked, and I stepped sideways to put more distance between us. He continued as if he hadn't noticed. "I feel bad saying this, but I'm kind of glad you don't know how to do anything. It means you can live here for a long time, learning and settling in. You'll have a great home here."

"You have a great community," I said, hoping he would leave it at that. We turned a corner and stopped at a door. Not a fabric curtain like every other entrance here but an actual door with a knob and keypad. I rapped a knuckle against the door's surface. Metal. "What is this place?"

"The defense lab."

I gave him a sideways look. "I thought weapons were banned here."

"Our defenses aren't weapons. Not in the true sense of the word, anyway." Coltrane covered the keypad with his palm and typed in his code, then there was a click. He turned the handle and held the door open for me. The lab was dark, but the baglight I still held quickly flooded the room.

It was much larger than any room I'd seen down here. The walls and ceilings were lined with metal. Tables upon tables, all full of trinkets and piles of materials and who-knows-what were lined parallel to the doorway. Several chairs—actual plastic chairs, not the woven ones—sat stacked in the corner.

Coltrane let the door close behind him and headed to the far table. "You wanted to know what my contribution was. I've been working on this since I was eleven." He picked up a long, slim metal device that was rounded at the edges and held it out for me to examine. A green light flashed at the top, and I caught a glimpse of wires protruding from the bottom.

I touched the smooth metal. "What does it do?"

He removed a section to reveal a black box with circuits attached. "This part here is the low-inductance capacitor bank. It discharges into a single-loop antenna on the top, then emits an electro-magnetic pulse."

"What's the pulse supposed to do?"

He shoved the square section back on with a click. "One push of this button and it can shut down any weapon or aircraft within half a mile or so, provided they're electric." He cradled it in his palm. "Pretty amazing, huh?"

"Got it. An EMP."

His grin faded. "Does NORA have these?"

"No, no. Well, maybe, but I've never seen them use one. They need electricity too much. They use it for everything."

"That's what I figured. Although I'm not a hundred percent sure it works. Since my mom destroys every weapon we come in contact with, I can't test it effectively. I'm pretty sure it'll do the job, though. It's shut down Domingo's wave shield over there several times." He pointed to a tall machine standing at the other end of the room. "Makes him so grumpy. I love it."

I looked around at the other inventions. Some were covered, but not all. "Are you sure we should be in here? I doubt your inventor friends would be okay with me seeing this stuff."

He shrugged. "What are you going to do? Run back and tell NORA we're trying to block their weapons?"

"I already told you. I would never do that."

He looked me right in the eye, his usual humor gone. "If you're worried about what people think, why not take out your implant? Find a contribution and present it to the elders. Then they'll have to accept you. I didn't bring you here to show off. I just wanted you to see that everyone has something inside them to contribute. You just haven't found yours yet. Once you do, I think you'll be really happy here."

He shoved his hands into his pockets and clamped his mouth shut as if he'd said too much, and the familiar pink in his cheeks returned.

If he was fishing for a promise, I couldn't give it. Removing my implant was the logical thing to do. But it also signaled that I wanted to be a part of all this. I was fascinated with this place and these people, but I wasn't one of them. My implant was the divider, the reminder that I didn't belong. The tether that kept me grounded to my goal.

A series of clicks sounded outside the door, and it opened to admit a guy of eighteen or nineteen. He had a tall, slender build and wavy blond hair that hung past his ears. He grinned when he saw us and leaned casually against the door.

A girl about ten years old with the same hair color trotted in behind him and gave me a shy smile.

"You know the security code?" Coltrane exclaimed. "Maxim, you're going to get in such big trouble."

"I have clearance now," the guy said. "And you don't see *me* bringing girls in here for make-out sessions. Who's the digit?"

Coltrane's cheeks burned a bright red. "I was showing her my project, and don't call her a digit. Amy, this is Maxim and his little sister, Mandie. He developed an intelligence line for his contribution a few years back. He gets news from traders passing by and reports it to my mom."

"And Coltrane *pretends* to work in here," Maxim said, striding closer. "Are you the girl he found in the desert?"

"That's me," I said, forcing a smile. Mandie stayed by the door, eyeing me curiously.

"Was it as dramatic as Cole made it sound?" Maxim asked, standing over me. "He said he fought off a brushfire, two dozen rattlesnakes, and an entire NORA unit to get to you."

"You are such a liar," Coltrane said, but he finally broke into a grin. "There were a dozen snakes at most. And for your information, my project is very important. It'll save lives someday."

Mandie must have decided I wasn't a threat because she stepped into the room and let the door close behind her. "My dad says Coltrane's invention doesn't work."

Maxim and I burst into laughter as Coltrane threw his hands helplessly into the air. "It does too work. If your dad would get me what I need, I could prove it."

"Doesn't look like that's happening, man," Maxim said. "I'm sorry, I really am. But don't you think you should spend your time on something else? Something you can actually demonstrate in front of the elders? I mean, we have a ton of people working on defenses. But there are needs in other places that need to be met."

Mandie moved from one table to the next, touching everything she could. She reached an empty bowl and peered inside. "Do you want to be an inventor?" I asked her.

Maxim frowned. "Mandie's training to play the violin. She'll be a musician, like our mom. And it'll be easy enough for her to find a husband, considering there are five boys for every girl her age."

I watched Mandie move to the next table, only half listening. "Do all the kids go to the same school here?"

"School?" Maxim looked confused. "You mean a single place for everyone to get the same education? That's an outdated way of thinking. Each child has different skills and interests, and those should be groomed in the home. Our parents taught us what we needed to know, right, Mandie?"

His little sister nodded and put down the coil of metal rope she'd been holding.

I bent over so we were the same height. Her cheeks were dotted with freckles, and her eyelashes were long and delicate. "Mandie, have your parents taught you how to read?"

"This is ridiculous," Maxim said. "Mandie, time to go."

"There's so much I have to learn about your community," I said, "but I'm wondering if that's something I can help with. Seriously, Mandie. Did your parents teach you mathematics—geometry, calculus, trigonometry? And science—biology, chemistry, geology?"

Mandie blinked at the onslaught, then shook her head. "I can read a little. But my mom taught me to play the violin. She said I'll be good enough to present before I'm fifteen."

An idea had begun to form, and I felt excitement pulsing through my body. "That's great."

Coltrane frowned, watching Maxim stride toward the door. "I'm not sure what all this is about, Amy. Intelligence isn't a contribution. I'm sure you'll find something that adds to the community."

I raised an eyebrow. Intelligence wasn't important? Then what about all these inventions? What room was there for Mandie and her young friends, if they weren't pushed to think?

"If all else fails," Maxim said, "you can sell us a few NORA secrets. That may be worth something. C'mon, Mandie."

I ignored Maxim and nodded to the girl as she followed her brother out. "Hope I get to hear you play the violin someday." She beamed back at me.

When the girl and her brother left, I handed the baglight to Coltrane. "I know what I'm going to do."

"What's that?" Coltrane asked warily.

"I want to be a teacher," I said. "Let's go talk to your mom."

10

VANCE

ood people of Blackfell, we thank you for your attendance at this momentous event," Mills said into the handheld amplifier. His voice echoed off the valley walls as the crowd quieted. We stood on a makeshift platform that jutted out from the wall, then dropped ten feet as the ground sloped toward the swamp below. Even from this high, I could still smell it. "Many of you have waited long for this. Perhaps you struggle to survive each day, suffering greatly as you mourn the loss of dear ones. It is our hope that those who have passed and those who remain can finally find peace with the capture of this man. I will now read the charges brought forth by the people against Vance Hawking, son of Iron Belt Hawking."

Someone clapped and shouted, and then the audience joined in. I picked out a familiar face here and there. There were no chairs. The settlers stood, some holding young children or babies, all watching me with disgust or anger. There had to be hundreds of them, maybe even a thousand or more. Even the dirt trail was full of spectators. Ju-Long stood off to the side of the platform, watching me like a mountain lion eyes its prey.

I was such an idiot. Ju-Long moved slowly, carefully, smoothly. Like a fighter. I should have seen it long before now.

"The first charge brought to him is defection," Mills said. "When his clan was attacked and incorporated into the New Order Republic of America, young Hawking chose to join them instead of fight."

"I did fight," I growled.

He talked right over me. "He spent two years hunting down so-called criminals who were simply settlers trying to survive, showing no mercy to his own clan members."

A few people booed and yelled. NORA had watched me closely for any sign of defection. I wasn't proud of my time in EPIC, but at least my family was safe. They were probably here somewhere. I swept the crowd, looking for my mother's face, but she must have been too far away.

"The second is falsehoods. When he discovered a movement to unseat the leader of NORA, he tricked his people into taking part, telling whatever lies were necessary for them to participate in his scheme."

"They weren't lies," I snapped. "I made a deal, and I kept it. Just ask Rutner."

The group of older men and women sitting behind Mills frowned, and a graying woman half stood. "The defendant will refrain from speaking or be removed."

I didn't want to be here anyway, but now that I was here, I needed some kind of plan. "The defendant is sorry," I replied, then nodded to Mills. "Carry on."

"And finally," Mills said, lowering his voice dramatically, "a charge so horrifying I can barely stand to speak it. Vance Hawking is accused of blackmailing four of his clan members into shooting off a missile— into the very square where his own people gathered to protest."

I snorted, but the audience began shouting at that. Some pointed, and others even shoved through the crowd toward me. Ju-Long's guards lining the bottom of the platform moved forward, talking to the audience. Most of the angry settlers were people I recognized. Many had been in the square, helping our desperate little group pull bodies out from under the wreckage. I frowned. These people really believed I would shoot a missile and then organize a rescue operation? What did I have to gain?

One thing was certain. It didn't take much for these people to believe what they were told.

"And now," Mills said, "we'll hear the prisoner's plea. To the charge of defection, what say you, Hawking?"

"Guilty."

The crowd cheered. Half of them, at least. Others nodded their heads but didn't react much.

"To the charge of falsehoods?"

I glared at him. "Not guilty. I told no lies."

There was murmuring, but no shouting this time.

"And to the charge of collaboration of mass murder?"

"Ridiculous."

A dozen or so people rushed the platform, shouting. Their words blended in with each other. "Liar!" "Terrorist!" "He's not sorry at all!"

The guards stood their ground in front of me again, but it was woefully inadequate. The assembly members, who sat in chairs behind me, stood and backed away. The audience shouted and screamed and moved forward in an angry wave. Then one voice stood out from the rest. Mills. "Silence!"

It grew quieter, and the front runners slowed, but didn't stop. Mills tried again. "You will stop this instant, or you participate in Hawking's sentence!"

The line of people stopped at the guards. One of them spat and missed my face, getting my chest instead. Right above the heart.

"I mean it," Mills said, his voice echoing across the crowd. "He will receive his punishment soon enough. Let justice be done for his atrocities. I feel as you do, but please stand down and allow us to finish the requirements of the law. The boy admitted his guilt on one count."

The louder individuals in the crowd stopped pushing their way toward the platform, but it was clear from their dark expressions they didn't trust whatever "requirements of the law" Mills had in store. In our clan, we handled things a little differently. Those protestors weren't backing down; they were simply waiting for their chance to see justice done.

Mills asked the assembly members to step forward and deliver their sentence for my admitted crimes, then handed over the amplifier. "His sentence is service," a stern-faced woman announced. "A lifetime of service to those he has wronged. For those with missing fathers and husbands, he will provide financial support. For the children, he will find worthy parents. He will right every wrong, seek those who are lost, and become the person he should have been."

Mills's smile slipped. It was obviously not the sentence he'd expected.

The crowd murmured, a few people more vocal in their reactions than others.

"That's not justice!" someone called out.

"Service?" a man shouted incredulously. "What kind of punishment is that?"

The shouts grew in volume, tripping over each other. The audience began to inch their way forward toward the platform again, some raising fists. I had to agree with them. This wasn't justice at all. If I knew it, they definitely knew it.

No matter what their assembly said or did, I was as good as dead.

An idea hit me then—something that could possibly buy me a little more time. Risky, but possible. I lifted my voice over the crowd. "A fair sentence. But with all due respect, I came here to be judged by the Hawking clan, and we have our own rules. In my clan, what you dole out is given right back. Since I caused so much pain to my people, I ask that they be allowed to return it."

The noise died as the audience gaped.

Even Mills looked puzzled. "You're saying you want to deliver yourself into the crowd?"

"Just my clan," I said. "I owe the others nothing."

I saw the emotions play out on Mills's face as he considered it, then hid a smile. He turned to the assembly. "What say you?"

"We do not return violence with violence," the woman said.

"It encourages anger and revenge," another elder hissed. "Take him back to the prison before the crowd gets out of control."

Mills looked unhappy, but he nodded. The guards grabbed my shoulders and started to pull me away, but I had already made my decision.

I swung around, knocking away their hands and leaped off the platform into the audience.

The crowd exploded again as I landed on an unsuspecting guard, sending him flying to the ground. He hit hard and I heard a crack. I rolled sideways, tucking my fastened arms, then jumped to my feet. The settlers completely surrounded me now. Adrenaline pulsed through my body, screaming at me to run. I could do it. Unless somebody had a stunner and incredible aim, I could fight my way to the trail right now.

But then I saw my mother. She stood with one hand over her mouth. The gray in her hair was more prominent, her eyes lined with wrinkles. Silent communication passed between us. Finally, she gave a slight nod.

I shoved away the instinct to run. The time would come, but not yet. Instead, I went against everything my brain was telling me and stopped. The crowd that pressed around me grew thicker and louder, arms jostling and pushing me around. Wylin Newport stepped forward, his hands already forming fists. He was the oldest son of Stuart Newport, one of the men we'd arrested on our last Meridian raid. Wylin's father had been executed on a public broadcast. Service wouldn't bring him back.

"Well?" I shouted toward him. "You've wanted to punish me for what I did. Here's your chance."

"Guards, stop this!" the assembly chair shrieked. The guards looked confused and conflicted; some bent over the unfortunate man I'd landed on. But none looked willing to leave their posts to protect a prisoner.

A few people hung back, but several seemed eager to take me up on my offer of revenge. They immediately formed a line. A figure pushed through the crowd and emerged, shoving his way to the front. Anton.

He sized me up and down. "You don't know how long I've wanted to do this."

"Didn't realize you were waiting for permission," I said.

Anton's face darkened and he took a step forward.

11

TREENA

Getting permission to start a school wasn't difficult. It was finding students that was the problem.

Lillibeth didn't seem very optimistic as we left the next morning to go recruiting. Now, after the fourteenth dwelling, I was beginning to understand her doubts. I rubbed a headache that had come on suddenly and ignored the ache in my ankle. "I don't get it. They look at me like I'm trying to kidnap their kids."

Coltrane grinned wryly as we made our way to the next dwelling. "Well, what would *you* do? A stranger shows up from an enemy country and says she wants to educate your kids. It's not like they'll hand their children over and say, 'Sure, just have them home by dinnertime.'" He motioned toward a doorway. "This is the Clapton dwelling. Their dad is a chemist and a friend of my dad. It's worth a try."

I clapped four times as I'd seen Coltrane do. A man swept the cloth aside and squinted at us. "Hello, Coltrane. How's your mother?"

"Doing great, thanks." He turned to me. "Mr. Clapton, this is our guest, Amy. She's working on her contribution and has something she wants to ask you."

The man stared at me, expressionless. Then he stepped out and squared his shoulders, letting the cloth fall closed behind him. "Kacey just came by and told me you were making the rounds. We're not interested in any NORA school."

"That's not it at all," I told him, knowing it was futile but determined to follow through. "I'm only teaching the basics of math and science, and maybe a little reading."

"We settlers know more about math and science than you digits ever will. I hope that someday we get the chance to show them who the real brains are. Sorry, missy, but you aren't teaching my kids." He turned to go in but paused in the doorway. "You know, Coltrane, some people are talking. They're worried about your mother harboring a NORA refugee."

"We've helped lots of travelers before, Mr. Clapton."

"Needy people, yes. Not a well-to-do NORA citizen." He eyed my Rating, and his eyes narrowed even more. "Some of us are wondering if the pact isn't the best thing for us anymore. We have families to think about. Tell your mother it's time for this girl to go."

"Sir," I cut in. "I mean your community no harm. They've been nothing but kind to me. I would never allow them to be hurt."

"There's something wrong with all this," the man said. "You could be a soldier sent to spy on us. Or worse, an assassin determined to kill us all so NORA doesn't have to lift a finger. And you dare come in here with that innocent act and ask to teach my kids? If I had my way, we'd find that snake and let it finish the job." He turned and went back inside.

Coltrane's jaw hung open. "Uh, wow. I'm sorry. I had no idea he would say that."

I put a hand on his arm. "It's not your fault they feel that way."

"I'll talk to my mom about this. I'm sure there's something she can do. Don't worry about them, all right? We've only covered one quadrant, and there are three others. We'll have better luck tomorrow." He started to leave.

Tomorrow. Another day gone. I hung back and pushed away the disappointment. Why did I even care what these people thought? My leg was healing. Lillibeth said the tissue damage was minimal and I'd be able to travel again within the week. The only thing keeping me here after that was the lack of supplies and my debt. But as long as the people didn't trust me, I couldn't solve either problem.

For the first time in days, I thought about Vance. He'd be busy helping his clan build a new settlement. Would they be safe this time? Would Dresden keep his promise to leave them alone? Did Vance even want me to come anymore?

I'd been wrong to hurt him. I couldn't let him move on without hearing what I had to say. The only thing standing in the way was a few hundred kilometers.

"There's something I've been wanting to ask you," Coltrane said as we walked. "There's this social on Friday. It's a yearly thing for all the quadrants, a really big deal. Dale always makes these apple tarts, and they're hot and sweet and absolutely amazing." He paused. "Are you listening?"

I barely heard him in the heaviness of my thoughts. I had a desert to cross. These people already thought I was a criminal. If it came to it, I could always steal some supplies and leave. Nobody would be surprised.

"Amy."

"Hmm?" I asked, trying to recall what he had said. "Oh. Apple tarts. Got it."

Coltrane sighed.

Maybe I was going about this school thing all wrong. An idea formed in my mind. "Can we stop by Ruby's on the way back?"

Coltrane shrugged. "Sure, why?"

Because she was an elder. Because she was kind, and she'd offered help if I ever needed it. But mostly because Ruby was the only person down here I could relate to, and I desperately needed her advice if this school idea was going to work. "Let's see if she's been baking."

Coltrane grinned. "You make me proud."

12

TREENA

Not only did Ruby approve of my school idea, but she told me to come back in the morning with a lesson plan.

"Your students will be waiting," she said as she handed me a pan of sweet rolls.

Ruby was true to her word. When Coltrane and I entered Ruby's dwelling the next day, four children were seated on the center rug, two girls and two boys. Mandie was one of them, and she grinned. The other kids' eyes widened at the sight of my forehead.

I looked up at Ruby, who hovered over the children like a proud parent. "I watch these kids each day while their parents are working. Last night I told those stubborn moms and dads that if a digit could watch them, another digit could teach them, and if they threw a fit about it, I'd be done tending forever. So here we are."

I chuckled, picturing that in my mind. "Hello, class," I said, setting down my supplies to sit with them on the rug. "I'm Amy. I'm so glad you came."

"Do you really get to teach us?" Mandie asked, her knees bouncing in her excitement.

"Why are people from NORA called digits?" a girl with brown skin and black braids asked. "Oh, I'm Clara, by the way."

"I'd guess it's because we wear numbers," I told her.

"What are they for?"

"Because they're playing a game," Mandie told her knowingly. "My mom says there's only one winner and lots of losers."

"Why did you leave? Is it because you lost?" Clara asked.

Coltrane cleared his throat and found a chair. I just gave them a grim smile. "I couldn't stay there anymore. It was time to find a new life."

"So you're going to stay here, then?" Mandie asked. "My mom says you should go back where you came from, but I hope you don't."

"I—"

"Have you felt rain?" one of the boys said shyly. "My mom says she felt it once."

"Do they have rain in South America?" Mandie asked. "Maxim says the drought is really bad here, but only here. He wants us to move. Maxim says in Europe everything's green and they have tall, skinny houses above the ground."

I shifted uncomfortably. "I'm not sure. Why don't we start with reading—"

The questions kept coming. "What are NORA schools like?" "Have you ever flown in a helicopter?" "Do they have oatmeal there?" "Have you ever seen a horse?"

I looked to Ruby for help, but she shrugged and turned away, heading for her kitchen in the corner. I was on my own.

"Students," I said sharply, and the questions cut off abruptly. "I'd love to answer your questions, but we have a lot to do today. Raise your hand if you can read."

They looked at me blankly. Mandie raised her hand.

"Okay," I told her. "How do you spell *run?*"

"R-E-N. But I'm serious about the horse thing. My mom showed me a picture once, and it was super big when you stand it next to a person. Horses used to pull carriages hundreds of years ago, when the women wore dresses in Europe. That's where the Nations for Peace convention meets."

Europe. Nations for Peace. So many strange concepts. Ruby was right—I had a lot to learn about the world outside NORA. Maybe I'd be getting more out of this than I thought.

As soon as she took a breath, I held up a hand. "I'll turn some time over to you at the end, Mandie, and you can tell us about Europe. Until then, let's talk about vowels."

13

VANCE

At some point in my life I probably knew the symptoms of a cracked rib. As clan chief, my dad required everyone to learn the basics of first aid by the time we turned fourteen. That was him, self-reliance personified. That attitude made him a great leader, and the people would do anything for him. It also made him really hard to live with.

Now, sitting cross-legged on my bedroll, there wasn't a single position that was comfortable. So far I'd tried lying down, standing, leaning back against the bars, and slouching. Even *breathing* hurt, all the pain blending together. I straightened my arms, letting them take some of my weight, sitting up straight, and taking shallow breaths. The pain was bearable now, at least.

It was hard to tell how long ago they'd dumped me here. I vaguely remembered the swaying of a stretcher and spit slapping into my cheek just before the prison door slammed shut. When I came to in the darkness, the spit was still there, dry and crusty. It was harder than it should have been to lift my arm and wipe it off.

I resisted the urge to take a deep breath, knowing the pain would bring me nearly to unconsciousness. If I lay down now, I'd never get back up. My body would become a part of the floor. Flesh to dirt, like my father. Alive one moment, gone the next.

I sat there, the debate cycling through my head over and over, when the door opened. Edyn entered carrying a solar-powered lantern. The sudden light sent a knife through my brain. I groaned and looked away, choosing to keep my arm where it was rather than shield my sight.

"Yuck," she said. "Your face is more colorful than an artist's palette."

Wanted a new look, I tried to say, but it came out as a groan.

She slammed a chair down in front of the bars, then plopped into it. "What in Hades were you thinking? Do you have a death wish or something?"

"I don't—" Pain lanced through my ribs at the effort, but I pushed through. "I don't have an obligation to most of those people. I don't care what they think."

"But insisting that our clan beat you up? Did it occur to you how arrogant that would sound?"

Black spots danced in my vision. Unconsciousness wasn't far off if I kept talking. It would be a welcome relief. "Worth a try."

"Yeah, well, here we actually have these things called laws. It's about time you listened to me, your *lawyer*. I'm trying to save your life, remember? Or do you struggle to care about the whole death-sentence thing, too?"

"If it gets me away from your shouting, then great."

"You say that, but I know better. You act like you don't care about anyone but yourself. Maybe that was true two years ago." Her voice softened. "But I thought you'd changed. Want to know what I see when I look at you?"

"Besides rugged good looks?"

"Potential." She leaned back and crossed her legs. "Wasted potential. Mills is a coward, you know. When they took me in two years ago, he barely cared about what was happening here. He was so focused on NORA and their queen—"

"Empress."

"Whatever. It was obsessive, how he focused all his energy on a civilization so far away. The settlers almost unseated him and put someone else in his place, it got so bad. But conveniently, these Asian dudes showed up and said their settlement had been destroyed and they needed a place to stay. Now they practically run the place for him, and nobody dares challenge him. Vance, you could be three times the man Mills is if you stopped doing stupid things."

"What I don't get is how he convinced so many people that I launched his blasted missile."

Edyn frowned. "Mills holds their livelihood in his hands. He's the person who assigns jobs and living quarters, if you haven't noticed. His biggest supporters get the nicest homes, the structures nearest the rim. New refugees start at the bottom and work their way up as they prove themselves helpful to his plans. So, no, they won't contradict him, even if they know he's lying."

"That's why our clan is living in mosquito-infested swampland?" I spat. "Because they're too new to be useful yet?"

"So you do care," Edyn said. "I wondered."

"Let me guess. You live near the rim because you're a *lawyer*. That's what lawyers do—use their clients' misfortunes to lift themselves higher."

"Everything I have, I've earned," she snapped as she rose out of her chair. "Just like you deserve whatever you get." She strode toward the door and began to push it open. "Oh, by the way, I saw your mom on my way here tonight. She was with Mills, hanging on his arm and laughing like he was the funniest man in the world. Just thought you'd want to know."

The door slammed shut behind her.

14

TREENA

By the third day of school, there were eight students. Many of them were the older siblings of my original students. They'd probably been sent to listen and report. I was careful to keep to the basics, as I'd promised.

On the morning of day six, Lillibeth examined my leg and then ran me through a few exercises as she did every morning. But instead of injecting it with healing boosters, she sighed. "Your leg is doing well. It will ache when you walk on it too much, but I think that may take months to go away."

"That's fine. Thanks for all your help. Then the only thing keeping me here is the debt, and I'm working hard on that."

She studied my face. "Have we treated you so horribly you can't wait to leave?"

"Of course not." She deserved a little more explanation than that, but I hesitated. "It's just that there's someone waiting for me."

"A boy. Someone you think you love."

The words stung, and I glanced away. "I have to get to him."

"Or what? Are you worried he'll find someone else?" She knelt on the floor so I'd be forced to look at her. "If you have to worry about that, then he's not the boy for you. I've seen so many young people make rash judgments after flings. They always regret those decisions later."

"If you're trying to get me to stay, I can't. I'm sorry."

Her lips pulled together in an expression of disapproval, but she nodded and gathered her supplies together. A dull metal ring shone on her finger today. I hadn't noticed it before.

"Is that your wedding band?" I asked.

She didn't look at it. "Yes. I still wear it on occasion."

I wanted to ask if she knew what had happened to her husband, but the look on her face stopped me. Instead, I asked, "Why do you wear it on your pointer finger? I thought it was tradition to wear it on the third finger."

"That's a NORA tradition. Here, the position of the ring on your hand tells everyone how serious your relationship is. Pinky means you're promised, but no further. Third finger means your intentions have been ratified by the elders, and middle finger means your contributions have been accepted and you're about to be married."

"Interesting." It explained the rings I'd seen on various fingers while living down here. "So the ring is because even though your husband is gone, you consider yourself married?"

"No body was ever found, so yes. I'm still officially married."

"But that isn't fair. What if you found someone else?"

"Since we're playing the 'what-if' game, what if my husband came home? It would make things awkward if I were married to two men."

"Yeah, but that's not likely, right? You should be allowed some happiness."

"Well, as harbinger, I have greater responsibilities than most." She stood and opened the medicine cabinet, placed her supplies carefully inside, and then closed it. The lock clicked into place. For the first time, I wondered why she locked it. There were no young children here. What if somebody needed medical attention and she wasn't around to open it?

Of course she locks it. Some medications can be dangerous. She's just being a good physician.

I stood and slipped on my boots. She watched me silently. Finally, I started to leave.

"Look, Amy," she said as I reached the door. "Forget that I'm the harbinger. Forget what Coltrane wants you to do. I just want you to *think*. You want peace, a new life, to be happy. We can give you all that."

"It's not that at all."

"But it is. You've proven yourself to be a good, decent, peaceable member of our community. Your contribution is changing minds all over the place. All you need to do is present your skills to the elders and you'll be accepted. Then the people will be forced to see you as you really are." She paused. "There are other boys here your age. Better ones."

"I need to go," I said. "It's nearly time for school to start."

She stood, frowning. "Just consider it. We'll talk later."

⸻

Today Mandie had come with more gossip about Belgium and the Nations for Peace. I gave her five minutes to recount what she'd heard, trying to focus on her words but understanding about half the references.

As she spoke, Ruby placed a glass vase on the table. Ruby had managed to fit several vines with orange flowers into it, and they cascaded beautifully down the vase.

When Mandie took a breath, I plunged in. "Thanks for the update. We're lucky you can get the all the latest news from Maxim. We'll practice writing our names again today." I held up the stick I'd been using to trace letters in the dirt floor.

"That's boring," Clara said, twisting one braid around her finger. "Everyone already knows my name. When will I ever need to write it down?"

"Well, what if you left this place? Out there, you'll need to know this stuff."

Mandie snorted. "Right. My mom won't even let me go up on my year day. She says the air is poisonous or something."

"That's ridiculous. I've lived out there my whole life. The air is bad in certain places, yes, but those areas are far away."

"Like three or five days of walking?" the younger of the boys, Calvin, asked.

I'd seen the images of war-torn Old America. Piles of bodies soaked in fuel, then lit on fire. Blackened cities and farms. Endless streets, abandoned cars resting bumper to bumper. Toxic lakes and rivers. "Like three or five months," I told him. "I don't know if you could even walk there."

"How did Old America fall?" Clara asked. "Will you tell us what happened?"

"I'm only here to teach the basics," I said with a shrug. "Your parents will tell you all about it if you ask them."

"No, they won't," Mandie said. "I even asked Maxim. Nobody will tell me anything. Please?"

I hesitated, remembering Lillibeth's warning. "If they don't want to tell you about it, then I'd better not."

"You said it yourself," Clara replied evenly. "We need to know writing in case we ever have to leave here, right? Don't you think we should know what's up there for the same reason?"

Fates. The children's faces were so eager, so interested. I looked at their older siblings, who were pretending to write words in the dirt or examining their nails, and made a decision. "I guess I can tell you a little about it. Just the history though."

"Yes!" Calvin said, settling back for a story. The older siblings perked up, and every eye in the room was on me. Even Ruby watched, though with a wary expression. She knew as well as I did that I was getting myself into trouble here.

I shoved away the dread. If their parents were upset, I'd take full responsibility. But this was the history of their forefathers. Even if I left this place tonight, at least I could leave these kids with something of worth. Mandie was right. They needed to know what had happened.

"Many years ago," I began, "there was a great war."

15

VANCE

The guards must have taken pity on me because they finally brought a physician. He muttered something about mosquitos and infection as he entered. I couldn't get my shirt off for the examination, so he sliced it open with scissors. There was a quick intake of breath as he examined my right side. It was completely purple and black. After feeling around, he ordered painkillers, healing stimulants, and what he called "proper bedding." It ended up being only an extra blanket and pillow, but it was better than nothing. Soon I was resting comfortably.

After two weeks of traveling, being forced to lie around was actually pretty nice. They gave me real food—usually dehydrated meat with rice and mashed-up vegetables on the side—and I could sleep as much as

I wanted. Problem was, I also had plenty of time to think.

For some reason, I couldn't get Edyn's words from the previous night out of my mind. *You could be three times the man Mills is.* Edyn, the girl who'd contradicted and criticized everything I'd done my entire childhood. When I thought of her, a specific memory surfaced.

I was eleven, which meant she was probably nine or ten. Mom had sent me out to the river for some clean water. The settlement's water reserve tank was high, but she didn't trust it. Sixty percent of the settlers had fallen ill in the last week, and she believed it was some kind of new bacteria in the water. As I shuffled my way along, carrying two metal pails, I grumbled about having to work all day and kicked a squirrel that didn't scurry away fast enough.

Edyn saw me do it. She put her hands on her hips like women do and glared at me. "You're a bully," she said.

I laughed at her. It sounded cruel even to me, but she'd caught me in a bad mood. "That's right. If you get in my way, I'll kick you, too."

"You'd never get the chance. I'm too fast for you."

"Right. I bet I can make it to the river and back before you even touch the water."

"You're on." She sprinted away, and I chased after her. The river was less than a quarter mile from the wall, but it was all downhill and the trail was too narrow to pass her. I mentally kicked myself for not starting first.

Edyn half slid, half ran down the hill and pulled up just short of the water. I trotted right into it a full second behind her, nearly running her over. She choked a laugh. "See? And you're older and taller than me."

"You haven't touched the water yet," I said, drawing one pail through the freezing river to fill it. "That was part of the deal."

"Don't you pretend I didn't win." She snatched the other pail out of my hand and sank it into the river, pulling it out full. "I'll tell everybody."

"They won't believe your scrawny little face."

"Whatever. They believe everything I say. You're the one who never tells the truth."

I dumped my pail of ice water over her head so fast she nearly fell over into the river. With a shuddering gasp, she stood there, fingers flayed, dripping water like a drowned cat. Then she let out a shriek that could rival a banshee. I yanked the pail out of her hand, filled it again in one swoop, and hurried up the trail.

But it was too late. Her screaming echoed across the forest. When I approached the crest, Rutner was headed down the trail. His face darkened when he saw me. "What did you do?"

"How do you know I did anything?" I muttered.

"Vance," he said with forced patience. "Where is she?"

You didn't mess around with Rutner. He was almost as intimidating as my father. "Standing by the river."

He shoved past me, but Edyn emerged from the trees and approached him like a zombie, arms out and wailing. "D-d-daddy! V-vance pushed me in!"

"I did not!" I protested.

"H-h-he did," she said with chattering teeth. "He tried to drown me because I beat him r-racing to the r-river."

"You're such a liar," I told her, but Rutner turned an icy look on me and pointed toward the settlement. I trudged away as her father removed his jacket and wrapped it around her. Then he picked her up and carried her up the hill behind me.

I forgot about the incident as soon as I walked in the door. Sick bodies lay scattered across every soft surface we owned. My parents had offered their home to the harder-hit patients since the physician himself was sick. Mom and Dad had given up their bed to three women who spent all night moaning and crying out in their sleep. I wasn't sure where my parents had slept. It looked like two more people had arrived since I left. I could see someone's feet hanging off my bed.

Mom saw me enter and took one of the pails. She noted the wetness beneath my boots. "I swear, Vance. When will you learn not to immerse yourself in the river every time you fetch water?"

"You gave away my bed."

She cupped my chin in her hand and sighed. "I know, sweetie. I'm sorry. It won't be for more than a night or two."

"Like the people in your bed were supposed to be? What about the ones on the floor?" My voice rose in volume. "You guys always do this. It's all about the settlers, not your family."

For once, my mother didn't know what to say. She let her hand drop. Her eyes were a muddy mixture of brown and gold, I recalled. They brightened in color when she was really tired. Like now. Her shoulders sagged as if she carried an invisible weight, and for the first time, I felt bad for my words.

"It is our pleasure to serve," Father's voice said from the other room. He turned the corner and stepped into view, brushing his hands clean. "The clan *is* our family. We're all on the same team. If we can help these people fight their illness, everyone will benefit."

I glanced again at the stranger in my bed. "Not everyone."

"Vance." Father bent down until we could see eye to eye. "This settlement is a refuge, a place where people can find peace and happiness. We're the lucky ones who get to serve them."

I didn't understand, but I was suddenly tired of the conversation. "I know. Sorry, Dad."

"Someday you'll understand." He put a massive hand on my shoulder and squeezed it. "In the meantime, I need your help. I'd like you to stop thinking about yourself for a few minutes and help us save lives. Can you do it?"

"Yeah."

"What was that?" he prompted.

"Yes, *sir.*"

Someone knocked on the door as I followed my father around the corner. Another sick person, most likely. An entire family sat propped against the wall, all pale and weak. It was the Ashby family. They had a dog named Clyde they let me play with sometimes— worthless for hunting but fun to chase around.

"Go find another blanket," he told me. "They're in the chills stage."

"There aren't any left."

"Go to the next wing and ask if they have any to spare."

"Yes, sir."

The front door was open. Mom was speaking with someone with her arms folded. I slowed and stopped. It was Edyn's mother.

". . . sure he didn't realize how cold the water was," my mother was saying. "Kids do stupid things sometimes."

"She could catch this dreadful illness!" the woman said. "If she breaks out in chills and fever, I'll be extremely upset."

"Simply being cold doesn't make one ill," my mother began. "It has to be bacteria or a virus—"

"Don't start. I expect that you'll take care of this and make sure it never happens again." Her statement rose like a question.

"Of course."

The door closed, and my mother turned around. She didn't look surprised to see me there. But the weight that pressed her down into the earth seemed even heavier. Her thin legs were barely able to hold her frail weight.

"I didn't push Edyn in," I insisted. "I only threw some water at her. She's just trying to get me into trouble."

Mom shook her head. "Edyn's mother and I were best of friends once, you know."

I kept silent. I had a feeling this wasn't about me anymore.

"When I had a son, and she had a daughter, I assumed it was meant to be," she continued. Mom reached out and smoothed my hair. "Neither of us expected to have such spirited children. It will be interesting to see how this plays out. I think the two of you will have many grand adventures together."

"With Edyn?" I said with a snicker. "I can't stand her."

She looked down at my wet boots, her lips pressed tight. I'd forgotten to take them off and braced myself for another lecture.

Instead, she turned and walked away.

16

TREENA

When I arrived at Ruby's for school the next day, I half expected my students not to show up. Surely they'd told their parents about my forbidden history lesson. Any minute now, Lillibeth would come charging in and demand that the school be shut down. But when I walked in, my students were already seated—every single one. There were several more, actually. Some of the older kids had brought their friends, and smiling children covered the walls of Ruby's dwelling, sitting wherever they could find an empty spot on the floor. We wouldn't fit in here much longer.

It's only a matter of time before they tell on you, I reminded myself as I greeted the kids. But until then, I would answer their questions honestly. They deserved that much, and I couldn't think of a better contribution in this place than that.

A few minutes later, Mandie was having her say about a bombing in Tokyo when Coltrane ran in. His eyes were wide, and he gasped for air. "We're under lockdown," he managed. "We need to get all the kids home right now."

The children gasped, and then there was mayhem. Older children reached for their younger siblings, all shouting and scrambling for the doorway.

"Lockdown?" I repeated dumbly. "What happened?"

"A helicopter."

"Choppers fly over us all the time," Ruby said, waving good-bye to Clara. "Shouldn't be a cause for concern."

"This one landed right above us," Coltrane said. "They're searching the ground. They seem to be focused on the abandoned town, right by the north exit."

Searching the ground.

Ruby swore under her breath. "Children, hurry, it's time to run home. Leave your belongings."

"Ruby!" Mandie exclaimed. "You said a bad word."

They were looking for me. I knew it then as clear as if Coltrane had said exactly that. NORA was on my trail.

And I'd led them straight here.

"Amy!" Coltrane said sharply.

"What?"

"I said I'll help Mandie get home. Can you find your way back by yourself?"

You've killed us all.

Everywhere I went, people got hurt. That was why I needed to leave this place. There had to be somewhere in the world I could go without endangering anybody. At that moment, all I wanted was Vance. I wanted to bury my face in his shoulder and have him tell me everything was all right. I wanted him to say it wasn't my fault, any of it, and tell me I wasn't alone.

It was time to leave.

"Yes," I finally said, and I realized that the decision was made. "I can get there just fine."

17

TREENA

I wandered several minutes before realizing that I had no idea where the exits were. We'd traversed every quadrant, some several times, but he'd never actually shown me how to get out. Remembering a previous conversation about the abandoned town being near the north exit, I kept heading straight toward the northern quadrant. It took almost half an hour to find it, but there it was.

A metal door like the one that guarded the defense lab loomed ahead, but someone was in the way. He sat with his leg extended across the door, the other leg bent at the knee, and his head tilted back as if asleep. Great. A guard.

I stepped forward, hoping he'd be asleep. But the moment I reached the door, he looked up. "Turn around and go back or you'll regret it." With a start, I realized it was a woman. She had short dark hair and broad shoulders, but her facial features were definitely feminine. She couldn't have been more than thirty years old.

"I'm Amy," I said.

"Violet," she said in a bored tone. "And, no, I'm not letting you out. I know exactly who you are."

Cursed numbers. Why hadn't I removed my implant? I decided to ditch the formalities and come straight to the point. "NORA is looking for me. If I don't go out and meet them, they may find your exit."

"If you come climbing out of our exit, then they'll definitely find it, don't you think?"

"Well, I won't do it while they're looking. I'm not stupid."

"You must be if you think I'll believe your lies." She pulled her legs in and stood, towering over me. "This door leads to a tube that goes upward. You climb the rungs and open the hatch overhead to get out. A girl climbing out of that would bring them onto us faster than a hummingbird's wings."

"I'll find a way," I said stubbornly.

"You'll stay right here and go down with us. Should've thought of that before you became a spy."

I wanted to punch the girl in her pretty nose, but that would only hurt my case. "If I was a spy, why would they be tracking me? Besides, there's only one helicopter out there. If they knew you were here, they would have brought the entire fleet."

"Okay, tell you what." She folded her arms. "I'm going to call Lillibeth. She'll send guards to take you away. But first, tell me you've never been trained by the military."

I shifted my weight from one foot to the other. "That's not a very accurate measure of loyalty. I'm here in peace."

"Then tell me this. Have you ever killed someone?"

You've killed us all.

Tali. Vallorah. A palace guard. Hundreds of people I didn't even know, citizens who were willing to risk their comfort and safety for change. They haunted my dreams, and now, here in the present, they held me in a tight grip. It was almost as if someone choked the breath out of me as I squeaked an answer. "Yes."

I had expected Violet to leap into action then, or at least try to arrest me. But instead her expression softened. "Me too, before I came here. I could tell. You have that look." She removed a radio from her belt and dialed. "Lillibeth? I have your guest right here. She says she wants to leave."

There was static, and then a voice responded. "Sending someone right away. Keep her there, no matter what. Do not let her open that door."

"Copy that." She clipped the radio back on and folded her arms again.

"I don't want to fight you," I said, feeling the desperation build. "But I have to get out there and stop them before it's too late."

"I'm afraid that's not an option. You can try to get past me, but that will only get you thrown into a cell. You're not the only one with training."

I looked at the door again, then at Violet. "I care about these people."

"So do I. Sorry, but you'll have to take it up with the elders. Or Lillibeth, although you'd have better luck reasoning with a viper."

I sat on the floor and leaned my head back against the wall as I'd seen her do, my mind racing. There were probably guards at all the exits, especially right now. How would I get permission to leave? The elders, with the exception of Ruby, would all jump to the same conclusions Violet had. And Lillibeth wasn't being very helpful.

Minutes later I heard footsteps coming down the tunnel. I stood, ready to argue, but then Coltrane turned the corner. He jogged toward us, holding a baglight. "Amy! They're gone. The chopper is gone." He reached me and pulled me in for a hug. Stunned, I stood there for a second and then pulled away. Coltrane's face was radiant. "They got in and left, and now we're safe. Come back with me."

Relief flooded my body. "We got lucky this time, but I still have to leave. They're looking for me, Coltrane."

"Don't be ridiculous. Why would they do that?" He waved to Violet, who simply stared after us, motionless, and then we headed down the tunnel again.

"I have to talk to your mom," I said.

"The community is still under lockdown, so she's busy right now, but she'll be back tonight. May as well come back and wait, then we'll clear all this up."

But as we walked back to the dwelling, there were several things I knew for sure.

First, these people were in danger as long as I was here. If NORA was desperate enough to send a chopper after me, they wouldn't stop looking until I was found. Second, I was a prisoner. There were likely guards at each exit, and now they'd be watching for me. Third, I needed supplies. Lillibeth was the one person who could change all that, and she was about to get an earful from me.

Time to go where I could never hurt anyone else again.

18

VANCE

Three days later my mother still hadn't shown up. I'd have some serious words with her when she did come. The thought of my mom dating again was bad enough. But of all the men in this settlement, she'd chosen that snake, Mills.

I'd almost prefer Ju-Long. At least he did his own fighting.

Near the end of the third day Mills and Ju-Long came by, bringing no less than a half dozen guards with them. Anton was among them. His usual loose T-shirt had been replaced with a dark gray guard uniform. Of course he'd sold us out the moment he got here. And somehow *I* was the traitor.

Mills stopped and examined me as I lay on my bed, one pillow supporting my injured side, cleaning dirt out from beneath my fingernails. "Stand up, Hawking. Or do you need to be carried like a sleepy toddler?"

"Kinda busy here," I said. "Make an appointment with my secretary outside."

Ju-Long clicked the lock and swung the door open. "You are being relocated. Grab whatever belongings you need and follow us immediately."

A guard grabbed my arm and yanked me to my feet. I shoved him away, holding back the gasp that threatened to escape as the pain hit. The other guards stepped forward. Most had the same Asian features as Ju-Long.

"My new place better be near the rim," I said through clenched teeth. "I always did like a good view."

"Oh, I wouldn't worry about the view," Mills said. "Cuff him, then surround him on all sides. Let's show the boy his new home."

It was basically a bird cage situated on the shore of the swampy lake—square at the bottom but tapered at the top. Shaped to fit a head and shoulders and not much else. It looked like a medieval torture device.

"Home sweet home," Anton said in a singsong voice.

I stared at it, then at Mills. "You've got to be kidding."

"Keeping you hidden away is no longer in our best interest," Mills said. "The people want to see you, to confirm in their minds that you are indeed the violent, bloodthirsty man they imagine."

"That idea certainly fits your agenda." My mottled face and bandages wouldn't help much. "And your assembly approved this."

"Our laws require you to be locked up, but they don't say where. The assembly cannot object." He smiled triumphantly. The guy had probably discovered that loophole in the law this morning. "You represent so much, young Hawking. This is far beyond you and your crimes. This cage is small, its metal bars tight and thinly spaced, you'll notice. But it is enough to contain even you. We are greater than any force that presumes to remove our freedom."

"I'm trying to take your freedom now?" I said. "That's a new one."

Ju-Long shoved me in. As I turned around to face him, he locked the door. I immediately saw why it had been shaped that way. It would be almost impossible to lie down. I'd have to curl up like a dog and sleep in a ball or simply sleep sitting up.

Neither way was physician-approved. I suspected that my painkillers and healing stimulants had come to an end as well.

"It's escape-proof, so don't even try," Anton said. "I designed it myself. Nothing but the best for my pal Vance."

"Nielsen," Mills said. "You stay behind. You'll be relieved at midnight."

"Yes, sir," Nielsen said.

"I'm happy to take the first shift, sir," Anton said.

Mills whirled on him. "I know you brought Hawking here, soldier, but that doesn't make you special. I will choose who I see fit, and that's the end of it. Understood?"

"Yes, sir." Anton's face went red.

Nielsen stood rigidly as the others left, including Anton. As soon as the group had climbed back up the trail, he let his stance relax. He pulled the front of his shirt up and over his nose, probably to filter the smell.

"Take a deep breath," I told him. "It's just you, me, and the swamp now. At least until people realize I'm here and close in for the kill."

He didn't answer, but the stiffness in his shoulders said he'd heard.

It wasn't as busy out here as I'd expected. People walked by occasionally, but they didn't stop to gawk. They seemed uncomfortable with my presence, actually. I caught a glimpse of the iron-belt symbol painted on a couple of makeshift tents. Cattle and goat droppings filled the road, and I saw the muddy figures of grazing sheep not far off. There were no fences between the humans and the animals. Soon curious heads peeked out of the makeshift shelters along the trail. Children.

One of them emerged from a shelter, looked both ways, then approached with a confident air. He was probably about five, with shaggy brown hair and no shoes. He held an open water packet in his hand. "Are you the terrorist?" he asked.

"Nope," I said, holding back a smile. "That would be Mills."

"Hold your tongue, Hawking," the guard snapped.

"Or what?" I asked. "It was so kind of Mills to move me here. It's almost as if he was begging me to tell people the truth. Don't you agree?"

The guard turned to look at the boy, then turned away, muttering, "They won't believe you anyway."

The boy came closer and handed me his water packet. There wasn't much left. I nearly refused it, but he grinned and sat cross-legged in front of my cage. I took a swig, noting that his feet were black from dirt.

The boy examined the bruises on my face. "My brother says you're a good fighter, but I saw some people beat you up. I don't think you're that good."

I choked and nearly spit the water back out. "That's because I didn't fight. I gave them permission to hit me." Twenty-two men and seven women had taken me up on it. At least that's what I remembered. Their angry expressions as they approached had gradually turned to guilt and disgust when they'd left me on the ground.

"Why?" the boy asked with wide eyes.

"Because I hurt them, so it was their turn to hurt me back."

"So now it's your turn again?"

I chuckled. Two more children made their way over, stepping with care as they watched me warily. "Nah, I don't want anybody to be hurt."

"They hurt me sometimes," the boy said. "When I knock on their door to ask for food."

"Who does?"

"The people with nice clothes. They hit my face and tell me to go back where I came from. But my mom says we can't go back because we have nowhere else to go."

I studied the boy. There was something familiar about him, but I couldn't place what. "Is your mother around?"

"She works in the water plant." He pointed to a massive building on the other side of the swamp. "My mom doesn't come back until nighttime."

"My mom watches him," a girl said. When I turned to her, she blushed but plunged on. "Mom says that if we came from somewhere else we'd be fine, but since we came from Iron Belt's clan, we're the feeted."

I gave her a sideways look. "The feeted?"

"You know. When somebody loses?"

"Ah." Defeated. I gritted my teeth and let my gaze sweep over the shelters lining the lake. The assembly and Mills pretended to have a grip on things here, but it was obvious they hadn't known what to do with so many new refugees. It wasn't that there were no resources, either. Some of the structures near the rim were a decent size.

The children moved aside for a group of men coming home from work. They were covered in black grime from their boots to their ears, and they muttered good-bye to each other as the road split off. One guy, his blackened face giving his white eyes an eerie look, glared at me. He whispered something to the man next to him. Great. This was exactly what Mills had hoped for—he'd placed a rabbit in a den of foxes.

"Time to go," I told the kids. "Thanks for the water, but run home now."

The children fought over the empty water pouch as they ran across the trail, cutting off the group returning from work. I straightened as the men approached. The cage would make defending myself difficult but not impossible.

The two men gave me a respectful nod and continued on their way.

I watched them go. Was it possible they considered my debt paid? Edyn hadn't thought so, but maybe my clan did. Even in this strange new place, our clan followed the old laws. We always would.

Rutner should've known better. This was no refuge. This was slavery in its truest form. If people here thought we were defeated because we'd come from NORA, they were dead wrong. We'd been scattered for a while, but we were back now, stronger and angrier than ever. You couldn't take everything away from a person without changing him forever.

I could see it now. The way my people moved— they weren't defeated at all. They were determined. Not beaten but biding their time. Waiting. Sure, there were a few sell-outs like Anton and Rutner, but for the most part, our clan was as proud as ever.

I watched the shaggy-haired boy disappear into the shelter with his friends. The trial was a sham. I already knew what the outcome would be. But I wasn't gone yet.

Maybe it wasn't too late to do something about it.

19

VANCE

I still think you're lying about that buck," Anton grumbled.

We were fifteen. Our parents had been letting us hunt alone for about two years. We knelt behind some forest brush with our rifles, facing each other, neither willing to be the first to scratch our legs where the itchy plants met flesh. It was a no-scratching contest, a game we'd played since childhood. That night I would go home and scratch every inch of my body, but for now, I couldn't yield and admit defeat.

"You saw the buck yourself. You even ate some of it," I said, keeping my hands clasped together so I wouldn't accidentally lose the game.

"Oh, I believe that a buck existed. I just don't think you're the one who shot it."

"Just ask my dad." That day was the reason my father allowed us to go on hunting expeditions alone. It was the first time my dad decided I was worthy of his trust.

"Your dad would agree just to protect your reputation. He doesn't want you to look bad."

I snorted. "You don't know my dad very well. He punishes me for every little thing."

"See, now you're lying again. I've seen what he does. He just tilts his head, like this, and taps his foot. Then he says, 'We'll talk about this later.' My dad pulls out his belt and takes care of business right then and there."

"Just because Dad won't discipline in public doesn't mean he avoids it." I didn't mention that my father had never struck me in that way. He was a strange paradox, a fighter who refused to fight. "Speaking of fathers, why did your dad take so long to agree to this trip? He didn't want to hand over his gun again?"

Anton's smile faded. "It's not that he doesn't trust me with his rifle. It's just—it's nothing."

"No, really. What did he say?"

"Forget about it."

"Because he's afraid you'll get eaten by a bear."

"You're such an idiot."

"Mountain lion? Or maybe a vulture."

"He was punishing me, all right?" He rocked back and sat on the rocky ground, stretching his feet out in front of him. Shoots of brown grass extended between his legs. "Last time we went out, I almost shot my mom. She was coming toward us, all quiet. I aimed at her thinking she was a deer."

"Your mom isn't *that* ugly."

"It's not funny!"

"Okay, okay. I'm just glad you didn't shoot her."

Anton set his dad's rifle against a tree and stretched. "Yeah, so am I. Dad shoved the barrel just in time, and I shot a tree instead. Then he took his belt to me and my mom both."

"So you're saying I shouldn't walk in front of you while you're holding that thing."

Anton let out a frustrated breath. "I shouldn't have told you."

"Well," I said, "now I know why my dad insists on the trigger sequence. I just thought he was being paranoid." Anton's frown deepened, and I sobered. "Just forget it. I'm pretty sure the rabbit is still in there. If we hurry, we can cook him up out here so we don't have to share."

"Some chief's son you are," Anton said, but he settled down on his knees again, looking down his rifle toward the bush. He absently scratched at an itch on his nose. I chose not to point it out.

I liked everything about the hunting—the thrill of catching sight of prey, the chase, and that one chance to make your shot count. But I hated the dead time in between. The waiting made me restless and irritable. We'd been tracking this animal for several hours now. Definitely too long for a rabbit that would only feed three people.

Suddenly Anton stiffened. "Did you see that?"

I lifted my rifle and looked down the barrel, ignoring the scope. I never used it. Nothing moved. "Did it run out?"

"Nah, it's still there. I saw some brown. Maybe it's testing us."

"Rabbits aren't smart enough for that."

"Shh . . . I'm concentrating."

"Trigger sequence," I reminded him. "No shooting until you call it first."

He rolled his eyes. "Ready," he whispered.

"Set," I said.

"Go." He paused for a second, then pulled the trigger. The rifle bucked against his shoulder, emitting a powerful blast. He leaped to his feet and yelped. "Yes!"

I didn't see anything, but I chuckled. Anton had never hit anything before, but you'd think he had taken down a grizzly.

He leaped through the brush and headed toward his kill.

"Be careful," I said. "It may not be dead."

"Oh, it's dead. And it's no rabbit. Check this out, Vance. It's got to be a buck!" He trotted toward a lump on the ground. I followed him, rifle up and ready, safety on.

He was right. Whatever he had shot was much, much larger than a rabbit. The brownish lump lay still on the forest floor.

"Oh no." He knelt next to it. "Don't tell me."

"A doe," I said.

He put a hand on the body. It had been a clean shot, right through the heart. A quick death. If it had been a buck, Anton would be hailed as a hero for the shot. But there was one animal that was off limits in the forest, and that was the doe. The recent deer shortage had the circle worried, and they'd decided last year to implement restrictions about what we could bring home.

Something else moved in the brush, and I raised my rifle, but Anton just shook his head. "A fawn. I saw it behind that tree." He kicked a tree branch, sending it sailing over a rock. "My dad'll never let me hunt again."

"We can leave it here," I suggested.

"Nah. The others will find it and figure out what happened. Besides, as bad as this is, wasting the meat would be worse."

I nodded. He'd echoed my thoughts exactly.

Anton sighed. "Well, may as well get it over with. Give me a hand, will you?"

I helped him lift it over his shoulders, the head flopping lifelessly to his right side. He gathered the legs in front of him and nodded to his rifle. "Carry that for me."

"Will do."

An hour later we pushed through the gates and into the settlement. Anton stumbled along behind me, exhausted and angry, deer blood dripping down the back of his shirt and matting his hair. The settlers who walked by brightened at the sight of fresh meat, but the older ones narrowed their eyes when they looked closely at Anton's kill.

When we reached the wing of the lodge where Anton lived, we had a crowd following us. Some just wanted the meat, but I knew others wanted to see what his dad would do when he found out what Anton had done.

"Let's take it to my place," I said.

"I'll get punished harder if I don't show him now," Anton said.

"What's going on?" his father's voice said, and he shoved the door open. Anton's dad, Jaxon Beck, was one of our best hunters. His face was browned and heavily lined from years of squinting in the sun. His eyes lit up with pride when he saw Anton's kill, and then his smile froze.

"It's a doe," Anton said quickly. "I didn't—"

"He didn't do it," I jumped in. "It was me. I didn't get a good look before I shot it, sir. I'm afraid to tell my parents."

Anton's father folded his muscled arms and looked me squarely in the face. "You will go home right now and tell the chief exactly what happened. There's only one thing I hate more than lying, and that's fear."

"Yes, sir."

Anton gaped at me. "But—"

"Don't try to defend me," I told him. "I appreciate it, but your dad's right. I'd better go face the consequences. I'll see you later."

Anton looked at his father, then swallowed. "Um, I'll hold on to the doe for you."

"One thing's for sure," his father said as I walked away. "Vance won't be getting an inch of that meat. Probably no dinner at all, if I know ol' Seb."

He was right, but that would only be the beginning. My dad would be furious. I'd never shot something before I knew what it was, not even when I was young. We just didn't do that. He would probably set me to work chopping wood or washing dishes in addition to the lack of dinner. He couldn't have his own son undermining the settlement's laws. In this instance, he had to be clan chief *and* a father.

Somehow it didn't matter as I made my way home. Anton was free to hunt again, and his untarnished reputation would continue to follow him around. He cared what people thought of him. I didn't.

As I sat there in my bird cage nearly five years later, I realized we were both paying for it in our own way.

20

TREENA

We need to talk," I said the moment Lillibeth stepped in.

She looked up, and I then felt bad for sounding so demanding. The woman looked as if she'd aged ten years today. Her eyes were pinched and haunted, her shoulders hunched. But then her expression hardened, and my defenses instantly went up again.

"You're absolutely right," she said. "Coltrane, go check inventory on our emergency supplies."

"I did that last week."

"Do it again. Can't be too careful."

"But, Mom—" he began, looking at me helplessly.

"*Go.*"

Shaking his head, Coltrane pushed the curtain aside and left. If a door had been there, he probably would have slammed it behind him. It couldn't be easy, growing up with this woman.

"Since when am I a prisoner here?" I snapped. "There was nothing in our agreement about me not being able to leave."

Lillibeth straightened, her eyes flashing dangerously. "You're subject to our laws, girl. Nobody leaves without permission from me or the elders. Even our own members are restricted to an outside visit but once a year, and that's under cover of darkness. You tried to walk out an exit in broad daylight during lockdown! With NORA soldiers swarming the desert above us, for stars' sake. What were you thinking?"

"I was trying to keep you safe!" My voice had risen to a shout now, but I didn't stop. "They're looking for *me*. I thought once they found me they'd leave your people alone."

"And you'd appear out of thin air, well fed and clothed, and they wouldn't question that." She nearly spat the words. "Stupid girl. You would have killed us all."

"I would never betray you." I raised my arms, then let them fall to my sides. "I'm not the type of person who would do that. Why won't anyone believe me?"

That hard glint entered her eyes again. "You're a digit. You'd sacrifice every one of us if it meant getting what you want."

"I—" It wasn't true. It wasn't. "If you only knew who I am, you'd let me go. My real name is Ametr—"

"Don't tell me!"

Her scream echoed in the small dwelling, and I expected people to come running any moment. "But that first day, you asked who I really was."

"I've changed my mind. The less I know, the better."

I practically laughed. "With NORA hovering over the exit? You're the harbinger, Lillibeth. We don't have time to argue about this."

"No," she said quietly. "We don't."

"So you'll let me go?"

"No, but I'd like to make an agreement. One that will benefit us both." She sat on my bed and patted it. "Come. Let's discuss this like adults."

I wanted to tell her that she was the one screaming, but I figured that might not be the wisest course of action. I sat as far from her as was physically possible. "I'm listening."

"Your options are limited with no supplies. You can leave and die in the desert, or you can leave and get captured by NORA. Neither one gets you wherever it is you were headed."

She was right, but I forced myself to remain silent.

"Or," she continued, "you can stay here for another day. Just through tomorrow night. Our exit was never discovered, and the helicopter left. The lockdown will lift, and life here will resume as normal. Oh, we'll double the guard and keep watch on the sentinel around the clock, but for the most part, the danger is over for now. Tomorrow night is our yearly community social. I'd like for you to attend. After that, if you still insist on leaving, I'll withdraw the guard and allow you to sneak out the south exit after dark. You'll 'steal' one pack of our emergency supplies for your journey. It will only last you a week, but it will have to suffice. Do we have a deal?"

I stared at her. "You're asking me to—to go to a party? But why?"

She stared at the ground. "It will be an important night for Coltrane. He's presenting his project to the elders, and I know he'll be crushed if you aren't there. My son means everything to me."

This conversation had taken such a strange turn I didn't even know what to say. "Fair enough."

"The last condition, however, is silence. You never tried to leave, and you have no idea what the helicopter was looking for. This conversation never happened. Do you understand?"

Something was wrong here. She wanted me to lie, to cover up the truth. Was this woman really asking me to put her community in danger for the sake of her son's party? "I get it," I said. "You don't want your people to know that we put them in danger. If they find out who I really am, they'll be livid."

"My reasons are my own. Do you agree to my terms or not?"

What other option do I have? If I didn't go along with this, I'd never get out of here and NORA would keep searching. Eventually they'd find us here. Maybe this really was the easiest way to protect the people. And if I could avoid NORA scouting planes, there was a chance I could still get to Vance. Everyone would get what they wanted.

I pushed away my doubts and nodded. "Deal."

"And by the way," she said, "I heard about your history lesson. You will teach only approved subjects tomorrow, or our deal is off. Surely you can heed my advice for one day."

I thought of Mandie. Who would answer her questions when I left? Maybe Ruby would continue their lessons in my absence. But I discarded that thought immediately. She'd never participated in our lessons. As an elder, she probably wasn't allowed. When I left, that would be it.

"Fine," I said, letting the guilt sweep over me. I was betraying those kids twice over. "One day."

I scowled at my reflection in the mirror. This was just not going to work.

The dress Lillibeth had loaned me was ten centimeters too long and—well, poufy. Everywhere. It was like carrying my bed around with me. Thick, striped, navy-blue fabric covered every centimeter of my body except my face and fingertips. Instead of coming in at the waist, it draped.

"I am not wearing this," I said.

"Oh, you look fine," Lillibeth said from behind me. She wore a green dress with a similar cut, only it looked somewhat normal on her. She had released her black hair from its braid, and it fell in gentle waves down to her waist. She came up behind me and reached up to touch my hair. I recoiled.

"Are you leaving your hair like that?" she asked in a casual tone, but I could sense irritation in her voice.

"I'm not trying to impress anyone."

"Well, I'd prefer if you didn't embarrass us, either." She held out the brush.

I took it and ran it through my hair. It caught. Maybe it had been too long since I ran a comb through it. I began brushing more vigorously. When I was finished, Lillibeth began pinning my hair up, twisting and then piling it at the top of my head.

She was nearly done when someone clapped their hands outside the doorway.

"Enter," Lillibeth said, pinning up the last wayward piece of hair.

Coltrane pushed the cloth aside and walked in. He wore a white, collared shirt and dark pants with a blue vest. How he'd gotten his clothes so clean in a dirt-filled cavern was beyond me. The thing that made my breath catch was the bouquet of wildflowers he held toward me.

For the second time in two days, I took the flowers and murmured a thank-you. These settlers had strange customs, but I could definitely get used to this one. "What are these for?"

"Beautiful girls deserve beautiful flowers," Coltrane said. "I think they're the same kind Ruby gave you." His voice was nonchalant, but his flaming cheeks gave him away.

I expected Lillibeth to snap at him for sneaking above to retrieve flowers, but she watched her son with a strange, secretive smile. Coltrane met her gaze and grinned back.

"What should I do with these?" I asked, holding them awkwardly. "I don't have to carry them around all night, right?"

"Oh, no," Lillibeth said quickly, reaching out. "Here, I'll take them. They'll look great in the front room."

"Wait," Coltrane said. He plucked an orange flower off the vine and tucked it into my hair. His eyes sparkled when he stepped away. "Perfect."

I looked myself up and down. "Perfect? I look like a swamp monster. This dress doesn't even come close to fitting."

"It may be a bit big for you, but it works. I mean, it covers everything that needs to be—stars. I'm going to shut up now."

I couldn't help but laugh. "I think that would be wise."

"Shall we go?"

I looked wistfully at my usual clothing, wadded up on the floor. Even a blanket wrapped around me would look better than this dress. But it didn't matter what I wore. By this time tomorrow I'd be getting ready to leave. This would be a good opportunity to say good-bye—even though nobody but Lillibeth knew my plans.

"Have fun, you two," Lillibeth said as we left. "I'll be right behind you."

21

VANCE

As it grew dark, traffic on the trail increased, but I was sick of watching. My neck and shoulders were sore from sitting straight, so I resolved to find a more comfortable position. My sore ribs refused to cooperate, but eventually I found that sinking to the bottom of the cage with my knees bent allowed me to adjust which bars held the weight of my back, which I rotated often. I hadn't grabbed a blanket from the jail. I regretted that now.

The sky from here was actually quite striking. The shaded bowl created an interesting effect, and the sun's last rays streaked across the sky in oranges and reds. Then they disappeared altogether, replaced by a uniform blue and finally black. It reminded me of lazy nights in the mountains with my parents, sitting around at sunset and discussing the day's events. It was a lifetime ago.

Maybe Mills was the reason my mom wouldn't come to visit. If he'd somehow convinced her that I really was the murderer he wanted everyone to believe—no, that wasn't possible. A lot could happen in two years, but she knew I wasn't a murderer. I thought of the way she'd nodded to me, giving her approval for our clan to take justice into their hands. Any other mother would have screamed and stood in the way, making excuses and pleading. But my mom had never been that way. She was too much like my father. She did what needed to be done.

I swatted absently at another mosquito, knowing as I did that it was useless. They were even worse down here than at the jail. My arms and face were already covered with bites. If I survived angry assassins, the mosquitos would get me for sure.

A couple walked by in the darkness, arms wrapped around each other's waists in a comfortable way. One of them stopped, and I heard a woman's whispered voice. Then she took the man's hand and dragged him over to my cage.

"See?" she exclaimed. "I told you."

"Welcome to the zoo," I said. "And you are . . . ?"

"Madilan. This is Carver." She pulled him the rest of the way, then he planted his feet and refused to come any closer.

I could make out a shorter man with facial hair. He shuffled his weight from one foot to another before he spoke. "Why'd they put you in a cage?"

"What kind of question is that?" Madilan asked. "I'm sorry, Vance, but he's nervous. We stopped by the jail yesterday trying to speak to you, but the guard wouldn't let us in."

A soft snore from my "guard" told me he was long gone. I turned back to the couple. "Well, my schedule is clear at the moment."

"You're younger than I thought you were," Carver muttered.

"I doubt you came to discuss my age," I said. "May want to get to the point before my secretary here wakes up."

"Your age doesn't matter," Madilan said. "Not really. See, the thing is, your father was about to do a wedding blessing for us when NORA attacked. But then we got separated, and we just barely found each other again, and I can't let anything split us up, and we just—" She looked up again, and the man nodded for her to continue. "Well, your father's gone now, and they don't perform the blessing here."

"They do a ceremony," Carver said, "but it's different. Just doesn't feel right when they say all the wrong words."

"Anyway," Madilan said, "we wondered if you would do it for us since you're Iron Belt's son."

I stared at her. "You want me to *marry* you."

"It sounds kind of ridiculous, I know," Carver said. "But we've discussed it, and there's nobody else we'd rather have do it. Despite what you did to land here, we respect your parents. It's right that you should do it in Iron Belt's place."

"What about Rutner?" I asked.

They looked at each other. Madilan spoke carefully. "Rutner is a good man, but he's busy."

"He's moved up top," Carver said bitterly.

"Sorry to disappoint you," I said. "But I'm not the clan chief. Nothing I say means anything."

"It means more than a settlement ceremony would," Madilan said. "Please. I know it's a lot to ask. But to us, you're still the next in line. Our marriage will never feel official until it's done right."

I remembered the blessing. I'd seen my father perform it dozens of times. He always wore his best shirt, the kind with buttons, and scrubbed his boots right beforehand. If these people were desperate enough to approach a beaten criminal in a cage wearing an unwashed, stained shirt and holey socks, the least I could do was go along with it.

"Fine. I'll do it."

"Thank you," Carver said with a smile in his voice. "I'll get a few witnesses. Just a second." He trotted away, then returned with three other adults, two women and a man. They positioned themselves behind the couple with big smiles.

Carver turned back to me and nodded.

I motioned for the couple to kneel. They did so, positioning themselves as close to the bars as they could. I put one hand on each of their shoulders as I'd seen my father do.

A memory of him pronouncing his blessing, his voice deep and powerful as he declared their love and commitment as official in the eyes of the clan, gave me a lump in my throat.

I swallowed it down and began.

22

TREENA

As we walked to the lab, we saw dozens of couples shuffling along with us. They wore similar clothing, although the women's dresses fit them much better than mine. I caught a glimpse of several rings on varying fingers. The shocking thing was how young some of the couples were. They held hands as they walked, looking comfortable and happy in each others' presence. A guy with light brown skin and black hair spoke to the girl on his arm, and she said something back, her words running together in a torrent of indistinguishable words. Spanish, if I remembered correctly. Integrants in NORA were required to learn English before they received their Rating, although I'd heard other languages whispered in corners. But this couple seemed completely content to let themselves be heard. It was beautiful.

I broke out in an instant sweat the moment we stepped inside the sweltering lab. It was hard to believe it was the same room I'd seen before. Instead of tables and lines of inventions, there were people. There was barely room for a few chairs along one wall. A few boxes stood stacked in the far corner, the only evidence of this room's usual purpose.

Music caught my attention. I stood on my tiptoes to follow it; it came from the back wall. I instantly recognized Mandie. She and her mother—Irina, I thought her name was—each held what looked like a shapely wooden contraption on one shoulder and an odd stick in the other hand. They ran the stick over the strings of the wooden instruments. Violins. A plain word for such an angelic sound.

I floated toward them, mesmerized. When I reached the corner, Mandie smiled at me. Her arm moved the stick back and forth with incredible grace. Her music soared like a bird taking flight, wavered a little, climbed still higher, and then plunged to a dramatic end just as her mother's song rose again, in perfect harmony. I felt myself moving, swaying with the tune.

"You like this song?" Coltrane said beside me. He watched me with a soft smile, warmth filling his gaze.

"It's incredible," I said. "I've never heard anything like it."

"It's not her fault," Ruby said from behind us. "They don't have music in NORA."

I whirled to face her. She wore a brilliant, sparkling silver uniform dress. It caught the liquid lantern glow, sending it a thousand different directions. Several stripes lined one arm.

A uniform dress. Old-fashioned in cut and style but definitely NORA-made.

I had stood in front of a mirror just weeks ago, gazing at my own sequin-lined uniform dress. I'd clung to the fabric as I shivered, convincing myself that it was the cool night air and not nervousness. Convincing myself that what I was about to do was right.

Don't think about that.

"What do you mean, NORA doesn't have music?" Coltrane asked. "Every civilization has music. It's hardwired into our DNA."

"Let me clarify," Ruby said. She didn't notice me staring at her dress. "NORA has *songs*. But with each generation, the usefulness of music in general has faded a little more. You see, in NORA, the 'harder' subjects and skills receive more points, like science and mathematics. And athletics, for some reason. But passions like art and music? They don't directly contribute to society, so they practically don't exist."

She turned to me. "At least that's the direction it was headed when I left. Would you agree, dear Amy?"

"Hmm?" I pulled myself out of my thoughts and watched Mandie take a bow. The song had ended. "That was amazing, wasn't it? I had no idea she could play like that."

"Maybe you can take lessons from her," Coltrane suggested. "Although you may have to trade for your own violin. I doubt her mom will let you touch either of theirs. She doesn't seem to like you much."

"Right." I grimaced at the look Mandie's mother gave me from across the room, as if she expected me to raise the fires of hell at any moment.

Ruby just smiled. "I remember that feeling, the first time I heard a violin. It was like falling in love."

Coltrane turned to her in surprise. "You've been in love?"

"Of course."

"You were married?" he asked. "I didn't know that."

"I didn't say I married him," Ruby said. "Although we probably would have married if . . ." Her voice trailed off as the violins began again.

"If you hadn't left," I finished for her.

Ruby bit her lip and looked away. It was a strange reaction for a woman in her seventies. She'd lived here for decades. Had it taken her that long to get over him?

"Maybe you'll find someone here," Coltrane said. "There's no age limit for presenting a mate to the elders."

Ruby put a gentle arm around his shoulders. "Such a kind thing to say. I'm afraid those days are gone for me. But, you, sweet Coltrane? I have a feeling that you'll find your own once-in-a-lifetime love someday."

"I hope so," Coltrane said, glancing at the opposite corner from the musicians. A few couples gathered over there, all around our age. I caught a glimpse of several rings. "Good to see you, Ruby. If you don't mind, we're going visiting for a bit before the presentations. Amy, come meet my friends."

"Um," I said, catching a glimpse of Lillibeth in the corner, speaking with some older adults. Those had to be the elders. "Are you sure? Don't you need to practice your presentation?"

"I'm not worried about it. Come on, there's someone I want you to meet."

Ruby smiled meaningfully, and Coltrane grabbed my arm, pulling me through the crowd toward his friends in the corner. They watched us approach. At the last moment, Coltrane's hand slid down my arm and grasped my hand in his. I blinked, then pulled my hand away, but the damage was done.

"Who's *this*?" a guy with close-cropped brown hair asked. One arm was draped around a girl.

"Hey, Kev," Coltrane said, then nodded to the girl. "Lacey. This is—"

"Wait, don't tell me," the girl said. She wore the same color blue as me, but her dress followed her curves and stopped just below the knee. "That's the girl you found, right? The one who got bit?"

"I'm Amy," I said, folding my arms so Coltrane wouldn't try to take my hand again. "Nice to meet you all."

"How romantic!" Lacey said. "You rescued her, then you guys fell in love. It's like a story. Is that why you're applying for a dwelling permit after your presentation?"

Coltrane looked at me. "That's not exactly—"

"What in the stars is she doing here?" a voice shouted from the doorway. We turned to see Maxim standing there. He wore a gray, collared shirt that emphasized his shoulders. He strode toward us, then stopped, towering over me and Coltrane both. His eyes bored into mine. "And here I thought Lillibeth cared about our safety."

"I do," Lillibeth said, walking over. "This is not the time, Maxim."

"What is, then? First you completely ignore my report about strangers setting up camp in the town—"

"We're discussing that. It's not your concern."

Maxim continued as if she hadn't spoken. "And then this. The girl should have been gone within the hour. And yet here she is, the leader of NORA, wearing that ridiculous dress like she belongs here."

The room went dead silent.

"Those reports are private," Lillibeth snapped.

"Except when you choose to ignore them and endanger us all," Maxim snapped. He pointed at me. "They're looking for her, and you know it."

Lillibeth folded her arms. "We don't know that it's her."

"What other green-Rated girl with short dark hair could it be?" Maxim said. "My intelligence network confirmed it this morning. They've offered a hundred Rating points to any citizen who brings her in. They're desperate. I bet once we contact their emperor and turn her over, he'll give us a permanent pardon. We won't need to hide any longer."

"You are not to discuss such things in public, Maxim," Lillibeth said. Her face was nearly purple with anger. "You'll scare everyone unnecessarily."

"They should be scared. They finally know the truth." Maxim walked over to his mother, who watched him, her face blank. She held her violin tightly to her side. Maxim continued. "Every refugee who passes by says the same thing. There was a protest in the capital city led by a girl with dark hair and a high Rating who claimed to be the successor."

My uniform dress was full of sequins. I didn't want to go dressed like that, where everyone could see.

"But they were arrested as soon as they reached the palace," he said dramatically, enjoying the attention. "The girl was pulled out of the group, and then the protesters got blown to pieces. She survived. The girl disappeared, and a new emperor, young and stupid as they come, took the throne." He leveled his gaze on me. "Guess she didn't care how many people died as long as she got what she wanted."

"You're saying that Amy is the successor to the NORA throne?" Coltrane asked incredulously.

"Was," Maxim corrected. "She's been replaced. But you can bet they want her back. Must want to put her on trial for what she did."

You've killed us all.

"Amy," Coltrane said. He grabbed my arm, and I recoiled from his touch. "Is it true?"

Ruby stood there watching me, a thoughtful frown on her face. The chef, Dale, stared at the ground, still holding a half-full tray of snacks. Mandie looked at me pleadingly, her arm tight on her violin. And Lillibeth watched me with her jaw clenched. Our secret was out.

When I didn't answer, Coltrane's voice was quiet. "I see."

Maxim smiled coldly. "Whatever she said to convince you that she'd live the pact was a lie. This girl is a murderer, and she deserves to pay for her crimes. Let me turn her in, and then we'll live like kings."

Quiet murmuring filled the room. Coltrane's cheeks were bright red. So much for his grand presentation. The music and laughter and conversation had ended. I'd ruined their party, just as I ruined everything I touched.

Even when I tried to help people, I ended up hurting them in the end.

I turned and stumbled toward the door, but Maxim caught my arm.

"Let her go, Maxim," Lillibeth said as I entered the tunnel. "Elders, if you'd join me in the corner. We have some things to discuss."

23

TREENA

My first instinct was to try another escape, but I had no desire to let the scene with that guard, Violet, play out again. Besides, I still didn't have supplies. I'd made a bargain with Lillibeth, and I'd kept it. It wasn't my fault Maxim had barged in and made all those accusations.

Or maybe it was. I'd been so blind, assuming nobody would recognize me.

Instead, I headed for Lillibeth's dwelling. It would be the first place she looked when their little meeting was finished, but I'd be long gone by then. All I needed were a few supplies. And a way to escape, of course.

Several turns before I got there, footsteps pounded behind me. I hid behind a corner until my pursuer trotted past, then relaxed. It wasn't Maxim. "Coltrane."

"Amy." He turned, but a frown had replaced his usual smile. "Or whatever your name is. You're leaving, aren't you?"

"It's Ametrine. Treena, actually. I'm sorry—I should have told you everything. I didn't think you guys would understand if you knew who I really was." And what I had done.

Coltrane came toward me. When I didn't back away, he lifted his hand to my cheek. "That's it, right there—that expression you wear when you remember. Regret. I've seen it so many times. I know I've only known you a couple of weeks, Amy, but whatever you are, you're definitely not a murderer."

His words seemed to melt something in my chest, something hard and cold. The emotions I'd dammed up for the past weeks began to surface, overwhelming my senses. I swallowed hard. "I couldn't face those people."

He let his hand drop. "I know you think they're mad at you—"

"Not them. I mean the NORA citizens, that night the bomb hit. All those people died supporting me. So many broken families, Coltrane. So much pain. I couldn't live in a palace while they suffered. Wherever I go, people are hurt."

He took a step closer, pinning me against the wall. "That's not true. You've made things down here a little better."

I snorted. "Yeah, I taught kids how to read and used up valuable food and medicine. That's basically all I'm good for down here."

"You can learn. There's still time."

I shook my head. He'd never understand. "Are they coming to kick me out soon?"

He hesitated for a brief second. "They can't. The pact protects you until you're proven to be a danger. We accept everyone, no matter where they're from and regardless of their past. Don't worry about Maxim, either. My mom will calm him down." Coltrane took my hands in his and looked into my eyes. "I want you to stay, Amy. With me."

I stared at his hands, gripping mine so tightly I couldn't pull away. "What are you saying?"

"As soon as we're promised, you're safe. You'll automatically become a member of the settlement, equal in every way, entitled to our protection." He stared at me, pleading, his eyes holding an intensity that made me uncomfortable. "My friends thought we made a great couple, and I was going to apply for a dwelling permit tonight. We can do it together—"

I jerked my hands away. "Are you asking me to *marry* you?"

"Coltrane!" a voice shouted from down the hall. Lillibeth.

He jumped to his feet, but the color in his cheeks was from anger, not embarrassment. "Never mind. Forget I asked."

"I don't—"

"Just forget it," he snapped.

"I just want to find somewhere I can never hurt people again," I said softly. "Even you."

Lillibeth came around the corner. She was sprinting. Alarm shot through my body as she pulled to a halt, breathing hard. Had they already made a decision? I'd lost my chance to sneak out.

"Sound the alarm." She gulped a breath or two, then managed to speak. "A full NORA squadron just landed. They've found us."

24

TREENA

Within minutes the tunnels were complete chaos. Women in dresses and men in pressed slacks held screaming children as they sprinted for their homes, pushing their way through the packed tunnels.

"I think they already know," I shouted to Coltrane over the noise. "Why sound the alarm?"

"It means we're evacuating," he yelled back. "Rather than hiding in our homes, we grab our supplies and meet in the emergency shelter."

When we finally got to Coltrane's dwelling, he ran inside. Seconds later an alarm sounded—a high-pitched tone that echoed down the hard rock hallways. The people crowding the tunnels started scrambling even faster, panicked. Bodies pushed by. Sobbing mixed in with the siren's wailing.

I came to a stop in front of the dwelling. NORA had come back with troops. That meant either they knew I was here or they knew there was a settlement underground. Neither one boded well for us. All the supplies in the world wouldn't help me now. Why hadn't I told Lillibeth no and left when I had the chance?

I couldn't save myself now. But I could save these people, and that meant I had to get up there. Now.

"Amy," Coltrane's voice came through the divider. "Come grab a pack. We need to hurry and get to the shelter."

"Actually," I said, moving the curtain to follow. "There's a change of—"

A low voice at my shoulder stopped me. "Where do you think you're going?"

I turned in time to see a kitchen knife plunging toward my stomach.

I leaped aside, redirecting the blade, and settled into fighting stance.

Maxim stepped back, then narrowed his eyes. "Definitely trained. I wonder if Lillibeth also knew that you're a soldier."

I kept my eye on the knife. It was slightly serrated, but not very long. "Put that down. There's no time for this."

"I couldn't agree more. Are you coming willingly, or should I hold this to your throat?"

"You're going to evacuate with the rest of them. I'm going up, but I'm doing it alone."

He adjusted the knife in his hand. "And let you run off the first chance you get? I don't think so."

I rolled my eyes. "If I go by myself, I'll tell them there's nobody down here. They won't believe that if you come along. Now get out of my way."

"Amy?" Coltrane called from inside. "I need you to carry a few things." He swept the divider aside and took a step out. He didn't see Maxim until it was too late.

Maxim turned on him. He plunged the knife into Coltrane's upper arm. Coltrane gave a choked yell and stumbled backward, hitting the side of the doorway. Maxim pulled the knife out and held it to the younger boy's throat. Coltrane froze.

"Let's try this again," Maxim told me. "You're coming with me, girlie, and you're doing it now."

Coltrane stared at me in horror.

I walked slowly over to him, my hands up. "Fine. I'll go with you. Just don't hurt Coltrane."

Maxim smiled and lowered the knife. Coltrane straightened, cradling his injured arm. Blood soaked through the sleeve. I tried to keep my face impassive as I approached. Maxim's knife thrust into Coltrane's arm had been wild, uncontrolled. The guy had no idea what he was doing. I stopped, keeping my palms forward and my eyes on the knife.

Maxim took a step toward me. I struck then, knocking his hand aside. I'd intended to dislodge and retrieve the knife, but it went flying and hit the wall. Maxim's face darkened, and he lunged for the blade, but I threw my leg out to trip him. He landed hard on his stomach and rolled over, his gaze murderous.

I didn't give him time to think. A tight fist to his nose yielded a sickening crunch. He gasped, throwing his hands immediately to his face, and sank to the floor again, lying on his back.

I hiked the dress up and grabbed the knife, holding it toward him it before Maxim could get any ideas. "Hurt Coltrane again, and I'm coming for you."

Maxim's eyes were fixed on the blade. After a moment he nodded, still clasping his nose, blood trickling between his fingers.

Coltrane still stared at me. "What *are* you?"

I took his hand and pulled him back into his dwelling. In the hallway behind us, Maxim grunted. A moment later, heavy footsteps pattered away. Good. I tossed the knife onto the bed and wiped my bloody hands absently on the dress.

Coltrane stared at my hands, then tore his gaze away. He eased himself onto the bed, then lifted his sleeve to examine the wound.

"Let me see," I said.

"I'm fine," he said through gritted teeth. "That was little more than a glorified butter knife. I just need some painkiller. Once I get to my mom, she can stitch it up."

"I'll get it. How do I get into your mom's medicine cabinet?"

"In her—her pillowcase," he managed, trying to unbutton his shirt. Dark blood soaked most of his sleeve. His shirt was definitely ruined, the one he'd washed and ironed and saved for what was supposed to be the biggest night of his life. Finally he grasped the collar and, with a mighty heave, ripped the shirt apart. He eased it off and then tossed it on the floor. "It's a round piece of metal."

I retrieved it and trotted back in. "How does it work?"

"Run it against the lock," Coltrane said, his voice more steady now that the shock had passed. Color was already returning to his cheeks.

The lock clicked when I touched the magnet to the cabinet door. The small metal door swung open. I dug through the bottles until I found one labeled "Pain," then swiped a clean syringe from the bottom shelf.

I filled it as I'd seen Lillibeth do. "I'm not sure where to inject this."

He eyed the syringe. "My shoulder. Here, I'll do it." He took it and plunged it just above his wound, wincing. After a moment, he pulled it away and handed it back to me, then took the roll of bandages I offered and began wrapping it around his bicep.

I stood there, uncertain what to do. I needed to get to the surface, but I didn't dare leave him here alone. This wasn't exactly the good-bye I'd imagined.

Coltrane finished off the roll and studied my face, his jaw tight with anger. "You didn't answer my question. What are you really? Is that what they taught you to do in NORA? Smash peoples' noses in?"

"Of course not. I was trained—" I stopped, realizing that explaining my time in the empress's special forces unit probably wasn't a good idea. "I never wanted to hurt anyone."

"Whatever." He stood. "I'm going to the defense lab. Time to test out my project. I don't care what you do. Just—don't do anything stupid." With that, he strode out.

I imagined a dozen men and boys retrieving their contraptions, excited and afraid at the prospect of actually using them. They were probably the ones who would face any NORA soldiers who broke in. A line of unarmed, hopeful inventors against an army.

An army I'd brought to them.

My eyes fell to the medicine cabinet, its door still open. Dozens of identical brown bottles were lined up in neat rows, all labeled with a careful hand. Lillibeth was prepared for anything. *Spanish Flu. Rabies. Viper Antivenom. Scorpion Bite.* I scanned the words carefully, then stopped on a bottle at the very back. There were two, actually, and they both said the same thing: *Rattlesnake Antivenom.*

I took one out and read it again, confused. Lillibeth said a rattlesnake had bitten me and that I'd used the last of the antivenom. But she had two full vials here.

An unsettled feeling filled my stomach, then anger. No, not anger. Pure, undefiled rage. Another quick scan of the labels failed to turn up a single tube of nutrition pills. I slammed the medicine cabinet door closed, not caring if it locked, and swiped the only baglight in the room. The golden light around me shifted with the movement.

Then I stalked out the door.

25

TREENA

The vent in the EPIC bunker in NORA had been tall and narrow, with handholds strategically placed to make climbing easy. The architects had obviously intended it to be an emergency exit if necessary.

The underground settlers, though, had no such contingencies. Their ventilation shaft was short and wide. Giant fans and thick filters filled almost the entire space. There was barely enough room to get around them if I plastered myself against the edge, ducked my head, and slid by. The fans were loud and powerful, and after squeezing past the second fan, I learned to squint to prevent the blinding dirt from activating my tear ducts. It was hard to decide which was worse—not being able to see, or the heavy dust coating the inside of my nose and throat. The only good thing was that it gradually ascended upward. If it had gone straight down, there was no way I could have climbed it intact. Especially in a dress. Why hadn't I changed my clothes?

"Idiot," I muttered for the tenth time. "I had to believe her." I sank my boot into something soft, then yanked it away, grateful for the thickness of the soles. Most of the dead animals in here were hard, but some were relatively fresh. The stench was nearly overpowering. To my relief, the golden baglight I'd stolen from the dwelling had already started to dim. There was very little in these ducts I wanted to see.

I lifted my dress to step over another unrecognizable lump of fur. Maxim and Coltrane thought I was leaving to save them. I'd intended to do just that, and I knew that was the right thing.

But Lillibeth had lied to me. She'd manipulated me, using me just like Dresden and Konnor and Mills. It didn't matter where I went—they were all the same. Or maybe I was the problem. I was too trusting. Maxim had accused me of wanting to run the moment I escaped. The entire settlement probably expected that. I was a digit, after all, incapable of kindness.

The last section of the vent went nearly horizontal, and I could see the gentle white glow of moonlight ahead. I paused at the opening and let the cool desert air soothe my aching lungs before climbing out. It felt so good to stand up straight.

The vent ended on a slight hill. When I turned around, though, the vent opening wasn't there. All I saw was a flat section of dirt. These settlers were serious about their camouflage tech. That also explained all the dead animals. I wiped my boots on the ground again for good measure, then looked around—and instantly flattened myself on the ground.

In the distance, NORA soldiers swarmed the desert like hundreds of angry ants. The abandoned town stood in the distance, barely visible in the night. A circle of lights, aircraft, and vehicles stood just outside it, circling something I couldn't quite see. The north exit.

I squinted and counted the choppers, tiny reflective lumps in the darkness. Fourteen or fifteen. It was impossible to count the troops. The soldiers clustered together as if waiting for something. There was no question now that they knew people lived underground. The only thing I didn't know was whether they thought I was still down there.

A core of hot anger sat in my belly, refusing to be extinguished. I paused to consider my next move, then realized I'd already made my decision. It had been decided the moment Lillibeth uttered her lying words.

I tossed the baglight back toward the hill, and it disappeared behind the camouflage tech. Then I hiked the dress up to my knees, turned toward the mountains, and ran.

26

TREENA

The mountains loomed ahead, black against a gray sky. A brown-red moon, nearly full, lit the dark wasteland before me. I shivered against the cold wind, impatient for my body to warm up. The only sounds were my boots pounding into the desert sand and my rhythmic breathing, heavier than it should have been. Sweat began to build in my hair, dripping down my cheek and curving under my chin. My injured ankle pulsed with a dull ache, intensifying by the minute. I used the pain to propel me forward. There was no time for rest, not with NORA desperate for my capture.

I tried to block out memories of the community I had just abandoned, but they kept seeping into my thoughts. Had they made it to the emergency shelter before NORA came knocking? Maybe Coltrane and Lillibeth were wrong about NORA. Maybe Dresden would negotiate with them, allow them to keep their home. Once they saw how peaceable those people were—

An explosion rocked the desert. Light flashed first, then the sound hit my ears, and I slid to a halt. A bomber plane turned overhead, then headed back for another pass. The bomb had hit near the hill where I'd just escaped.

No.

Fates. They were bombing the entire valley, starting on the far end. Trying to drive the settlers toward them. Whatever the soldiers had been waiting for, it seemed they had run out of patience. The attack had begun. And hundreds of innocent people below ground were about to meet their deaths, shelter or not.

It's not too late. You can still turn yourself in. Even if it didn't stop the attack, it could at least buy a little more time.

But if I went back to NORA, I was as good as dead. There were hundreds of witnesses and thousands of people who wanted justice in the deaths of their loved ones. I'd be executed, probably by punishment mode. But that wasn't as painful as the realization that I'd never see Vance again—never find myself in his arms or lose myself in his kiss. He'd never know I loved him.

I wrapped my arms around myself for warmth, still standing there, thinking of Ruby's disappointed frown when she'd found out who I was. Maxim's accusations echoed by Lillibeth's skepticism regarding my motives. The entire community's suspicion. The shock in Coltrane's eyes as he asked, "What *are* you?" The two vials of antivenom, hidden at the back of the medicine cabinet. I had every right to run away and find peace.

A lock of hair had escaped from where Lillibeth had pinned it. I brushed it out of my face and caught something rough. I fingered it, then pulled it out. Coltrane's flower. Ruby's favorite.

Perhaps you were on the wrong journey. Ruby's words. Dear, sweet Ruby.

The bomber jet grew louder overhead. There was little warning. The blast hit just north of the previous one. Light flashed and the ground rumbled beneath my boots. They were definitely trying to drive the settlers out. Coltrane had been confident in the community's engineering, but there was no way it could withstand this.

Digit or not, I couldn't let them die.

I cursed and sprinted back the way I'd come, waving my arms in the sky like a lunatic. "Stop!"

Overhead the noise of the bomber jet grew louder again. I waved more frantically and increased my speed, but I couldn't pick my way very carefully in the dark. I tripped on my dress and fell, then jumped to my feet again, hollering to the jet. Any minute now, the soldiers would see me. They'd call off the bomber and come to get me. If I could just make myself known. The first bomb site was just to my right now.

The jet shot by overhead. There was no way the pilot hadn't seen me. I put on a new burst of speed, stumbling through the pain in my ankle. "Please! Stop!"

A distinct whistle sounded in the night, and then the ground exploded in front of me. An incredible force threw me backward, and I flipped once, twice. My head whacked into something hard, and the blackness closed in.

I shook my head and forced my eyes open. I lay sprawled on the ground, my face coated in dirt. A horrible high-pitched ringing played on repeat in my ears. I forced enough air into my lungs to speak, but nothing came out. Or maybe I just couldn't hear myself talk.

The desert was unrecognizable in front of me, torn up like a giant had hacked it apart with a shovel. Thick smoke blew sideways with the wind, but it was still too dark to see much else. If NORA was still out there, I couldn't tell. I raised my head to look for the bomber jet. Either it was gone or the smoke was too thick to see it coming again.

I pushed myself to my feet and nearly fell over. I tried again. This time I stood slowly and let my head adjust. A few steps, and the smoke cleared for a second, just enough for me to see people coming in my direction. Running.

They wouldn't be headed this direction if the bomber pilot was still a threat. The settlers below were safe for now.

The soldiers encircled me with stunners, at least forty of them, all wearing serious and determined expressions. I raised my hands in surrender. As they grabbed me roughly, locking my wrists together and saying words I couldn't hear, I sighed with relief.

27

TREENA

ORA's camp was a harsh white under the brightness of a dozen work lights. The camp did indeed surround the north exit. Several soldiers stood around it with their stunners trained on a round hatch in the ground—a three-foot-wide metal opening. They'd apparently found a way to disable the camouflage feature.

The soldiers dumped me at someone's feet. When I looked up to face my captor, I nearly fell over. "Mom?"

"Oh, honey," she said with a gasp. Her eyes were tired, and she threw her arms around me. "I'm so glad you escaped those awful people."

"What in the fates are you doing here?"

She pulled away. "They asked me to help with the search. I can only imagine how hard Dresden's appointment must have been for you. What Konnor did was unforgivable." She combed her fingers through my hair, which had flopped down into my face. "I didn't realize you felt so strongly about the throne."

"You honestly think I left because of some tantrum?"

She hesitated. "Well, it doesn't matter now. Let's get you home and safe. Are you injured? What—what in the fates are you wearing?"

I looked down at the sleeves of Lillibeth's dress, damp with dark red stains. Coltrane's blood. "I'm not hurt."

"I can't believe you survived down there for so long." She turned to a female guard. "She needs some privacy to change. I brought a clean uniform for her. It's in the second chopper, over there."

The guard grabbed four others and then motioned me inside the helicopter as my mom had instructed. The women didn't speak as I dressed, but I felt their eyes on me, every inch of me, until my uniform was zipped up. It felt a little baggier than usual. I hadn't quite gained back the weight I'd lost in the desert.

They secured my wrists in front of me the moment I finished. I looked at Lillibeth's dress on the floor, torn and stained almost beyond recognition. One of the women kicked it aside as we stepped out of the chopper.

"Mom," I said when we reached her. "When are we leaving?"

She pursed her lips. "Commander Denoux has something he wants to take care of first."

NORA's general and councilman of war. The man who had smiled at my arrest just weeks before. "He's here?" I looked around, but he was nowhere in sight. "What are we waiting for?" Her eyes met mine then, and my stomach plummeted. The pity I saw there was like a slap to the face. "*No*. No, Mom. I won't let him do it!"

She shook her head. "Things are a little complicated right now, Treena. If we'd found you wandering in the desert, that's one thing. But you uncovered a civilization hiding just hours from NORA's borders."

"They're peaceful, Mom. They don't even allow weapons. You have to help me!"

Another pause. "Treena, calm down. You need to act like an adult here for a moment."

"You didn't question my adulthood when I was the successor," I hissed. "Look, those people saved my life when I got a snakebite. They fed me and gave me a bed to sleep in and offered to let me stay there forever. If the commander thinks I'm going to help him destroy these people, he's wrong."

"I'd think long and hard about that," Commander Denoux said, stepping out of a nearby chopper. My mom jumped out of the chair and stood next to me, eyes on the ground.

Denoux sat down in the newly vacated chair like it was a throne, legs crossed. He faced me. "We're not asking for you to shoot anyone, Ametrine. All we want to know is the layout of the settlement."

I spoke through clenched teeth. "Not a chance."

He sighed, the type of sigh that meant I was being unreasonable. "You're in a very precarious position here, young lady. You're defending a group hostile to our nation, which will not bode well for your trial."

"I don't care about that, and they're not hostile."

Denoux nodded to a guard. He locked my mom's hands behind her, pausing for a moment to connect her bonds to her techband. She continued to stare at the ground, not looking surprised at all.

The message was clear: Mom wasn't here to help. She was collateral. Denoux was using the same threat on me that he'd used on Vance. And why not? It had worked on Vance for two years.

Vance. I'd traded my chance to see him to save the settlers, and now I wouldn't accomplish either.

"Treena, just tell them what they want so we can go home," my mom said quietly. "Nobody will think less of you once you've done your duty. There's something big happening. Dresden needs your help. Maybe after the trial you can take the throne back—"

"I don't care about the stupid throne!" I snapped. I was angry—angry at my mom for letting herself be used, angry at Denoux for trying to use me, and at the settlement for making me care. It would be so easy to turn them over. But they didn't deserve this. "Hundreds of people have already died trying to help me, Mom. I'm not letting hundreds more suffer the same fate."

"That sounds very dramatic," Denoux said. "But it comes down to this. All you're doing is postponing what will happen anyway. You can minimize losses on our end by answering my questions, or you and your mother can die with them. Your young emperor friend will have to deal with it."

I pushed away the panic spreading through my limbs. "Dresden and my stepfather, Councilman Dowell, would never believe it. You can't hurt my mother without them realizing what happened, Denoux. It would be the end of your career."

He considered that, studying me with those dark eyes of his. "Be that as it may, you have no such protection. I've looked forward to ending you for a very long time. Now, I'll give you one last chance. Tell me how many people live down there, or you'll join them in death."

"You may as well put me right back into that hole, because I'm not helping you."

His face darkened. It was the same expression he'd had the day Vance had confronted him. "Have it your way, then," he said slowly. "Milton and Jentry, dump her down the hatch, and then blow it all up."

28

TREENA

The soldiers looked stunned.

"Sir," one soldier said. "We haven't located a second hatch. We won't be able to retrieve any survivors if this entrance is destroyed.

"Survivors were never the objective," Denoux said. Then he motioned to the soldiers on either side of me. Two of them grabbed me by the elbows and began pulling me toward the hatch while a third jabbed a stunner into my back.

My mom gave a sharp intake of breath. "No! Treena, there's still time. Just tell him, and we can go home. Do it now!"

"I can't," I called back to her.

The guards surrounding the metal hatch stepped aside, their stunners still aimed at the opening.

"Ametrine, just tell them," my mother shouted. "You're not saving any lives by throwing away your own!"

"I'm so sorry, Mom," I called back to her. "I love you."

"Ametrine!"

"It's still locked," a female soldier said as we reached the hatch, muttering something that sounded like "Why doesn't he just shoot her?" She retrieved a laser tool and activated it with a low hum. "Stand back while I slice the—What was that?"

"What's wrong?" the guy to my left asked impatiently.

The woman stared at the hatch for a moment as if listening, then pulled on the handle. The hatch lifted open, revealing only blackness. "What the fates?"

The man frowned. "You said you tried it."

"I did," she snapped. "It was locked before." She bent over the hatch to peer inside, and then screamed as her legs followed her up and over, disappearing into the darkness. Her shriek echoed from the shaft and then ended abruptly.

It was locked before. It only took a second for me to figure out what had just happened. As my guards tightened their grip on my arms and leaned over to see inside, I thrashed to the side and yanked myself free.

The soldiers grabbed at me again, shouting, but I had already closed half the distance to the hatch. I ducked just as a shot whooshed over my head, sending my hair flopping forward again.

"Incoming!" I yelled as I leaped, arms extended in front of me, still locked together. As I jumped into the dark tube, feet-first, another shot flew by and grazed my fingers. It stung so badly I missed my chance to catch the opening with my hands to stop my fall.

I threw my feet out and tried to catch something—anything—to halt myself, but there was just air. Had I misjudged the situation? I'd assumed someone had opened the hatch from the inside, which meant there had to be a ladder. But now I was freefalling to my death, just as the soldier had done.

Just as a horrified scream burst from me, I felt arms close around me and tighten, catching me at the armpits. The man grunted and guided me to the side. A rung materialized beneath my foot, and then another one under my hands. I set my other foot down to help support my own weight, and let my eyes adjust to the darkness.

"Good to have you back," Coltrane said beside me with a chuckle. "Although next time you decide to leap into a thirty-foot tube expecting me to catch you, maybe give me a little more warning first."

A million questions fought to escape at once, rendering me speechless. Coltrane hadn't gone to the shelter with his community. He'd come back. Exhilaration and dread settled deep in my stomach.

"Quick, close the hatch," I whispered. "They're going to toss a bomb down any second."

"Oh, no they won't," he replied. "Get ready to see something seriously awesome." He turned and climbed up, then shoved a fist through the opening above. His shout hurt my ears. "Back away, or I'll use this!"

The shouting of soldiers above quieted. I squinted upward at the object in his hand. The weapon disabler?

His thumb curved around the device as he pushed a button. I covered my head with one arm, ready for an explosion or a light or *something*. Coltrane ducked, holding his device high out the hatch.

Nothing happened.

The shouts began again. Coltrane pulled his hand back down and stared at the disabler in disbelief.

"Shut the door!" I hissed.

He grabbed the hatch lid and swung it down just as the barrel of a stunner appeared. The lid slammed closed with a deep metallic thud.

"Hurry and lock it!"

Too slowly, Coltrane pulled on the handle, then forced it sideways, wincing as he did so. I felt instantly guilty. I'd completely forgotten about his wound. The metal hatch began to vibrate. They were shooting at it.

"They're going to slice it open," I said quickly. "We have to get out of here *now*."

"I can't believe it didn't work," he muttered. "I was so sure."

The banging on the hatch above stopped. Seconds later the whirring of a motor sounded. The slicing had begun.

"Come on!"

"I am," he snapped. I could barely hear him over the shrieking metal above. I focused on working my way down the rungs. It was tricky with my wrists locked together.

Half a minute later something dropped from above and clattered its way down the metal tube, hitting the ground with a *plop*. From the sound, we were about three meters from the bottom of the tube. If the bomb was standard, we had five seconds.

Five.

"Time's up," I called, grabbing Coltrane's leg. Then I jumped, pulling him with me. He yelped as his hands tore free.

Four.

We hit the ground and rolled, thankfully avoiding the explosive. What had been a deep ache in my ankle was now agony, but I forced myself to my feet.

Three. "Run!" I shouted, then stumbled over something in the darkness. The NORA soldier's body. Coltrane followed, stepping carefully around it.

"Hurry!" I shrieked, wishing more than anything that Coltrane had brought a baglight. I felt around the wall for an opening and found a doorway. The door was still partially open. I shoved my way through it and heard Coltrane do the same just behind me.

Two. He slammed the door closed, then took my arm and pulled me behind him. The darkness didn't seem to bother him in the least.

We turned the corner. The tunnel exploded behind us.

Dirt dumped onto my head, and I felt something hard slam into my back, but I managed to stay on my feet. Coltrane was still running ahead of me.

"Don't stop!" he yelled. "Everyone's in the emergency shelter. We're the last ones."

"What were you thinking, Coltrane?" I shot back. "You just tried to take on the entire NORA army by yourself. With a plastic circuit case, no less."

"If my disabler worked, it would be way more powerful than a stunner," he said. "Anyway, you weren't doing so well. Thought you could use some help."

"How did you know that?"

"The sentinel," he said simply.

Fates. Coltrane had probably watched me run away, then come back. "I tried to stop them."

"I know."

We ran in silence for several minutes. Every step sent daggers up my leg, and soon I was limping so badly

I could barely cover distance. We slowed to a walk. I couldn't help but wonder what was going on above us. Had Denoux already reported to Dresden that I was dead? What did my mom believe?

"This emergency shelter of yours," I said. "Are you sure they'll even let me in?"

He paused. "No. But I'm not going in without you."

The shelter's entrance was situated inside the defense lab. The lab looked much as it had last night, the tables cleared away. The only difference was that the boxes full of stored projects had been torn into and lay on their sides, scattered throughout the room. A hatch slightly smaller than the one I'd just come through lay open in the corner.

Lillibeth stood outside it, a look of profound relief on her face when Coltrane walked through. Her smile froze when she saw me.

"She escaped, Mom," Coltrane said, heading for the hatch. "We're the last ones." He lowered himself down. I did the same, giving Lillibeth a long look. The stunned look on her face was almost comical.

"By the way," I told her, "I saw your other vials of antivenom. You kept me here on purpose. I hope you're ready to explain to us why you did it."

Her shock turned to horror as I lowered myself down the ladder.

Coltrane was waiting for me at the bottom, a new baglight in hand. "Is my mom coming?"

I looked up. "I don't see her. Maybe she needs a minute. Do you want to wait?"

"Nah. She knows where to go."

The air was much cooler down here, and the tunnel echoed strangely. It sloped downward for what felt like several hundred meters. That definitely explained how the settlers had survived the bombings above—this shelter of theirs was extremely deep.

I tripped on the uneven ground several times before deciding to keep a hand on the tunnel walls at all times. I kept looking behind me, but Lillibeth didn't appear.

We'd been walking for about twenty minutes when we reached some black plastic bins bolted into the walls like the medicine cabinet had been. "What's this?"

"Good old-fashioned dynamite," Coltrane said proudly. "As soon as everyone is accounted for, they'll seal this tunnel off. Even if the soldiers decide to stop bombing and come down to investigate, they won't be able to follow us. It should buy us some time."

The tunnel ended at a thick metal door. When Coltrane swung it open, my jaw dropped in awe. The cavern was massive. Metal beams reinforced the ceiling in a dome shape. It reminded me of the dome at the block in Olympus, but this was twice the width and packed with people. There had to be hundreds of them, all sitting against walls or propped up against each other. Most still wore their nice clothes from the party. Young children struggled to get away from their parents while older siblings clung to each other. The adults were somber. We weren't out of danger yet.

Many heads turned toward me as I stepped inside. Mandie broke away from her mother and threw herself at me. "You're here! Maxim said you weren't coming back."

I reached around her for a hug, eyeing her brother as he approached. "Guess he was wrong."

"Absolutely not," Maxim snapped, making his way through the crowd. He pulled Mandie away from me. "She is *not* supposed to be here."

Coltrane faced him. "You have no right to talk, Maxim, after what you did."

"I don't know what you're talking about."

The exchange was barely audible over the growing noise. Several others had begun to yell at me as well, motioning toward the door. Women scrambled out of the way with their young children as two men approached, squaring their shoulders. The room was chaos now, with choruses of "Throw her out!" and "Traitor." I recognized several of my students dotted in the crowd. The children looked at the floor. Clara had tears streaming down her cheeks. Mandie returned to her mother and picked up a long black case, clinging to it like it was a shield. Her violin, probably.

The men stopped in front of me. Coltrane tried to step between us, but I moved him aside and faced them. "You can throw me out, but first let me say this. NORA's not interested in prisoners. They're bent on extermination this time. I know what your feelings are on violence, but you may not have a choice. You'll probably have to fight your way out of here."

Everyone began talking again, arguing, shouting, and I knew my pleadings were useless. Even if they wanted to defend themselves, they had no weapons but the experiments from the lab.

"You were the heir to the NORA throne," Maxim said. "What makes you think we'll believe anything you say?"

"I don't actually care whether you believe me or not," I snapped. "They sent me down here to die. I don't particularly want that, and I'm assuming you don't either. So let's figure this out together."

Ruby appeared and put a gentle hand on my shoulder. "Why didn't you tell us who you were?"

"I should have," I admitted. "At first I thought you'd throw me out or turn me in. Then Lillibeth said I had to stay until I paid off the last vial of rattlesnake antivenom I used. When I realized NORA was looking for me, I tried to leave." I turned to Lillibeth, who had just walked up behind me. Her face was a mask. "Lillibeth said she would help me escape if I waited until after the social."

Ruby turned on Lillibeth, arms folded. "You told us we had plenty of antivenom left."

The ground rumbled beneath our feet. The bomber jet again. Dirt streamed down upon our heads, and I instinctively covered my head, but the cavern held.

"Mom?" Coltrane urged.

Lillibeth swallowed and squared her shoulders. She'd probably been planning this speech the entire walk down here. "You have to understand the situation I was in. My position is a contradiction in terms. I'm required to accept all travelers, no matter their past, but also protect us from harm. When I saw the girl's number—Rating, whatever they call it—I had to make a decision. I assigned Coltrane to follow her around and report to me about her activities, looking for any sign of malice." I met Coltrane's gaze, and his eyes flicked away. "Then," Lillibeth continued, "I began to notice something. Not only did the girl follow the pact, but for the first time in years, my son was happy. He woke up early to be with her, told her stories, and offered to run errands. Before that, he'd been so quiet and sad I could barely get two words out of him."

I raised an eyebrow at that. Coltrane, depressed and withdrawn? But then I realized what she was saying. Coltrane stared at his mother, stunned, his face reddening.

The crowd began to murmur to themselves, and Lillibeth plunged on. "I know it sounds horrible, but please try to understand. Coltrane grew up without a father, and the other girls his age are promised. I'm all he has, and when I'm gone—well, I wanted him to have a chance at happiness, the joy I had with his father." Her gaze swept the crowd. "I truly didn't believe the girl was a threat. I've served as your harbinger for many years. But I'll always be my son's mother, and I swear my actions were out of love. I know nothing I can say will make everything right. I'm terribly sorry for the wrongs I've caused, and I officially resign as harbinger."

The group was still. Horror and humiliation filled my body as I thought about all the times she'd encouraged me and Coltrane to be together—the walks, the tour, her insistence that my relationship with Vance was superficial. The flowers. Lillibeth had smiled through it all, giving encouragement and nudges wherever necessary.

"Mom," Coltrane said, his face redder than I thought possible. He pulled away and let her arm drop, then faced her. "You say it was out of love. But you never asked me what I wanted. Is it too much to ask for me to live my life without being pushed in whatever direction you wanted me to take? Did it ever occur to you that I'd want to marry a girl who wasn't *forced* to be with me?"

"Coltrane—" she began.

"No," he snapped and turned away. "Look at this. Look at what you've done. And you dare stand there and say you sacrificed your settlement because you're a *good mother*?"

Lillibeth's face twisted in pain, and she looked at the ground. The crowd murmured.

Coltrane lifted his jaw and turned toward the watching settlers. "Fine. I second her motion that she be removed from her position. Let the next person in line take her place."

Rumbling shook the ground again. The desert would be unrecognizable when we got out of here.

"Don't you think we should do this later?" Ruby asked, her face concerned. "They're bombing our homes as we speak."

"No," Coltrane said, looking at his broken mother. "I think this is the perfect time."

"I agree," a man called out.

"Do the elders concur?" Coltrane asked. His voice was hard. He seemed to have grown five years in the last hour. I couldn't imagine what he was feeling right now. He'd lost his home, his mother had betrayed him and everyone else, and he'd been embarrassed in front of everybody he knew.

"Aye," several voices said.

Ruby shook her head. "No."

"Aye," Lillibeth said. Her voice quivered, and the crowd quieted again. "We have nine votes in the affirmative and one in the negative. The motion passes. Do the elders have a choice for harbinger?"

"We do," a balding man said. "We've known who the next leader would be for several years. Ruby, lead us well."

A gasp escaped my throat as Ruby stepped forward. I'd assumed that since Ruby was a digit she'd be near the bottom of the list. But she didn't even act surprised. She reached up and squeezed Lillibeth's shoulder. The two women stood like that for a moment, looking at each other, silent communication passing between them.

"I'm going to check the sentinel," Coltrane said, walking to the other side of the room. He rummaged through a box and pulled out another contraption.

"It won't do us much good now," someone muttered.

The ground rumbled again, more violently this time. A sharp crack jarred me to the bone. The room seemed to tilt, then right itself. Screaming began again from the group as the families gathered against the walls, clinging to their loved ones, kneeling and covering their heads.

"That was too close," Ruby muttered.

The earth stopped shuddering, and we stood frozen for several minutes. It felt like an hour before we dared move again. The explosions had stopped.

Just as I was beginning to relax, Coltrane swore, staring into the sentinel screen. "Mom, you'd better get over here. Quick."

29

TREENA

Ruby shot a startled look at Lillibeth, then the two of them made their way over. The device's screen cast a light blue sheen over their faces. Their eyes widened, and Lillibeth covered her mouth.

"Folks," Ruby said. "I'm afraid the soldiers have uncovered the west exit. They're streaming in now. It's the only corner that hasn't been destroyed. If they find the defense lab . . ."

She didn't have to say it. The soldiers would note the lack of bodies and assume we were hiding somewhere. The hatch was easy to see. They'd be here within minutes.

"Is everyone accounted for?" Lillibeth asked quickly, her face spotted with pink.

"Yes," Maxim responded, stepping forward. "Everyone's here." He gave me a look that said, *Even those who shouldn't be.*

"Then it's time to seal the tunnel." Lillibeth walked over to the metal door and swung it closed. It slammed shut, the sound bouncing sharply off the walls. She secured the bolt, then opened a box in the wall. The settlers watched her with solemnity.

The weight of the moment settled upon me. "But once it's sealed, you won't be able to get out."

"We have enough food and water for two weeks," Ruby said. "We'll have that long to find another solution."

"Ten seconds," Lillibeth said.

I counted down silently. Others looked like they were doing the same. The woman next to me wept quietly into her husband's shoulder. As I approached number one, parents covered their children's ears and bodies protectively. But one passed, and there was nothing. Then five seconds, then ten, then half a minute.

"Something's wrong," a man said. He strode over to the box. "Show me the sequence."

"It's correct," Lillibeth said. "Just didn't work. It's an older system."

"We'll have to send someone out to manually activate the switches," Ruby replied quietly.

The room grew silent again.

Maxim was the first to speak. "That's easy. There's only one person who doesn't belong here." His gaze locked on me. "Coltrane will get over her eventually."

"None of this is Amy's fault," Ruby began.

"How can you say that?" Maxim snapped. "*All* of this is her fault. Remember, this girl led protestors to their deaths and then ran away. Send her out before it's too late."

A squeaking sound echoed through the room, and then a clang. Every eye turned toward the door.

Lillibeth was gone.

"Mom!" Coltrane shouted and scrambled for the door. When he reached it, he pulled on the latch.

It didn't budge.

"Help me!" he hissed to a man fiddling with the box.

The man shook his head. He growled in frustration. "She put a time delay on the lock. I can't change it."

Coltrane pounded on the door. "Get back in here! We can talk about this."

I joined him at the door. A soft voice, barely audible, floated in from the outside. "I owe them this much. I'm so sorry."

Coltrane's breath caught, and then he started kicking the door as well. "You know I didn't mean what

I said. You're a good mother. We're a team! I don't need a girl to make me happy, Mom!"

"I hope that's true," the voice came back. "I love you very much."

A strangled cry escaped Coltrane's throat as he threw himself at the door. "Don't do this! Don't you dare do this!"

I opened my mouth to interrupt, to tell Lillibeth that it wasn't necessary. I didn't have feelings for Coltrane the way they both wanted, but it still sliced me in the gut to see Coltrane hug the door like that. He didn't deserve to lose his home and his mother all in one day.

"Lillibeth, please," I called out. "Come back in. There's got to be another way."

"Stand back," Lillibeth called. "Just in case."

"Wait!" I shouted.

And then the blast came.

30

VANCE

It was still dark when I awoke. My body felt cramped and sore from lying in fetal position on a slab of metal. I sat up and banged my head. The iron bars rang a victory call. The jail cell had been luxurious compared to this. Maybe Mills had hoped I'd slowly go insane in here—not from exposure or boredom but from cramping muscles and the inability to stretch.

Then I smelled the smoke. It was what had awoken me, I realized. A ribbon of red and orange flickered on the other side the lake. It was barely visible through the dark haze of early morning, but I'd know it anywhere. Fire. Here, in the valley.

I gripped the bars of my prison and squinted, trying to identify the source. It didn't look like there were any buildings over there—no, wait. The fire was already spreading upward, carried by the wind, most likely. It swept from building to building, devouring wood like a dragon, growing brighter even as I watched. How was it spreading so quickly?

Trying to remember my march down into this mountain, I mentally traced the trail all the way up. The fire was headed straight for the larger, newer structures—the loftier citizens' homes. Mills probably lived up there.

I glanced around, looking for the guard, but he was nowhere to be seen. Went home as soon as his shift ended, probably. Or maybe Mills had ordered him away, hoping someone would kill me and spare him the trouble.

My hands gripped the bar, and I took satisfaction in squeezing until it hurt. Those higher settlers wanted me dead, every single one of them.

I could sit back and watch. Easy as falling back asleep. I was in no danger, and neither were my people. It was the settlers who were the problem, and surely someone would discover the fire any second now and raise the cry. They could use a bit of humbling anyway.

The smoke was heavier now, but it still reminded me of home. The smoke that had whirled amongst popping flames and brought me delicious smells of breakfast as a boy was the same smoke that had eventually filled the camp with the scent of death. That scene was about to repeat itself tonight.

I owed my accusers nothing.

The smoke swirled in front of me again, stinging my eyes. The fire nearly doubled in size with each passing minute, and the wind seemed to carry the smoke across the lake and straight to my cage. It reminded me so much of home that it hurt. The last time I'd seen my dad, it was through haze like this. He was a good man. He didn't deserve to die. He would have raised a cry by now.

The realization sent guilt like pain down my spine. What had I become?

"Fire." It came out as a croak. I cleared my throat and tried again. "Wake up! There's a fire!"

Six calls and the dark structures finally stirred. I didn't stop yelling until several people, all men, emerged from their doorways and headed my direction. I pointed across the lake.

One of them stopped dead in his tracks and took up my cry. "Fire! Somebody sound the alarm."

Everyone on this side of the lake was awake now, and I heard the shout being carried above us. A crowd gathered around my cage. "I can't believe they haven't woken up yet," someone muttered. "That's got to be louder than a stampede and hotter than hell."

"Probably all passed out from a late night partying, like always," a woman said. "Serves them right."

"Who's in charge of the alarm?" the first man said. "We're wasting time!"

"Now, wait a second," the woman said, looking guilty. "The divide will keep us safe. We don't need to worry about no fire. Let them suffer a bit and remember that they's people just like the rest of us."

Several murmurs from the crowd made me frown. She wasn't the only person who felt that way.

The man stiffened. "You can't be serious."

"Why not?" the woman snapped. "You can bet they wouldn't say a word if the fire was on this side. They'd dance with joy to have us gone."

"Just curious," one man said. He approached my cage and stopped in front of the door. I recognized him from somewhere but couldn't quite place him. "I wonder why this boy decided to raise the alarm, seeing as how he's doomed and all."

Dozens of pairs of eyes turned to me. I shrugged. "It's true that they deserve what they get. But if we let them die, we're no better than they are."

"This ain't about philosophical stuff," a man grumbled.

"At the very least," I continued, "they'll lose their homes. You really think the higher settlers will let you keep your shelters while the higher settlers use rocks for pillows?"

"They'll have to fight us off," someone said.

"And it'll be war. More people dead. Details can be worked out later, but lives can't be replaced."

Shouts echoed from across the lake. Someone had noticed the fire—finally—and raised the alarm. People began streaming out of the hazy buildings.

"Grab buckets, cups, bowls, anything that can hold water," I said. "Cross the divide and get yourselves wet in the lake. Form a line from the water up. Try to get above the fire line if you can and either remove the dry vegetation or wet it down. It may not do much, but it's all we've got at this point. Just *stay wet*. Wouldn't do to lose any of you. Remember, the better off they are up top, the better off we are down here."

The familiar man cocked his head as if examining me under a glass but finally shook his head. "Well, Hawking has a point. Let's get moving."

And they did. They actually went. The crowd grumbled, and I got more than one dirty look, but they went. The group filed back into their homes to retrieve containers, and then it began. Some swam across the lake; others ran around. They arrived at about the same time and sprang into action.

I watched them from my cage, just as helpless now as the night my world burned to the ground.

31

VANCE

When the sun came up, the fire had been beaten back. It wasn't completely out. I could see lines of people dumping lake water onto it. The heavy smoke turned white as it thinned and died. It had been three or four hours at most. The entire settlement seemed to be there, a huge black swarm of exhausted workers. It was hard to tell the high settlers from the lower ones from this distance, and it was probably hard for them too. I knew their faces and clothing would be charred and blackened. They'd fought a battle together and won. It was a double victory.

"I heard what you did," a voice drawled.

I turned to find an older man with a trimmed mustache and an expensive-looking dark blue jacket. He held a wooden cane in one hand but barely leaned on it.

He looked down a bulbous nose and smiled. The only way to tell was the faint movement of his mustache.

"What did I do this time," I grumbled, "blow up the moon?"

"Nah, I mean last night," he said. "I been talking to your people, and they told me. You rallied the lower sections to come help when they resisted the idea."

"Forgive them for not racing immediately to the rescue, but it's tough when you upper settlers treat them like trash."

"That we do," the man said, not sounding sorry at all. He caught me looking at his jacket and nodded. "I stayed late at a friend's. Tried to go home this morning to find the south side of my house completely charred. They woke up my daughter and got her out in time. She's fine."

"Good." I wasn't sure where the guy was going with this.

"My daughter is deaf. If your people hadn't broken in and grabbed her when they did, she may not have woken up in time. You saved her life."

"*I* saved nobody. I stood here and watched the whole time."

"You're locked away, Hawking. If free, you would've helped like you did when the missile hit. Rumors can be powerful, you know, and most of them are about you."

"Let people say what they want."

He pulled something out of his coat pocket and set it on the floor of the cage. I picked it up. A yeast roll, white and fluffy and still soft.

"It's a noble thing you did," he said. "Some people are wondering when you're going to challenge the governor for his position."

I felt my eyes widen. This man was halfway to the loony house. "I'm just happy nobody's put a bullet in my head yet."

"We need someone who can see past all the lines we've drawn between ourselves, boy, and that's you. 'Course, I wouldn't challenge him until you're sure to win because the losers always disappear."

I watched him for a moment, but the man seemed sincere. "You're saying he kills them off."

He shrugged. "Not right away, but eventually, all mysterious-like. Anyway, just thought I'd plant the idea."

Then he plodded his way up the trail again and disappeared into the smoky haze covering the valley.

32

TREENA

The settlers slept in the cavern that night, piles of shivering bodies strewn amongst blankets and rolled-up clothing. Infants and sobbing children sounded here and there, but my mind had learned to block them out. What it hadn't learned to block out was the huddled figure sitting with his back against the door. Coltrane hadn't moved from that spot in ten hours. He hugged his knees, head down, his torn and bloody shirt still visible from where I sat. Once in a while a shudder racked his body. Dozens of settlers had filtered past to give him a hug and wish him well. I'd just walked away.

I couldn't face him.

The dream came again that night. As always, hundreds of bodies littered the ground, their eyes fixed on me. The empress laughed. Tali lay silent, her body twisted among the wreckage of a building.

"You've killed us all," the group said as one.

"Death follows me," I whispered, "but I don't cause it."

"You've killed us all."

"I've never wanted anyone to die!" I burst out in frustration. "I'm not the one who did this. Why won't you leave me in peace?"

The bodies watched me, unblinking.

Suddenly Tali was right next to me. Instead of the bald, broken body in the ground, she was the way I remembered her—choppy dark hair, slightly smudged uniform, a smile lighting her eyes. "You're smarter than that, Treena," she said. "You know we're not talking about the bomb."

I sighed. "What is that supposed to mean?"

"We are the people of NORA," she said simply. "You didn't kill us with explosives. You killed us when you left."

Ruby shook me awake, her eyes red-rimmed and swollen. I wondered if she'd slept at all. She held an orange-yellow quilt tightly around her shoulders, and I recognized it as the divider that had hung in her doorway. "Amy, dear, wake up."

"What's wrong?" I asked in alarm.

"Nothing." She chuckled. "Well, everything, but let's not get technical here. The settlers will wake soon, and they'll expect a plan. I believe I have one. But I need your input."

I rubbed my eyes and glanced at the figure blocking the door. Coltrane lay on his side, his back to me, one arm extended over his head. The sight was like a punch to the gut. I looked away, swallowing hard. "What help would I be?"

"I found the excavator," Ruby said. "You see that pile over there, covered with the tarp?"

It was just a dark shadow, but I nodded.

"If we can get it to work, we can carve out a tunnel to the surface. I'm assuming that's why Lillibeth stored it in here. But I'm not sure whether NORA will be waiting for us out there." She hesitated. "And since I haven't set foot outside in many months, I need to know if there is anywhere safe left for us to go."

"How long will it take?" I asked, eyeing the mound.

"Two or three days, if we work through the night. Assuming we can get it to work. I'm fairly certain Coltrane knows it inside and out, considering how that boy worshiped the engineering plans his father left behind."

I resisted the urge to look toward the door again. "The other option is waiting it out, rationing food and then trying to bust through the wreckage from the bomb. But even if we can get through, which I doubt, we'll be stuck in the middle of the desert with no supplies."

"If they've left the cafeteria intact, we can scrounge what's left."

I shook my head. "The cafeteria is gone. From what I could tell, this was the last area left untouched, before Lillibeth—" My voice sounded strangled. *Focus.* I cleared my throat and tried again. "Personally, I'd forget about the tunnels and create a new route, straight east. Do any of the sentinel cameras still work? Maybe the network can help guide us to a hill where we'll be covered."

"That was my thought as well. And now the other question. Where do we go?"

"You meet up with the other refugees. They're building a settlement high in the mountains. You should be safe with them if you can get there."

She nodded. "If there's one thing this group is good at, it's surviving. What about you, Amy, dear?"

I looked at Coltrane's still form again. "I don't think I'm welcome here. I'll scout ahead and leave a trail for you."

She cocked her head. "What of your family?"

My mom's desperate shrieking seared into my mind. She probably thought I was dead. I closed my eyes against the pain. "I made my choice when I left. I can't go back now." What was it Mom had said? Something about Dresden needing me. Right. I bet he did.

Ruby glanced at the door and then patted my shoulder. "Lillibeth was a good leader and a dedicated mother. I believe she knew exactly what she was doing when she locked that door behind her."

My voice was hard. "Coltrane already lost one parent. She was all he had left."

"Coltrane is a survivor, like his father. I think she saw that." She gave a wry smile. "And you, dear Amy, carry a heavier burden than one person should be expected to shoulder. Do not take guilt that belongs to others. When you're my age, you'll have enough of your own."

I stood, looking away, anywhere but at Ruby's face. "Tell me what I can do to help."

Ruby hesitated. "I don't think the people should know you're involved. But I do think there's one person who needs someone, and I'm pretty sure he's faking sleep right now." She glanced at the door, then walked away.

It took several minutes for me to gather my courage, but I finally made my way over to Coltrane. At first I thought Ruby was wrong. Coltrane's side moved up and down in a steady, silent rhythm. The shudders that had rocked him last night were gone. He'd finally found a little peace in sleep. The last thing I wanted to do was take that from him.

As I turned to leave, he spoke, still facing the door. "It should have been you."

His words knocked the air from my chest, and I found it hard to answer. "I know."

"We were fine before you came. Maxim's right. NORA would've never found us, and my mom would still be here."

And they'd all be safe in their beds, anticipating another eventless day working away at the contributions. "It's true."

"But it's not really your fault, is it?" Coltrane rolled over and sat up. The same gentle eyes that had pleaded for my love yesterday were now hard as steel. "You didn't force your way down here." His voice was bitter. "It's because of me. I should have let you die."

"Coltrane—"

"Enough," he snapped. "I can't take back the past, but maybe it would be better if you left." He stood and strode toward the dark mound, stepping carefully around sleeping bodies. Ruby had begun sliding the tarp off the excavator, and he headed in that direction.

"But—" I moved to follow, but he turned and gave me a sharp look. I stopped in my tracks.

Coltrane's words had stirred a few people awake. Soon hundreds of settlers would begin their day, the first of many without a home. Today Ruby would propose that they make their way to the mountains. They wouldn't like it, but they had little choice. Denoux probably suspected we were dead, but I knew without a doubt that NORA would be watching the desert closely. Survival was our priority now. There would be time for looking back later.

I sat next to the door now, taking Coltrane's perch. The ground was still warm from where his body had lain. My dream came back then, hitting my mind with staggering force—Tali's insistence that it was my leaving that had killed them. What in the fates was that supposed to mean? Surely she wanted me to find happiness, especially when the only thing that awaited me in NORA was pain.

She doesn't want you to do anything, I reminded myself. *It was a dream pulled from your subconscious. Tali is dead. She's not telling you anything. Ever again.*

So much death. I hugged my knees like Coltrane had, taking over his somber vigil near where his mother had spent her last moments and trying desperately to push away the darkness in my thoughts.

33

VANCE

The guard didn't return all that day. When the adults returned in the late morning, coughing and dragging their feet in exhaustion, some of the older children greeted them on the trail with a makeshift breakfast. These kids had nothing but their clothes and possibly a tent made of canvas or old fabric sewn together, yet they gave away their food with a smile. Their breakfast looked like hard, dry pancakes.

"Want one?" a boy asked.

I turned to find a familiar face. Selia Dunstrep's son, the one I'd arrested in Olympus weeks earlier.

He beamed and held out a pancake. "They're hard and not sweet at all, but edible. I already had one."

I accepted it and took a bite. His description basically covered it. "Thanks," I said through the food, then swallowed. "So you got out."

"Yeah. My brother says he gave you his water packet yesterday. I've been watching you. Doesn't look like anyone's giving you food or water, so I figured I'd help."

"That was your brother?" The boy and his family had escaped NORA, at least. "Is your mom around?"

"No, she works at the—"

"Water plant. I know."

He watched me shove the last bite into my mouth. I savored it, letting the crumbs melt in my mouth before swallowing. It made my mouth dry, but, hey, it was food.

Finally he spoke again. "You need a guard. The other one left."

"I'm fine. Don't worry about it." The kid acted like I was a family friend, not the guy who had arrested him and his mom.

"Then I'll just hang out here for a while," he said and sat down on the hard ground, settling in and looking upward at the sky. "My brother's swimming, but he's crazy. That water is disgusting."

This conversation was so bizarre. "You remember who I am, right?" I asked.

"'Course."

I wiped my mouth with my sleeve. "I don't see why you're giving me food, then."

He turned to me. "My mom says NORA brought out the worst in all of us. Now that we're here, we can be ourselves again. Figure that applies to you as much as anybody."

I wasn't sure how to respond to that, so I sat back and let silence fall once again.

***

That night I awoke again, but there was no smoke in the air this time. I strained to hear something, anything, in the darkness. Selia's boys had taken turns "guarding" me all day, but they seemed to be gone now. Good.

I had nearly gone back to sleep when a foot stepped quietly in the gravel. If they'd walked by quickly, I wouldn't have woken up at all. I'd gotten used to sleeping with people striding by. The alarming part was how soft the footsteps were. Like someone was sneaking up on my cage.

I kept my eyes closed and steadied my breathing, ears perked for the slightest sound. There it was again, a tiny click of two rocks grinding underfoot. Closer now . . . maybe five feet.

My eye opened a crack. Still no guard. The cold night chill had settled upon my skin hours ago. Nobody else was awake.

The sound stopped. It was silent for so long I wondered if I had dreamed the sound. I turned to check.

Moonlight glinted off a metal surface. A knife, headed straight for my throat.

I recoiled and grabbed at where the handle should be, but the attacker had turned it, redirecting it at my chest. I gripped his hand and ducked, shoving his arm hard against the bars. He grunted but didn't let go of the knife.

I clung to it with both hands now, trying to peel it free, ducking below the attacker's hand. He closed his fist around the knife and sent a downward punch. That was harder to avoid. I wrapped his elbow as it entered the cage and snapped it sideways. He gasped, finally dropping the knife.

I scrambled for it, feeling along the floor of my cage. Clouds covered the moon tonight, withholding the light I so desperately needed. I caught the corner of the knife and accidentally swept it out of the cage.

My would-be assassin's outline was black as he moved around the cage toward where the blade had fallen. He held his injured arm with the other. "You will pay for that," he growled in broken English.

"After you," I snapped. My hand finally found the knife through the bars and yanked it back just before the man leaped for it. I sliced a nice line in his arm before he pulled back. Not deep, but enough to make him think twice.

He reached into his jacket and took something out. A pistol.

"Probably should have started with that," I said. "Unless you were trying to keep all of this quiet. I guess I can see the appeal if you're not intending to get caught."

He pulled the hammer back and aimed the gun at my chest. "Do not worry. I won't."

I'd had plenty of guns aimed at me. It wasn't tough to dodge if you did it just before they pulled the trigger, forcing the shooter to readjust his aim. But this time I had nowhere to go. I couldn't even stand up straight, much less leap to the side.

I threw all my weight forward against the cage. It balanced at first, resisting my weight, then started to tip forward. A sharp crack split the air as wind rushed past my face. I flung myself against the bottom as the cage fell onto its side. My attacker took a step forward, put one foot on the cage to keep it from rolling further, and aimed it at my head.

I kicked the floor with all my strength, using both feet at once. I wasn't sure what that would accomplish—maybe knock out the base, or knock his foot free, or even make him pause. But it propelled me to the top of the cage just before his shot went off. My shoulder jerked, and blinding pain slammed into my consciousness. I gritted my teeth. "Hey, everybody wake up!"

The man cursed in Chinese and aimed again.

"What's going on?" someone shouted. A woman. Her footsteps pounded through the gravel toward us.

"Rot in hell," the man whispered. Then he lowered the gun and placed both hands on the cage—and pushed.

It tilted again, then the cage started to roll. I was a limp doll. Each rotation caused me to land with a thud on the ground. The pain in my shoulder was blinding. Somewhere I became aware of a splash. And then water everywhere.

Water.

I shook myself awake as my head became submerged. I hadn't had time to take a last breath. I instinctively kicked, then waved my arms—and nearly blacked out again from the fire in my shoulder. My head hit the top of the cage. It was still intact, a solid grave sinking downward in the blackness of this watery world.

I grabbed the bars again and pushed them with all my strength. They held, just as they always had. I leaped upward and kicked the top where it curved, but my legs moved in slow motion and glanced right off the bars. I tried sticking my good arm through the bars and flapping downward, anything. But the cage continued its slow descent—in this darkness, the only way I could tell was by the increasing pressure in my ears.

My lungs burned nearly as bad as my shoulder now. Soon they would give way, and I would inhale a chestful of water. That would be the end, the moment the water doused the fire in my chest forever.

A strange clarity came over me then. I'd heard people say drowning wasn't a bad way to go. The brain calmed itself, offering comfort as the life-giving oxygen faded away. You simply went to sleep. But what I experienced now was anything but calm. Something inside me was screaming. *No!* it protested. *Not like this. This is not the end!*

Why not? I argued. My trial was nearly here. Mills had won already. I would be executed, a quick bullet to the chest.

Because I still want to fight.

The truth sank into my heart like the cage into the belly of a mountain. I wasn't done. My mother was being tricked, my clan was suffering. I couldn't let Mills get away with this. I was the only one who knew who Mills really was. Which meant I was the only one who could stop him.

I had to survive somehow.

My body began convulsing, my lungs trying to take control of my brain and gasp for air. I held it in with the last bit of consciousness I could muster, still straining against the bars to slow the cage's descent.

Then something happened. White flashed in my eyes, then away, like a flashlight.

The cage jerked.

I strained to see something in the darkness, but I could only feel movement. The cage tilted one way, then the other, and it slowed. Had I reached the bottom?

No, I was moving upward again. There was noise beside me, bubbles, like someone blowing out air. The light was back, shining in my face. I strained my eyes against it and reached out, catching hold of something. A person. There was someone out there, fingers grasping the bars from the outside.

The cage lurched, sending me against the bars, where another arm held me in place. Two people, one on each side. Lifting my cage upward.

I tilted back toward the center of the cage and looked up. Blue moonlight rippled above us like a watery sky. The surface. It was too far. I couldn't make it. I just—had to—

Everything faded.

34

VANCE

think that did it," a woman's voice said.

My insides rushed up and out my throat, burning and suffocating. I coughed and spat, my body shaking.

I was lying on my side. My hurt shoulder lay limp, and I fell onto my back and gasped.

"You're one lucky son of a—er, gun," a boy said. A tan blanket was wrapped around his shoulders, and he shivered but wore a triumphant grin on his face. Selia Dunstrep's talkative boy from yesterday. The older boy also wore a blanket, but he looked somber.

A lantern sat nearby, and I heard the sound of water behind us. The lake that had tried to kill me. My cage lay partially submerged in the water, the top torn cleanly off as if with a powerful laser.

The woman who had spoken at first sat back and put something down. A plastic cup with a bulb, some kind of respiration device. "Never thought I'd have to actually use that thing," she murmured.

Her face was slightly more tanned and her hair a darker brown instead of the blonde I remembered, but I knew instantly that it was Selia.

She gave a grim smile. "Better get these wet clothes off, or you'll die anyway."

The clouds had parted in the night sky above us, revealing thousands of brilliant stars. I was alive. Water lapped against my feet, but I barely noticed.

"How do you f-feel?" the younger boy asked.

I couldn't speak. A low moan escaped my lips, and my teeth began chattering. The pain hit again full force.

"He's in shock," the woman said. "Let's get him inside. Do your remember the hold I taught you?"

"Yeah. Clasp hands under him, right?"

It took them a minute, but they figured it out and lifted me over their shoulders, sending a new wave of pain ripping across my shoulder. I must have blacked out again because I woke up shirtless and covered in blankets.

"Don't move," Selia said. "I didn't realize the shooter got you." She turned and muttered something about clean bandages.

My body shook violently, but my mind was clearing. I'd arrested this woman and sent her family to the work camps. I had betrayed her in the worst way, and she'd saved my life. She was probably the woman who had run out and startled the shooter, too. "Thanks," I managed.

She gave a wry smile. "You owe me big after this. My poor boys are chilled to the bone. They had no change of clothing, so they're stark naked under their blankets. I'm sure they'll be back when they're decent."

"That man. He didn't—hurt you?"

"Don't concern yourself," she told me. "The shooter ran off after he shoved you in. I figured saving you from the lake was more important than chasing him down. You're lucky my boys were able to find you in all that water." She fingered a bandage, lowering it onto my wound, then pulled it off again. "The bullet may still be in there. We'll have to get a physician. I only had a year of medical training."

I reached up with my good arm and grabbed her wrist. "Why did you help me?"

She sighed. "I've wondered the same thing. Maybe it's because I've been talking to people. Maybe I see a little bit of your father in you after all, or I remember what you were like as a child." She put the bandage on the wound and pressed down. "Or maybe it's because we were better off as NORA prisoners than as settlers here. And you know what I think?"

I gasped at the pain, then managed, "What's that?"

"I think that, bad or good, you're the only one who can save us."

35

TREENA

The excavator broke out of the ground three days later. We sent scouts out to investigate, but they returned within the hour. NORA was nowhere in sight.

We traveled all day before finding a ravine that would give us shelter. I tried to pull Ruby aside to tell her good-bye, but she was too busy attending to important matters to talk to me.

While everyone settled in for the night, I sat against an outcropping of rock, gazing out at the never-ending hills and weeds that stood between us and the mountains. It was like I remained in limbo, forever between worlds. Not a child, not an adult—not a NORA citizen, and yet, not a settler either. This must have been how Vance had felt, working for the government that had killed his father and destroyed his way of life.

I felt eyes on me in the darkness. When we had emerged from the shelter this morning, Ruby had reminded everyone that the peace pact was still in effect. Violence would get someone kicked out. Her meaning was clear. I was off limits. Maxim's eyes had bored holes in me as she'd said it.

It was kind of Ruby to try, but I didn't belong here. I knew it as well as they did. I'd scout ahead and leave a trail for them, even though not a single one of them would thank me for it.

As if listening to my thoughts, Ruby emerged from the heat and stood over me. After a moment, she lowered herself down, slowly, as if in pain. Her bony thigh rested against mine as she settled back against the wall with a groan.

"Are you okay?" I asked, growing alarmed.

"My bones are angry with me today," she said. "Getting too old to sleep on the hard ground. Although I guess it's better to be on top than underneath it."

I wasn't sure if she meant the tunnels or death. Or both.

"There's something I've been meaning to ask you about," Ruby said. She pulled something out of her pocket and held it out.

I gasped. "My ametrine stone! Where did you find it?"

"It was in the box Coltrane brought me on my birthday. I think Lillibeth found it and put it in there, not knowing it was yours. I wondered if it might belong to you."

"It was gone when I woke up in her dwelling." I took it from her and rubbed the smooth surface. "Thank you."

"I wonder . . ." She held up her hand. On the third finger, she wore a ring with a red stone. "Have you noticed this? It's a ruby."

Her meaning sunk in, and I threw my arms around her, maybe a little too tightly. "We're related!"

Ruby returned the embrace. "I was going to get to that eventually, but there you have it," she said, her voice muffled against my shoulder. "Who are your grandparents?"

I pulled away, trying to remember what Jasper, my biological father, had said. "My grandfather's name was Alex, I think. Alex James. He died when my dad was young."

Ruby closed her eyes against the words. "Alex was my brother. He was nineteen when I left. I hope he had a happy life. I never did get the chance to say good-bye to him." She went quiet for a minute, then came back, giving my shoulder a squeeze. "So I'm your great-aunt, then, and this stone is your family token."

"The Peak family tradition." I paused. "I'm leaving, Ruby."

She gave me a sharp look. "You're running away again."

"I can't live like this, knowing what they've lost because of me. I wish I could just forget."

Ruby's expression changed—it became raw, pained. She gazed distantly at the desert. "Certain memories will never fade. You'll forget what people looked like or what they said or what you ate. But the moments you try to forget are the ones you never can. Like a broken arm—not life threatening but painful enough to remind you they exist."

I studied her. "Do you dream about life in NORA?"

"Every night." She looked down. "I dream about my mother. Her features have blurred in my memories, but I remember how it felt when she braided my hair, her nails running through it and catching on the ends. She said I didn't use enough smoothing cream. I hated the stuff. It made my hair smell strange."

I chuckled. "It still does. You'd think they would have improved that by now." It had been a very long time since I'd used it. Weeks? Years?

"And then there are the bad memories," Ruby said, her voice low and quiet. "I'd love to forget my twenty-six months as a Rater."

I sat taller. "You were a Rater?"

Ruby nodded. "When the Academy approved me for the program, I thought I'd burst with happiness. I had everything I ever wanted."

"Why did you leave, then?"

Her expression fell as sorrow lined her eyes. "A discovery. Something I learned about some of my coworkers. Something so horrible it clutches my heart to think of it even now." Her voice was tight. "I had an urgent question and went to find my mentor, a man I respected like my own father. It was during the frenzy, the last month before Rating Day, and I thought he'd be reviewing files in his office."

She stopped, and I leaned forward, not wanting to miss a word. But Ruby didn't seem to want to go on. She wrung her hands, grasping them together and then spreading her fingers and doing it all over again.

"Did you find him?" I coaxed.

"I found him." Her expression hardened. "He was in his office, but he wasn't alone. A girl—" A sob caught in her throat, and she looked away. I wrapped an arm around her. She stiffened, but she didn't pull away. "A girl was with him. They were—she was on his lap, and his hands were all over her. Her uniform was unzipped to her waist, and I could see her white bra from the doorway."

I felt sick. "He bribed her."

"He *threatened* her." Ruby sniffed, but her eyes were hard. "An hour with him, and her Rating score miraculously rose ten points. I checked. If she had fought him—well, I imagine that's where many of our 'surprise' yellows come from. I started looking into it. It took some doing since the girls never talked, poor dears, but I eventually uncovered several other Rater colleagues with the same 'perks.' So I gathered my evidence and went to the Rating Councilman himself, Herbert Montgomery."

"And?"

"He fired me."

"He *what?*"

"Said I was imagining things, making false claims, and said he'd reassign me immediately with a huge Rating reduction. He said I'd be sent to a work camp if I told anyone about my findings."

I sat back and swallowed hard. NORA could never admit to their system's faults, no matter how awful. For all I knew, girls were still being faced with that choice. I thought back to my Rating Day a lifetime ago and how desperate I'd been to score well. It had been life itself to me. What would I have agreed to? "No wonder you left."

"That, my dear Amy, is just the point. The people who haunt my dreams are not those horrible men. It's the girls. Those precious, scared girls who thought they had no choice but to obey their masters, those men who wielded fate in their filthy hands." She turned to me, suddenly fierce and determined. "I can't remember what my own mother looked like. But I remember every detail about the girl. She had beautiful brown hair, curly and long, and a round face. I'll never, ever forget the look she gave me. The pleading in her large eyes, the desperation. She's the one who comes to my dreams. She's the one who haunts me." A single tear trickled down one cheek, but Ruby didn't brush it away. Her face was steel. "She looked to me, the only person who could have done something, for salvation. And I left. I *left*."

"You tried, Ruby. You went to the councilman himself."

"I was a coward," she snapped. "I caught a glimpse of the difficult journey ahead, then gave up after a single step."

I wanted to tell her she was wrong, that she was a good person, a victim of NORA just like anyone else. But that felt wrong somehow. Ruby had lived in torment for over fifty years. Nothing I said would change anything. Instead I wrapped my arms around her for a hug. She clung to me like my mother used to, and my breath caught at the warmth in her embrace.

"You've a long life ahead of you, Ametrine," Ruby said. "I know you've seen more pain and darkness than a sixteen-year-old should." She pulled back and turned

259

determined eyes on me. "But I see greatness in you. Where I failed, you will continue until all is set right again. Leadership is in your blood." She patted my shoulder. "Get some sleep. If you still want to leave in the morning, I'll set aside some supplies."

———•◆•———

I couldn't sleep. I finally sat up and looked around. The desert floor was dotted with black shadows, all settlers asleep with their families. A few guards stood at the edges, keeping watch, but I wasn't sure what they were supposed to do if NORA came. They had no weapons.

With a grunt, I stood and headed toward the nearest guard, then blinked in surprise. It was Violet.

"Headed toward the latrine," I told her, and she hesitated briefly before nodding. But when I made my way down the slope and around the hill, I stopped and hugged myself, rubbing my arms for warmth. I felt like I could breathe here, away from all the accusing eyes. This was the first time I'd been truly alone for a very long time.

No, I'd been alone for weeks. I'd just been surrounded by people. One of the two people who had shown unconditional kindness would probably never speak to me again, and I couldn't blame him.

My thoughts began to grow fuzzy as I stood there, staring at the empty desert. I turned reluctantly back toward the camp—and froze, squinting. Some of the stars in the distance had just disappeared, then reappeared again in turn.

"What the fates?" I muttered. I followed the phenomenon in a line. There it was again, moving fast. Something dark against the sky. I strained to hear, but there was no sound.

I stared in the direction it had gone, unblinking. It wasn't a chopper. Some kind of scouting plane designed for stealth? Had they seen us? The aircraft continued on its eastward course, and then I lost sight of it in the darkness. If it came in for another pass, we were in big trouble. Panic welled up inside me, and I turned to run back and warn the settlers.

And bumped into someone.

"Amy," someone whispered.

"Coltrane? What are you doing out here?"

"Well, I was going to use the latrine, but then I saw something really weird. Did you see it too?"

"Yeah. Was that the aircraft you saw the night you found me?"

"Maybe."

"We have to warn them. That thing might come around again."

He shook his head. "I don't think so. It was moving too fast to be a scouting plane. Besides, it was headed straight for the next town."

"There's another city out here?"

"They're all over the place."

We strained to listen in the darkness, closely watching the sky overhead. My heart pounded so loudly I wondered if he could hear it. "Coltrane, I'm so sorry—"

"Don't."

An awkward silence followed, and then I straightened. "I'm going to follow it."

"You're going to *what?*"

"We have to know what that thing was. Maybe there are soldiers ahead, setting up a trap for us."

"And you'll walk right into it and make a bigger mess of things."

His words stung, but I shook my head. "I'm still going. You can come if you want." I started walking.

"Fine." He trotted up beside me. "But for the record, I think this is a bad idea."

"You're probably right."

We walked for the next hour in silence.

36

VANCE

I sat on a pile of blankets and old bandages and struggled to pull my boot on. It was still a little soggy, and the leather had shrunk. It refused to allow my foot entrance. Pain lanced through my shoulder as I pulled harder, and with a sucking sound, my foot finally slipped inside. I picked up the other one.

"There you are," Edyn said, holding the flap of the tent open. "Mills is throwing a hissy fit. He thought you escaped." She wore a pink blouse and black trousers that fit her curves perfectly. Her blonde hair fell in soft waves past her shoulders. While I'd been recovering from a gunshot wound, she'd been curling her hair. Typical Edyn.

"That's the plan," I told her.

"Hmm. Must be tough work, trying to get yourself killed. Need a hand with that boot?"

"Nope." The second foot slid in without a problem. I shoved myself to my feet and ducked out of the shelter and into the sunlight.

"You're going out like that?" she asked, following me out.

I looked down and remembered my shirt was gone, torn and discarded in the mayhem last night. The bruises from my run-in with the clan had turned yellow and brown, and my shoulder was heavily bandaged. "I've seen plenty of men go without shirts here."

Her mouth curved downward into a petite frown. "True, but none of them look quite like you at the moment." She gestured at my chest. "I'm not sure whether you'll send women swooning or screaming."

"As long as they're out of my way, it doesn't matter." I wasn't sure how I'd get to the rim in broad daylight, but at the moment I didn't care. I started for the trail.

She jumped in front of me. "Where are you going, exactly?"

Selia was nowhere to be seen. Even the usual neighborhood kids were gone. I'd overslept. "I'm not sticking around until Mills figures out where I am. I'm going to find my mom and sisters."

"And then?"

"Then we're out of here."

Edyn gave a dramatic sigh and folded her arms. "Someone tried to kill you last night. Aren't you curious to find out who it was?"

I looked past her to the trail. "Everyone wants to kill me. Some are more patient than others."

"Vance," she said, grabbing my arms to keep me in place. "A few days ago I would've told you to run. But things are changing. We need you. I've talked to dozens of settlers in the last two days, and most of them are on your side. They respect you. At the very least they feel sorry for you."

I chuckled. "Back home you always felt bad when we brought home meat for dinner. You'd go on about the poor elk or rabbit whose life had been snuffed out. But in the end you ate it anyway."

She flinched. "I don't eat meat anymore. I'm a vegetarian."

"So you kill vegetables instead of animals. My analogy stands." I started to push past her, but she put a gentle hand on my chest. Her expression had changed from irritated to open and vulnerable. Her lips were the same soft pink as her shirt, and I had to tear my eyes away.

"I want you to stay, Vance," she whispered. "Please listen to what I'm saying. I think we can get you off for the murders."

"I didn't murder anyone."

REBECCA RODE

"I know that, and soon everyone else will too." She leaned in, her body right up against my stomach. "There's nothing out there for you. Your family has a comfortable home, Vance. I know you think our clan is being treated unfairly, but we can figure that out. Besides," she whispered, her lips just inches from mine, her voice trembling, "now that I have you back, I don't know if I can let you go."

Edyn's head tilted upward, and she slid her hand up my chest, carefully avoiding the bandage. Her fingers reached my unshaven jaw, then curved around to my hair. It sent a shiver down to my feet.

"You don't know what I've gone through," she whispered. "To spend years defending you, hearing horrible stories from refugees about what you're doing in a place I've never been. All the nights spent wondering if you thought of me, hoping you didn't find someone else but also hoping you weren't alone. And now that you're finally here in front of me, you can't wait to leave."

Edyn, Rutner's daughter. This was what our parents had wanted. I still remembered my mother's secretive smile when we went off to play and the way my father asked how she was doing at dinner, as if he hadn't just seen her hours before. If NORA hadn't attacked, we'd probably be a couple by now.

But that was another life. Even now I thought about Treena—the way she'd run, determined and

266

unarmed, from a group of men twice her size. How she gripped her necklace when she was worried. At her orientation, she had tried to cover up the fact that she'd found smugglers. Treena, the successor to the throne, had chosen to protect a young girl she didn't even know. In her first hour in the empress's task force, she'd done what I hadn't been able to do in two years.

Then I'd given her my heart, and she'd smashed it. Why was it so hard to remember that part? Treena didn't care for me. She'd chosen bliss with Bike Boy.

"At least give me a proper good-bye," Edyn said, and shoved her mouth onto mine.

Her lips were soft and warm, and I tried to relax. Her hands wrapped around my back as her head tilted sideways, pulling me closer as our mouths moved together.

I wrapped my arms around her waist, determined to enjoy this. Frustration pulsed through my body, and Edyn seemed to like the intensity with which I held her. I told myself it was because I was in the moment and not angry at Treena.

It wasn't until Edyn's hand brushed the bruises on my side that I pulled away with a grunt.

Her hand flew to her mouth, but she couldn't keep the smile away. "Oh! I forgot. I'm so sorry."

"I'm not."

Edyn wore a mischievous look. She slid her hand down my arm and wrapped her fingers around mine, then gave me a quick kiss on the cheek. "We'd better find you a shirt. Then I'll talk to the assembly, see if they'll order Mills to let you stay in the jail again. That cage idea was ridiculous anyway—"

"Nothing's changed," I told her, my voice a little breathless. Guilt settled heavily in my gut. I pushed the sensation away. I'd done nothing wrong. "I want nothing more than to make things better for our people here. But I can't do that from prison."

Edyn's eyes were big and round. "What do you have in mind?"

I opened my mouth to speak, then noticed movement behind her. A large group was making their way down the trail, all dressed in dark gray uniforms.

I cursed and pulled Edyn behind a nearby tent.

"I see your language hasn't improved much," Edyn muttered.

"Tell me about Rutner," I whispered, ignoring her comment. "Where does he fall into all this?"

She stiffened. "My dad won't help us."

My father had trusted Rutner with more than his life. The Rutner I remembered would do anything for our family. He was solid, like the center of the earth. If he wasn't willing to help, that was a bad sign.

"If you could just talk to him, tell him the situation," I said.

"No." She clenched her jaw and looked at the ground. "My dad was very affected by his time in

NORA. He's made it very clear that he doesn't want to be involved."

"Affected? But he was fine when I saw him last." He'd been there for negotiations between EPIC and my clan. Besides his dark looks and flat tone when he spoke directly to me, I hadn't noticed anything amiss.

"Please, Vance." Her tone was flat. "He won't help us, and that's that."

I shook my head and peered around the tent fabric. It was definitely guards, all Ju-Long's men, and they were headed this way. If they'd been sent to look for me, I needed a better hiding place. They were sure to keep an eye on the trail as well. Blasted Edyn. She'd chosen to have this conversation at the worst possible time.

Edyn put her hand on my cheek and turned my head toward her. "There's got to be another way. If only we could get everyone to work together."

"They did, once," I said. "During the fire. Everyone jumped in and helped . . ." I trailed off. The fire. It had sparked in the bushes a full hundred yards away from the nearest house. A person could easily have hidden in all that vegetation. Besides, the placement of it—exactly where the south winds would hit and push the flames upward—it was too much to be a coincidence.

"Someone started that fire on purpose," I said.

Edyn froze, then looked away. "Who would intentionally set a fire in a place like this?"

Someone who wanted to hurt the higher families and help me at the same time. It was placed right across the lake from me, in a place I'd be sure to see it. "Someone who knew I'd wake everyone up and rally them to fight the fire."

She stared at the ground. "A few people here would know you well enough for that."

I took a step back. "But it wasn't any of them, was it?"

"It's over with, and nobody got hurt."

A barely controlled rage built inside me. "How dare you, Edyn. How dare you take peoples' lives into your hands like that."

"You know *nothing* about this!" Her voice shook, but there were no tears in her eyes. Something new, something cold, glimmered in her beautiful blue eyes. "You've always been so arrogant. How do you even know it was for you?"

I stared at her. "What was it, then, some kind of twisted justice?"

"You really are clueless." She shook her head. "Look, Blackfell has no term limits on leadership. They serve until one of two things happen: they die, or someone challenges them for the governor position. My father knew he wanted to challenge immediately after his arrival, but he didn't think the locals would accept him. He thought that planting evidence of Mills's hand in a wildfire would help his case. Unfortunately for him, he didn't take your new living arrangements into consideration. They doused the fire too soon. Nobody's found the evidence, and now everyone thinks you're some kind of hero. You have a way of complicating things, Vance Hawking."

Everything she'd done was in her father's name. And now she was stalling, preventing me from leaving. I was such an idiot.

I shoved her away. "Yeah, well, it turns out that I don't like being used. Keep your political games and stay far away from me, because if I ever see you again, I'm telling everyone what you did."

"Then we'll go down together," she snapped. "When you start thinking with your brain again and not your ego, send for me. In the meantime, I'll be doing what's best for you." She stepped around the tent. "Guards! Vance is over here."

37

VANCE

With a stream of colorful words, I ducked into the tent, scrambling for a weapon. There was nothing but clothing and blankets and a few spoons.

"Come on. Not even a knife?" I grumbled as the footsteps outside grew louder. Edyn stood in front of the tent, yelling and pointing. I lifted the back of the tent and sprinted out, headed for the next one over. The thin fabric wouldn't provide much cover from a bullet, but it was better than nothing. The ache in my shoulder sharpened as salty sweat burned into the wound. It had been way too long since I'd run, and the days spent huddled behind bars had taken their toll.

I stumbled over a rock and nearly landed on a child playing in the dirt. His mother yanked him back, wide-eyed, away from the crazed, shirtless man with a wrapped shoulder running across their camp. I jumped to my feet and turned—just in time to see a guard raise a pistol to my face.

The mother screamed. The guard blinked, and his finger hovered above the trigger for a fraction of a second.

I changed direction and barreled into someone, toppling us both to the ground. Arms grabbed at me as I leaped up and scrambled away, but more bodies and more hands tore at my bandages and slashed at my hair.

"Secure him!" Ju-Long's voice snapped.

My body was sluggish, like fighting through mud. My sore shoulder was on fire now, shooting pain down the left side at every movement. I pushed through it, trying to force the wall of bodies to make way so I could slip by, but for every soldier I downed, two more were there to take his place.

Someone wrenched my arm behind my back for a wrist hold. As I twisted and pulled away, I caught a glimpse of Ju-Long's irritated expression. He stood rigidly, arms at his sides, waiting impatiently for the wayward captive to be subdued.

I was too slow. A set of arms grabbed me from behind just as cool metal clamped around my wrist. I got a punch in before they got the other arm in, but the cuffs just enraged me further. I bowled over several men on my way to Ju-Long, ready to trample him as well.

A small smile crossed his lips. Just before I reached him, someone caught my leg, sending to me the ground. Since my wrists were fastened behind me, I couldn't catch myself. I landed right on my sore shoulder. With a groan, I rolled over onto my back.

"Only a fool keeps fighting when he knows he is beaten," Ju-Long said. He motioned for his men to lift me up. Someone grabbed my injured shoulder—roughly—and I gasped in agony.

"Wait!" a voice cried. Selia ran down the slope, a panicked look on her face as she pulled a younger man along by the elbow. She pulled up, breathing hard. The man shook her off and wiped his sleeve.

"You can't take him yet," she gasped. "I just found the surgeon. He needs to remove the bullet from his shoulder."

Ju-Long glanced at my bandage. "My report doesn't mention a gunshot wound. I was told he rolled his cage into the lake in an escape attempt."

I snorted. "Is that what Mills's assassin told you?"

Selia turned back to Ju-Long. "How could you leave him alone and defenseless, especially down by the lake at night? I'll have words with the assembly and Mills about this."

Ju-Long's surprise turned into a slow smile. "Do what you must." He nodded to his soldiers. "Back to the jail with him." They shoved me forward.

"Didn't you hear me?" Selia exclaimed. "The boy needs a surgeon, or that wound will get infected. I traded my own bedding for the operation."

"A waste of time and effort, I'm afraid," Ju-Long said. "This boy won't live much longer."

She looked as if she wanted to push the issue, but I jumped in. "Thanks for your help, Selia, but I'll be fine."

We turned onto the trail that lined the lake, headed for the jail. Most of Ju-Long's guards were Asian, and they held me tightly as we walked, not speaking. One man's eye was nearly swollen shut, all purple and black. He glared at the ground.

"I've been gathering witnesses, Hawking," Selia shouted behind us. "Just hold on. Soon the entire settlement will know the truth."

I looked behind us at the turn.

Edyn was gone.

38

TREENA

I t took nearly an hour to reach the city. I crept toward it, bent over, hiding behind mounds and crawling on my hands and knees in places. Coltrane followed my lead.

Finally, we reached the outskirts. Several structures in varying stages of decay dotted the desert, surrounded by broken up concrete that had once been roads. But I didn't see the strange black aircraft anywhere.

"Maybe it's inside the city," Coltrane suggested.

I shivered, remembering the last time I'd set foot in an abandoned town. "I'm not going inside any buildings. Maybe it flew over the town and kept going."

"Let's go in there," Coltrane said, pointing to what looked like a fueling station. "We should have decent cover, and it looks down on this part of the city. You never know."

I looked at the dark and looming structure. "Fine, but warn me if you see any skeletons."

Coltrane laughed quietly.

"I wasn't kidding."

"Sorry."

We walked carefully past the concrete pieces and went inside. It had been looted decades before, rows of empty shelves overturned and wrappers littering the floor.

I situated myself at a counter and looked out, wincing as Coltrane groaned. He'd put his elbow in something sticky on the counter. I shushed him and peered out the empty windowpane.

A black aircraft sat across the way, taking up nearly every centimeter of what had once been a six-lane street. A hovercraft with four rotors at its sides. Dark figures carrying boxes descended a side ramp and went into a building, sending shadows dancing across the road. From the way the figures stooped as they walked, it was evident the crates were heavy.

The two men with lanterns were there. They pointed and occasionally stopped someone, but if they were talking, I couldn't hear anything.

The building they entered was one of the larger ones, still intact and windowless. Somehow it had survived a lifetime of desert heat and windstorms.

These couldn't be NORA soldiers. They would have secured the area and worked in broad daylight, bold and unafraid. Sneaking around at night was not their way.

Who else could they be?

Settlers. My heart quickened at the thought. Maybe they knew where to find Vance. If they had secret aircraft, they could travel to and from the mountains easily. A few more passengers wouldn't be a problem, and our trip would be a matter of hours, not weeks.

I felt a leap of excitement at the thought. I could be with Vance by this time tomorrow.

But something wasn't right. If the settlers could travel by air, why hadn't they done it before now? They could have transported the NORA refugees in shifts rather than forcing us to cross the desert. And why would the settlers keep cargo here, so close to the border?

One of the men raised his arm and yelled something. I strained to hear, but I couldn't make out the words.

Another figure shouted back. A woman. Her words made no sense either. Their voices rose and dipped in an unfamiliar way. Definitely not English.

We watched for several more minutes as the aircraft was unloaded. Then thirty or so soldiers flooded out the door and up into the cargo bay, packing themselves in where the crates had been.

I leaned forward as the aircraft lifted off the ground, but again, it barely made a sound. More of a high-pitched whine. It lifted straight into the air, hovered for a moment, then turned and disappeared into the darkness, going the opposite way it had come.

I slumped, disappointed. I'd hoped to get a better look as it passed overhead. It probably had distinguishing features or a logo, at the very least. Now I'd never know who those people were.

The building they'd just filled with boxes stood unguarded, silent as every other structure in this abandoned town.

"Stars, that thing was huge," Coltrane muttered, shaking his head, still staring at the blackness where the aircraft had melted into the sky. "So, did you get your question answered?"

I barely heard him. My brain was hard at work, trying to piece everything together. No guards. At least, none outside. Surely they'd left someone inside. Whatever their cargo was, there was a lot of it.

Something big is happening, my mom had said. Was this related somehow?

"Amy?"

I turned to Coltrane and pursed my lips, unsure how to explain what I was about to do.

He folded his arms. "You're going closer, aren't you?"

"I have to know."

"You're a raving lunatic, Amy. Really."

"I've been called worse." I crept around the wall and headed for the exit.

He gave a growl of frustration, but he followed.

———————

I tried to imitate how the soldiers had moved, smoothly and quietly. I imagined someone training a stunner at my head every time I ran out into the open, but there was no sound. We rounded the building and approached from the back, just in case. The night air was perfectly still. The moon emerged from the clouds, bathing the building in an eerie blue light.

"Okay," Coltrane said, and I winced at the noise. "What's your plan?"

I held a finger to my lips and motioned for him to get behind me. There was a door on the back side, but no windows. An old sign hung sideways, covered in dust and shadows. I tried to pick out the words.

Hamilton Credit Center

Please enter on other side

A familiar nervousness hung heavy in my stomach. I'd felt this way before missions as a member of EPIC. My life had been at risk each time, yet I'd survived.

You were surrounded by armed soldiers, I reminded myself. This time I was essentially alone and weaponless. Facing an unknown enemy.

Coltrane was right. I really was insane.

I hesitated, looking back at the road we'd traversed. We could turn back now, and nobody would think the less of me. Except me. No, if NORA soldiers were setting up bases in abandoned cities, we needed to know it. And if it wasn't NORA—we *definitely* needed to know it.

I picked up a piece of broken tile, aimed, and tossed it at the door. It fell short. I grabbed another. On the third try, a piece struck the door and bounced off. We leaped behind the corner again and plastered ourselves against the building.

Nothing. Nobody came out with stunners or rifles. Not a sound.

This time I found a rock about the size of my fist. It sailed true and hit the corner of the door with a *whack* that sounded like a gunshot. That would be impossible for any lurkers to ignore. We hid around the corner for a full five minutes while I gathered my courage. Coltrane must have seen the determination on my face because he gently touched my arm. "You don't have to do this."

"Yes, I do." I started to turn away.

He grabbed my arm, forcing me to face him. "Seriously, Amy. If you're worried about my settlement,

282

don't be. They know better than anyone how to survive in the desert."

"That's not it at all."

"Then what, your fellow NORA citizens? I thought you didn't care about them anymore."

I'd never stopped caring about them. I wasn't loyal to the government; I was loyal to my neighbors and friends, people who followed the script and did everything they were supposed to do without knowing why. People whose lives were being examined under a microscope and manipulated by people with strings. They deserved better. Someone had to help them.

I already tried. I'm done with that now.

Instead of replying, I strode around the corner and headed for the door. Coltrane sighed and followed. I made it to the door and stopped. There was no doorknob.

I went around to the front and listened closely. No sound. This door had a knob with a fancy-looking keypad. A red light blinked at the top corner.

A quick yank of the doorknob confirmed that it was locked.

"Password," an automated voice said with an accent. Strange.

"It's voice-activated," Coltrane said.

"No kidding." I yanked on the doorknob again, and the red light began flashing faster. "Is this all that's guarding this place? An automated lock?"

"Password," the accented voice repeated.

"Uh, Amy?" Coltrane said.

"Just a second." I tapped at the lock, but it seemed secure. A beeping began from the lock. Slow, but then it began speeding up.

"Amy."

"There's got to be a way to break into this." I felt around the mechanism for an opening or a way to key in a code. There was nothing. It was a sleek, modern-looking device.

The beeping quickened even more.

"Amy!" Coltrane shouted. He grabbed my arm and yanked me away.

We stumbled down the front step, landing on the ground. I leaped to my feet and whirled on him. "What was that about?"

"I know what that beeping is! We have to get out of here!" he said, scrambling to his feet. He grabbed my arm again and pulled me after him.

I yanked my arm away. "Stop that. What—"

An explosion rocked the night—an incredible force picking me up and throwing me backward. My legs flew up over the rest of me, and I tumbled before landing in a heap with my face in the broken concrete. Several smaller explosions sounded off, and then the night was lit by an eerie red hue. Heat singed my back. I turned slowly around.

The building was on fire. Flames licked the open doorway. What had once been the porch was now engulfed.

"Stars," Coltrane breathed. "That explosion was too big to be chance. There had to be explosives in there." He looked around, then back at the fire. "Great. People are going to see this for miles around."

A detonating defense mechanism. Those soldiers would rather lose their precious cargo than allow it to be discovered.

"Let's get back," I said.

Coltrane's expression was grave. "You don't have to tell me twice."

39

TREENA

We hadn't made it two kilometers before the scouting planes showed up. They had nowhere to land, so they circled the abandoned city. I knew choppers wouldn't be far behind.

"We've got to warn everyone," Coltrane said as we ran, breathing hard. "I think you really pissed NORA off by destroying their weapons base."

"I don't think that was NORA," I said thoughtfully. Nothing fit. What would they have to gain by storing ammunition out here? If they wanted to attack the settlers, they'd do it with bombers. Ground weapons were practically useless to them, especially so far from everything. And that strange aircraft . . .

"Of course it was," Coltrane said between breaths. "Who else would it be? And now they're going to descend upon this valley. We've got to get everybody out before we're discovered."

That much was true. My chest burned with pain, and my limping was more pronounced as the minutes went on, but I blocked all that out. I'd brought more danger upon Coltrane's people, and I had to make it right.

The settlers were scrambling when we got back, shoving half-folded blankets into their packs and soothing the children.

"Where in the dying stars have you guys been?" Maxim snapped as we approached. He whirled on Coltrane, avoiding my gaze like I wasn't there. "Don't you realize there was a huge explosion?"

"We've got to leave," I said, suddenly swaying with exhaustion. My leg throbbed, pulsing with each beat of my weary heart. "NORA is on their way. You've got to get over those hills before they reach the town."

"How could you possibly know that?" Maxim said.

"We saw them arrive," Coltrane cut in. "They're mad about the weapons storage we blew up."

"You *what?*"

I groaned inwardly. Coltrane wasn't helping the situation. "We didn't mean to. There were soldiers out there, so we went to investigate."

Maxim's expression was murderous. "And now you've brought their army down on us a second time!"

Irina, Maxim's mother, caught sight of us and strode over. Several others walked up behind her, all elders, their eyes all trained on me. "There you are. When we awoke and found you gone, the elders met in discussion."

Uh-oh. "You're throwing me out."

"You've got to go," a man said. I recognized him as the one who had tried to fix the explosive mechanism in the emergency shelter. "We have decided you're too big a threat to remain with us. You've only confirmed the wisdom of that decision."

Coltrane folded his arms and glared at me but didn't move away. "Did Ruby agree to this?"

Irina pursed her lips. "Ruby is still resting, but it doesn't matter. The vote was unanimous."

"Coltrane," I said softly. "It's okay. I meant to leave by now anyway."

"But the pact!" Coltrane insisted. "You can't—"

"Coltrane." I put a gentle hand on his shoulder. "I'm going."

"I'll come too," Coltrane said.

"No," Irina and I both said at the same time. She clamped her mouth shut and gestured for me to continue.

"Thanks for believing in me," I told him. "But they're right. I'll only put you in more danger."

"Let's move out!" a man called, and the people began shuffling after him, families and packs in tow.

"You can't wander out there alone," Coltrane protested.

"I'm heading toward the mountains. I know the settlers weren't sure about Ruby's plan to follow the refugees, but I hope you can talk them into it. Maybe I'll see you again soon."

The old Coltrane would have opened his arms for a hug, but now he just stood awkwardly, looking at the ground. Then he swung the pack off his back and dug through the pocket, pulling out a handful of water packets and a tube of nutrition pills. "I don't have much, but these will help you last a few more days."

"What about you?"

"The elders won't let me starve. I never liked those pills anyway. They make me sick."

I gratefully took his offerings, ignoring the eyes of hundreds of refugees following me, and stuffed them into my pockets. I caught a glimpse of Ruby gathering her things. She moved slowly, carefully. "Take good care of Ruby. She's not doing well."

"I will."

There were no belongings to retrieve. I headed back to the trail, watching the night sky thawing to the east. A new day had begun. Soon it would send heat and sun beating down upon my head. The farther I got while it was still cool, the better.

For the second time in weeks, I didn't look behind me as I stepped out into the open desert.

40

VANCE

My trial was the next evening. I wasn't sure why Mills was even going through with it. My appearance—disheveled, unshaven, my arm in a sling—was enough to convince anyone I was a half-crazed murderer, even without the dozen guards that stood within arm's reach, ready to grab me if I leaped into the crowd again. He had an entire bench of "witnesses" behind him.

The bench on my side of the platform was empty.

The audience stood back from the platform this time, whispering as the proceedings began. This time, though, the anger I'd seen in their faces was replaced with something else. Wariness. It wasn't much, but it was something.

"You stand alone," Mills said. "Where is your representative?"

"I represent myself," I said.

Mills smiled, showing rows of straight teeth. "Very well. In that case, with your permission, honored ones, we will begin with the prosecution."

"Naturally," I muttered.

Mills began to pace as if collecting his thoughts, then he lifted the amplifier to his lips. "Assembly members and respected people, you've settled here to give your families the best possible chance at life. That is your right, and it is our pleasure to welcome you. We've enjoyed many decades of peace. Until today. Today, we have before us the most dangerous criminal our jail walls have ever seen.

"Last time we met, Hawking kindly demonstrated the horrors of a barbaric justice system. You watched it happen. Now, I ask you to consider his character. Is this the type of man we'd like to welcome into our delicate way of life? Can we trust him to keep our laws and our secrets? Can we look at this man and say with a surety that he is on our side?" Mills turned to look at me, his eyes dark. "Today young Hawking's true character will be revealed. Witnesses, I ask each of you to stand in turn and tell us what happened three weeks ago, on that night of horrible devastation. Please keep it to five minutes each."

One by one, they came forward and took the amplifier before accusing me of ditching my clan instead of going with them to the square. That part was true. The accounts ran together, one after another, all reliving the gruesomeness of the scene when they'd come upon it. Surprisingly, Anton never stepped forward. I had expected him to be first in line for the attack. Instead, he simply stood behind me, frowning, his arms folded.

Mills cut them off at the same point every time, the moment where they described the aftermath. He didn't want the assembly to know what came after that. If they knew how I'd coaxed the bystanders to come help, how we'd worked together with NORA citizens to save lives, it wouldn't help his case. My hands slowly formed into fists, and I ground my teeth.

Then four men I'd never seen before took their turns, all with red scars on their foreheads. They'd taken their implants out recently. Each one said I'd threatened him, even going so far as to blackmail the last one, and then helped them escape the electrified border wall after giving them instructions. They said the bomb had been right where I left it, buried in the hills outside NORA, and that it had belonged to my father and we'd stored it all this time, just waiting for the opportunity to take out our anger on the NORA government. Their testimonies were so outlandish that I snickered several times.

When everyone had spoken, Mills took the amplifier back. "Before I turn it over to the *defense*," he said with a smile, eliciting chuckles through the crowd, "I have one more witness. Dean Rutner, please come forward."

There was movement in the crowd. I caught a glimpse of Edyn's face, and then Rutner emerged. He climbed onto the platform and stood in front of the witnesses, far from me, his steely gaze on the crowd. My father's most trusted friend wouldn't meet my eye. Rutner had always been respected by the clan, a hardworking and generous man, but he had a hard edge when crossed. In NORA, he'd kept track of the locations of our clan members as best he could, which was why I'd approached him in the first place. He was best equipped to contact them as part of our deal. They'd help Treena get the throne, and she'd let us all leave. It hadn't taken much coaxing to convince him.

But if the witnesses had already testified about this part, why did Mills think it was so important Rutner confirm it as well? Edyn's words came back to me, her warning about her father's agenda, and I shook off the feeling that something was not right.

"I knew the Hawking family well," Rutner said. "His father was a decent man, and Vance was raised with the best they could offer. I had almost as much a hand in his upraising as his father did. So believe me when I say it gives me no pleasure to tell you this, but for the sake of justice, it must be done." He raised his voice. "I've been gathering evidence since the beginning. There is no doubt that Vance Hawking is a traitor. The real question is why. He has said he was only protecting his family. But if that's the case, why has his own mother refused to visit him since her arrival? I think it's because she knows he's guilty." He frowned at the audience, and I followed his gaze to my mother's face. She, like most others in the crowd, was watching me. When our eyes locked, she looked away.

"A settlement like this operates upon a foundation of trust. And even before our clan was separated, we saw a pattern of reckless, challenging behavior from Vance. As soon as he could, he turned against us and exercised his newfound power. To answer Mills's question, no, this is not a man we want standing with us."

There were several nods in the audience. It didn't matter that it was the word of one man. The fact that the one man was Rutner changed everything. I met Edyn's gaze. She scowled at me as if to say, *Now do you want my help?*

Mills took the amplifier back. "Thanks for your testimony. We'll now let Vance's representative call his witnesses." He smirked. "Oh, dear. Looks like he has neither one."

"Yes, he does," a voice called out. Selia's. She came running forward. The guards helped her onto the platform, and she stood between me and the edge as if forming a wall between me and the crowd. "He calls me as a witness."

The senior elder leaped to her feet faster than she should have been able to. "You cannot simply jump up and offer your testimony. You must be called. This is ridiculous."

"I call Selia Dunstrep," I said and waved a hand like a performer. "Please tell us your story."

"Thank you," she said. There was a smile pasted on her face, but her eyes glinted with anger as Mills reluctantly handed her the amplifier.

"Weeks ago I sat on a transport train," she began, "headed for the work camps. I was a prisoner, arrested by Vance Hawking. I had the task of comforting my children, telling them everything would be all right when I knew that it wasn't. My children were about to be fostered out, sent to live who knows where, and I faced a lifetime of hard labor for the crime of buying food for my sick and starving children. Like most of you, I chose Vance as the target of my hatred."

Her voice softened, and she looked down.

"But settlers, that was incorrect. It was wrong of me to do what was right for my family and then expect Vance not to do the same for his. The moment our settlement fell, we have all done exactly the same thing—protected ourselves instead of each other." Her voice rose, sharp and accusing. "Some of you noted the bulging pockets and darting eyes of your smuggling neighbors. Rather than protecting them, you called in the tip and received a reward. And don't pretend you banded together when we came here, either. Tell me why some of our clan live up top, while others languish near the bottom? I tell you this. If Vance is guilty, then we are all guilty."

"What about the missile?" someone called out.

"Only the witness may speak," the elder snapped.

Selia's head raised, her jaw set. "I have done my own research, Rutner, and mine is far more than an opinion. I know exactly what happened that night. Vance Hawking intended to run. Who of us would stay in that situation? He went all the way to the border wall before overhearing the missile plan. It would have been easy for the boy to shrug it off and leave us on our own. I don't know what changed his mind, but he came back. Vance put himself in the path of a *missile*, knowing where it would land, trying to save us all. He arrived too late and jumped in, trying to help the injured and dying, organizing rescue efforts. Mills asked about his character. I tell you, that is exactly it. Iron Belt's clan, if this is what you saw, please raise your hands."

At first nobody moved. But then I saw one reluctant arm go up, then another. Soon there were three times as many hands as there were witnesses on

Mills's bench. None of the witnesses raised theirs, but a couple of them nodded.

The guards muttered to each other behind me, and I turned to see Edyn climbing onto the platform. "Forgive me, assembly members, but I was detained. Please allow me to take it from here. Selia, are you finished?"

Stunned, Selia nodded. "I am." She gave me a pitying look, then jumped down from the platform.

I whirled on Edyn. "I told you—"

"To be on time." She shrugged. "I know. Sorry I'm so late. If we've heard from all the witnesses and examined all the evidence, allow me to make a closing statement."

"I don't need your help," I told her.

She flinched, but her smile barely wavered. "I told you that I'd save your sorry life one way or another. Let me do this one last thing for you." She turned to the crowd. "The second accusation is that Vance coordinated a missile attack on the people of NORA. We've had testimony on both sides of this issue. Although they cancel each other out, I'd like to say this: not a single member of his clan was hurt. Not one." She looked pointedly at the assembly. "Those who were killed were citizens, not settlers. If anyone has jurisdiction for those actions, it's NORA. Not us. The ridiculous accusation of mass murder should be dropped altogether." She turned and handed me the amplifier. "Now it's your turn, Vance. They need to know whose side you're on."

The crowd murmured. I raised it to my mouth, adjusting it in my grip. It was difficult with my arms chained at the wrists. "Those who have never worn numbers call us beaten, defeated. But I'll tell you what I saw while I was on the other side, fighting to keep my family alive."

The audience was silent. Even Mills stared at me, expressionless.

I paused, gathering my thoughts. "I saw people who waited, who fought pill sickness and dirty looks and hard labor. I saw kids who were spat upon, who held their heads high anyway. When we walked out of those borders, I saw survivors who had faced war and come out victorious. I saw people who did whatever they had to in order to survive." I stared them down, face by familiar face. "We all had to adapt, some more so than others. But we made it. NORA did not destroy us. They tried, but they did not succeed. I am not your enemy. I didn't try to destroy you. But someone here *did*." I was practically shouting now. "Why is Mills so eager to have me convicted when none of our clan was hurt? That is the question you should be asking yourselves. Where was he on the night the missile launched? Who are his friends, these people who have mysteriously arrived and been integrated into your way of life? How many of them live here, and why? Mills is right. We are in danger. But I am not your enemy."

The audience was quiet. I could see the realization fall upon them all at once. Their gazes went from me to Mills and back again.

Mills stepped forward. His smile had slipped. "Assembly, are you ready to give a verdict?"

The silver-haired woman stood. "We are."

The audience stilled. They hadn't even discussed it. Edyn frowned and shot me a worried look.

"We find the defendant guilty on both counts."

The audience exploded. Shouts and enraged screams filled the air. The crowd pushed themselves forward toward me and the assembly, and guards moved to block them, their weapons up.

"Order!" Mills called out, unable to hide a smile. "Order!"

Edyn leaned over. "I was afraid of that. This trial was just a formality. They knew all along what the verdict would be."

I nodded. They just hadn't expected the audience to see right through it. It was ironic. We had convinced most of the people of my innocence, but it didn't even matter.

Most of the people.

An idea sparked in my head.

"We will now sentence the convict," Mills shouted above the noise. "Stand down now, or you will be forcefully removed!"

"I have something to say," I said.

My words cut through the noise somehow, and the audience backed off and began shushing each other.

"The defendant's testimony has already been given," the woman said.

"Let him speak!" someone shouted, and Mills's head snapped toward the crowd. When it was quiet again, the woman opened her mouth to continue.

But I jumped in, speaking loudly so everyone could hear. "I declare a challenge to Mills for leadership."

41

VANCE

I knelt on the floor of my cell, forcing myself not to flinch as the surgeon picked away at my wound through the bars. The guard had allowed him in but refused to unlock my cell for the operation. He dug a little too hard, and a sharp pain stabbed through my body.

"Hold still," he muttered.

I grunted, feeling sweat drip down the back of my neck. The guy was lucky there were bars between us.

Selia stood in the corner, arms folded. "I haven't quite decided if challenging Mills was brilliant or very, very unwise."

"I suppose it depends on how this plays out," I said.

After I had declared my challenge, Rutner had stepped forward and declared his as well, glaring at me all the while. I had forced his hand before he was ready.

The crowd had lost control after that, everyone shouting at each other and throwing their support behind one person or the other. The commotion had thankfully convinced the assembly to postpone my sentencing until the election was over. Mills and Rutner had already begun making personal visits to the people. And here I sat, in jail, having my insides dug out with a knife while the surgeon searched for a bullet. The pain pill barely touched it.

Edyn spoke from the corner, where she sat cross-legged. "I'm just mad I didn't think of it first. Even if you lose, your challenge will buy you more time."

"Don't pretend like you care," I said. "You're the only reason I'm still here."

She glared back, leaning forward. "I'm not sorry. If you'd gotten away, Mills would have won. Everyone would know that he was right about you."

"That's happening anyway, thanks to you. Jumping in at the end of the trial to defend me doesn't magically make it all better, Edyn."

"You don't have to understand it, Vance, but you do have to be civil." Her mouth tugged a little, and I knew she was feeling guilty but refused to admit it. The girl was so exasperating.

"And what does your father think of all this?" I asked.

A little of the fire went out of her eyes, and she sat back again, her legs still tucked beneath her. "He'll get over it. Meanwhile, we need to figure out how to talk the assembly into releasing you under guard for a few hours. You have some visits to make."

"Edyn, you're taking this way too seriously. You can't really think they'd elect me."

"Not the upper settlers, no. But the lower ones might. They're mad, Vance. Even ask Selia—Mills is far too class-focused for them to ever climb out of the swamp as long as he's in power. You're their only chance, whether they like you or not. You have to go talk to them."

"It's true," Selia said. "You'll lose a lot of votes to Rutner, but that can't be helped."

I started to shake my head, then stopped when it tugged on my injury. The surgeon pulled away and sighed in exasperation. "This would be so much easier if you'd lie down and *hold still*."

"Vance isn't the type to lie down," Edyn said with a slow smile.

I tried to sit still. "If Rutner and Mills are visiting people, let them. I want to have a meeting instead."

Selia cocked her head. "You want everyone to come see you in prison? The guards won't let them in. It was hard enough for me."

"Then Edyn can hold the door open, and I'll shout really loud. Whatever gets the message across." I gave Selia an apologetic look. She was already too involved in this. "Do you mind spreading the word? We'll meet tonight after dark."

Selia's head shot up in surprise, but then resolve filled her expression. "I'll make the arrangements."

"There," the physician said, rocking back and wrapping his tools carefully in soft paper. "Got it. You're lucky the bullet was intact. If it was in pieces, you'd be halfway to death by now."

I already was. By this time tomorrow I'd either be sentenced to death or elected governor of the settlement. I'd never been one to settle for a mediocre life.

The physician fumbled through his tools. "You'll need a few stitches to close it up, but I don't see any sign of infection. Just be careful with that arm from now on, or you'll tear the tissues beyond repair."

"Thanks," I said. I'd already gotten a lecture about fighting the moment he walked in, which was laughable at this point. Whatever happened, we were way beyond hand-to-hand combat.

One way or another, it would all end tomorrow.

42

VANCE

That evening, Edyn came in, her face exuberant. "I got you permission to stand outside the jail for the meeting. Secured and guarded, of course, but definitely better than nothing."

"How did you manage that?"

She shrugged, but I could hear the excitement in her voice. "A little studying. Turns out that they can't legally keep you from speaking to anyone, or it invalidates the election results." She cocked her head. "Why are you looking at me like that?"

"I just can't believe you did it."

She grinned. "I know. You won't believe the crowd Selia has gathered. They're on their way now. People from up top, the middle, and down low—everybody together, all ready to defend you. They believe you,

Vance. I'm glad they finally see in you what I've seen all along." She stepped forward and took my hand through the bars. "Maybe our parents knew something we didn't. Maybe we need each other." Her face was so close now I could feel her breath. "This could actually work. You will overthrow Mills, and I'll be at your side. We'll make this the most powerful settlement that ever existed, and you'll be the one who made it that way." She smiled. "NORA will shake when they know you rule Blackfell."

My skin crawled. I'd never heard Edyn talk this way, but something about all this was wrong.

"This has to work," she murmured, "because we were meant to be together." She reached a hesitant hand up to stroke my jaw.

I pulled away, turning my back on her. "Edyn, thanks for all you're doing, but I can't talk about this right now."

"We don't have to talk." She leaned forward and lowered her voice to a husky whisper. "You communicate very well without talking."

I turned to look at her again, taking in her soft lips and the curls she'd obviously spent a lot of time on this morning. Her hair fell over delicate shoulders. Edyn was well built, everything a woman should be. And she looked at me as if she'd give me everything if I asked.

But as I looked at her, the usual uneasiness crept into place. "The other day was a mistake."

Her body stiffened. "I can help you get over her, Vance. She's not here. I am. We need each other." She leaned forward through the bars.

I confronted the reluctance in my mind, that feeling that said I shouldn't trust Edyn. I couldn't trust Treena either. She'd taken what I'd given and shoved me away. Besides, Edyn was right. Treena was gone forever, and Edyn was right here in front of me. Most any guy in my position would choose this.

Her words echoed in my mind. *NORA will shake when they know you rule Blackfell.*

I didn't want to rule anyone. If Edyn didn't understand that, she didn't know me at all.

I shook her off and headed to my bedroll, then sat down to put on my boots. "If they're headed this way, we'd better get moving."

Disappointment lined her features. "Fine. I'll get the guard to let you out."

But before she could leave, there were pounding footsteps outside. Ju-Long slammed the door open, followed by several guards holding lanterns. Anton came in last, frowning.

"What's going on?" Edyn asked. "We have permission from the assembly. You have no right to—"

"Rutner is dead." Ju-Long announced.

I stared at him. Edyn gave a startled gasp and stumbled backward. "What?"

"Poisoned."

"Dead?" Edyn said softly. "But—he can't be."

"I am sorry." Ju-Long's expression was anything but sorry. "His body was found on the floor of his home just thirty minutes ago. A physician was called, but it was too late."

Edyn put her hand over her mouth and leaned against the wall. I had a feeling it was the only thing holding her up. It was hard to see her shatter like this.

Ju-Long's face softened as he watched her. "His body has been taken to Mills's suite. You may visit him there."

She nodded, turning a sickly white, and wrapped her arms around herself. Anton opened the door for her and held it as she stepped through. Then she was gone.

Poisoned. If the fool hadn't declared his challenge, he'd still be alive. I could only hope that Mills wouldn't try the same tactic with me.

"Tell those idiots outside to go home," Ju-Long said to a guard. "Hawking is restricted to the prison tonight on suspicion of murder."

I swore. "How did I poison him from here? Do enlighten me."

"The timing is rather convenient," Ju-Long said. "You've been hosting visitors in the jail, sending runners to do your bidding all day. It's a matter of time before we discover it was one of your followers."

And until they planted evidence to that effect. This was the last piece in Mills's game, his move to unite the last of the stragglers against me. My clan respected Rutner, just as I had. If they thought I was responsible for his death, they'd kill me themselves.

It was brilliant.

Anton met my gaze, then looked away. Surely he knew what was happening here. Mills was killing off our clan members now. This had gone way beyond a simple trial.

"It won't be long now, Hawking," Ju-Long said, and then he shoved his way past his guards, who filed out after him.

Anton gave me a long look, as if wishing he could say something. For a moment, I saw the friend I'd grown up with. Then he shook his head and followed the crowd, letting the door close softly behind him.

43

VANCE

The next morning Selia Dunstrep stood uncertainly outside the bars, one hand rubbing her other arm. "I'm so sorry. I tried."

"I know."

"I'm sure the people know it wasn't you," she said. "Poor Rutner."

"But the assembly members don't, and they're the ones who count."

Her expression hardened. "In all my years in the circle, I never saw political maneuvering like this. I wonder what your father would have done right now."

I'd wondered that myself, many times. He wouldn't have gotten himself into this situation. He was too smart for that.

Selia looked at the floor. "Well, I'd better get back. They'll be having the vote soon. I have a few more people to talk to before then. Whatever happens, just know that your clan believes in you, at the very least. You'll die as Iron Belt Hawking's son and no less."

There was a stab of tightness in my throat. "Thank you, Selia. That means a lot to me."

That evening, the guards escorted me out of my cell. Eight of them. They locked my wrists and chained my ankles, forcing me to shuffle awkwardly along the trail toward the group area above. Mills was taking no chances tonight.

The valley was filled with people again, all waiting for the vote to be announced. Their votes had been counted for the last four agonizing hours. They hadn't allowed me a vote, of course.

Edyn was conspicuously absent.

They sat me in a chair at the opposite end of the front, my guards settled around me like a human cage. I started to stand, but a guard grabbed my injured arm and shoved me back into place. Pain lanced through my shoulder.

"As you know," Mills began loudly, "there were three contestants for the position of governor. Our beloved Dean Rutner was murdered yesterday. Ultimately, the vote has now been cast between Vance

Hawking, the convicted mass murderer, and myself. We will now announce the results of that vote."

The head elder stood and handed a paper to Mills. He opened it and held it out in front of him. "The people have voted. They have decided that I will retain my position."

A smattering of applause echoed across the gathering. It was nothing like the shouting and protesting at my trial. Nobody was surprised.

"Given the situation," Mills said, "and considering that for the first time in history a convict has issued a challenge, I move that we sentence the convict now instead of tomorrow." He smiled wryly. "It will save you all a trip."

A few people chuckled. The assembly chairperson nodded her approval.

Mills spoke louder. "I now turn the floor over to the assembly."

The spokeswoman stood. Her voice was shaky, but her frail frame held up proudly. "The convict and challenger, Vance Hawking, has been found guilty of grievous acts of murder and terrorism. He is a threat to the safety and unity of our people. He speaks of peace, but his actions display anything but. We had considered charging him with conspiracy to murder Dean Rutner as well, but as he has already been convicted of multiple other deaths, we feel it unnecessary. What is necessary, however, is to carry through on our responsibility as lawmakers." She cleared her throat. "Vance Hawking, please stand."

The guards grabbed my arms and yanked me up. I felt something in my shoulder tear.

"You are hereby sentenced to execution. Tomorrow morning, you will stand in front of the firing squad. Thank you all for coming."

44

TREENA

I almost cried with relief when I found the trail in the foothills. It was half covered in desert brush, and the gravel disguised how many people had passed here. But someone had left a note behind, a square cloth stabbed carefully onto a cactus. A symbol. Two squiggly lines with a square in the middle. A bird?

My weak stomach leaped inside. After a weeklong trek through the desert, rationing Coltrane's food pills and water packets until my hunger became a constant hollow pain, I'd spent two more days scouring the foothills for a trail. Whatever this symbol meant, it was the first sign of humankind I'd seen in a long time. I tore off a piece of my sleeve and tucked it behind the cloth in case Coltrane's settlement had decided to follow after all.

The trail sloped upward gradually, then became more steep. Tumbleweeds and cacti gave way to bushes and small trees. When I stopped that night, the valley behind me spread out like another world, brown and dead. NORA was out there somewhere, along with Dresden and Konnor and Commander Denoux. It felt like years since I'd seen them all.

I climbed the rest of the next day, spent the night shivering under a tree, and then walked all the following day. The trail wove through thick trees and heavy shade, and my journey became a blur of sage-green and brown. Though foggy, mind was constantly aware of leaves rustling in the wind and the never-ending ache in my sore leg. A few times I heard animals, but it didn't worry me. I'd already survived a snakebite. If a larger animal decided to make me dinner, it wouldn't get much more than a small, slowly-starving girl. Occasionally there would be a tree with the same squiggly picture I'd seen earlier, carved as if by a sharp rock.

And then the trail ended.

The meadow had once been full of long grass, but it had been trampled down. Empty food and water packets littered the ground, and a child's shoe sat overturned near the edge. I picked it up and studied it. It was NORA-issued, a light tan, but the sole had been worn nearly through.

I followed the edge of the clearing, looking for the trail to pick up again. Whoever had camped here had obviously moved on. They had to be up higher—near the peak, maybe. Surely there was some sign of where they'd gone. I searched the trees for more symbols.

Nothing. No trail.

I sat on a rock and dug through my pack, hoping some nourishment would help me think. There was only one water packet left and an empty pill container.

I could do this. There had to be a river or stream up here somewhere, and there were plenty of animals. I'd eaten meat before. Of course, I hadn't had to chase it down. Even if I knew what to do with a dead squirrel, there was no way I could catch one in my weakened state.

I slid off the rock and lay flat on the rocky soil, too exhausted to do anything else. My thoughts were like a dozen threads of different colors weaving together and then exploding into shards of memories. The mysterious, shadowy figures at the abandoned city and their strange boxes. The underground settlers and their peace pact. The orange flowers, crushed into pieces in my pocket. Had it all been for nothing?

That night, with the leaves rustling and forest animals scurrying around me, the nightmare changed. It took place at what remained of the palace in NORA, hundreds of bodies littering the ground like bent and seeping food packets. On the ground in front of me lay the empress, her body broken. Her mouth twisted into a smile. "You think you've won here, but you haven't. Their lives were far better under my rule than they are now."

"Dresden is smart," I told her. "He won't change what needs to be changed, but at least he knows what he's doing."

"And they'd be worse off with you in charge?" Tali snapped, standing next to me, beautiful and alive. She was standing now, her arms folded, a smirk on her face. She chuckled. "Treena, quit being so dramatic. You tried to help, and it didn't work. So try *again*."

"You don't get it. I only hurt people."

Ruby appeared. She looked younger, full of energy and life. "You're a leader. It's in your blood."

Dresden appeared beside her, wearing his new emperor robes. "Please come back. Something big is coming, and we need you."

"What's coming?"

He looked directly into my eyes. "You already know."

It came to me then. Those strange soldiers in the desert with their quiet aircraft and choppy language. They weren't NORA soldiers trying to ambush the settlers, as Coltrane had thought. They were foreigners trying to conquer NORA.

And I'd left them exposed and unaware.

I looked at the group. With the exception of the empress, I loved all of them in their own way. And they believed in me, every single one.

If I tried again, I'd probably fail, maybe even make things worse. But if I quit now, there was no chance of them getting better, either.

I closed my eyes and clenched my fists, face turned to the sky. "I can't do this alone."

"You won't be," Tali said. "There are more people on your side than you know. Go now, before it's too late."

I startled awake and threw my arms over my face, rolling away from the source of the storm. A sudden wind picked up dirt, leaves, even rocks, and threw them toward me like a tempest. So loud. I stumbled to my feet and away before I realized it wasn't a storm at all. It was a chopper.

It looked like a military model but was painted gray, the same color as the sky. I stepped farther back as the chopper began its landing sequence. It hovered a meter above the ground, then centimeters, then hit the ground. The door opened before the motor cut out, and a team of civilians leaped out, ducking to avoid the still-moving blades.

I sighed with relief. No uniforms. These had to be settlers. "Do you know where the settlers have gone? I came to join them, but . . ." *But I've changed my mind.* The realization settled into my chest. Sometime between last night and this morning, I'd decided to try again. As soon as I could gather the supplies, I'd return to NORA and warn them about the impending attack.

"No way," a man said, slowing as he approached. He stopped in front of me, eyes wide. The rest of them circled me. "You guys, this is the runaway successor. The one who destroyed the palace."

One of them reached for my arm, but I jerked away. "Don't touch me."

"This scrawny thing?" a woman said. "I didn't recognize her under all the dirt."

"Trying to seek asylum with the people you tried to kill, girl?" the first man asked. The others grabbed my arms and fastened them behind my back. I felt metal against my wrists and heard a click.

"I didn't try to kill anyone," I said, although the empress flashed in my mind. "We're on the same side. You don't have to treat me like this. I don't want to stay with the settlers anyway. I have to get back."

"Oh, no you don't," the woman said. "You're coming with us. You can rot in jail with your traitor friend until they put a bullet in your chest." She started forward, and I found myself being half pushed, half carried toward the chopper.

"I'm not a traitor!" I said, knowing it wouldn't do any good. "I really do have to get back. There's a war coming, and NORA doesn't even know it!"

"You better believe it," the woman said. "Declaring war on outlanders. That new emperor is really full of himself. They deserve everything they get, if you ask me. Now, climb up, or I'll throw you in. I can't wait to show Mills who we found."

45

VANCE

I was four, maybe five years old, when I went to my first funeral. Even now I could remember nearly everything about it except for who it was that died.

We stood in a straight line, waiting to pay our respects to the dead body. The settlers moved somberly, slowly. Alfred Tornough played the trumpet, his tune depressing but very, very loud. I remembered thinking that the sound would wake the dead person up and wondering if that was the point.

It was cold and windy, and I wore a coat that was too small. My mother had hoped it would last through the rest of winter, but the sleeves were so tight I couldn't even fold my arms. She'd buttoned it all the way up today. All I could think about was what she'd do if I unbuttoned it. Maybe just the top button or two, the ones tightest against my throat. Surely that wouldn't be so bad. I looked up at her. She was gazing off into the distance, her eyes rimmed red. I immediately went to work on the top button.

When we reached the body, my father nodded respectfully to the woman standing beside the casket. The brave smile she'd worn until now faltered a little as my mother reached for her and they embraced. Quiet sobs burst out of the woman, and her shoulders shook as my mom stroked her hair.

I'd gotten the entire coat undone, yet it remained tight against my body. My father leaned down and picked me up. The dead man wore none of the winter clothing we did, but a traditional brown, collared shirt and trousers to match the earth he was about to enter. His hair was uncovered, thin on top and long in back, and tied neatly with a red ribbon. He'd never worn his hair like that before. If he were alive, he'd tear it out and throw it on the ground. In fact, he looked as if he'd wake up at any moment and perhaps do just that.

I wrapped my arms around my father's neck. "He's creepy," I said.

He chuckled quietly. "No need to be afraid. Someday all of us will look like that."

"Even you?"

"Even me. We take the bad with the good, the end with the beginning. But don't worry. Your end won't come for a very long time."

"How can you know for sure?"

He hesitated, then a sure smile spread across his face. "Well, I suppose I don't. But that's what every parent hopes for. You have a long, full, exciting life ahead of you."

I gazed down at the body. "Did it hurt?"

"I don't know. I'd guess death only hurts for a moment, and then all the pain is gone forever. No, not gone. I think that pain—the hurt we feel as we go—I think it gets left behind and spread around to those we love."

"So if nobody dies, there's no hurting. Right?"

He gave a wry smile. "I think life can hurt as much as death, Vance. It's just a different kind." He reached down and squeezed the dead man's arm, muttering a good-bye under his breath. Despite my expectations, the dead man didn't open his eyes and swipe my father's hand away.

He didn't move at all.

My mother came to the jail that night. She didn't bring the twins. A gray wool blanket was wrapped tightly around her shoulders, and she hugged it to her as if it were holding her together.

Her face was pinched and drawn like a pair of pants she could never quite get to release its wrinkles.

When her gaze fell on me, I felt my throat tighten. Now she came. Now of all times.

"I'm not ashamed of you," she said immediately. "I know what Rutner said, but he was wrong. I've never, ever been ashamed of you. You did what your father would have done."

The pain in my throat intensified, and I found it hard to speak. "Why did you stay away?"

"I—I've been spying on Mills." Her words ran over each other in their haste to escape. "The men who enforce Mills's laws are Chinese. There are more of them than we initially thought, and they're increasing as our food supply diminishes. They're coming in from somewhere, Vance. They aren't refugees. I thought if I pretended to date Mills, he would take me into his confidence." She hung her head. "But then you arrived, and things got complicated, and I just—I felt I'd better stay away until things were resolved, putting in a word for you here and there. I've been so proud of how you've handled yourself, Vance."

"Well, you got your wish. Things are definitely resolved."

Her composure broke, and she sucked in a sob. "I've spoken to so many people. I thought we had it."

"Do you live near the rim, Mom?"

She lifted her head to meet my gaze, then looked away.

"Our people are suffering, and you're sucking up to Mills. It's good to know you aren't ashamed, but, frankly, I'm not sure I can return the favor."

"You're not listening." Her voice was hard as she approached the bars. "There's a reason the upper class lives up near the rim, Vance, and it's not because they're farther from the lake. It's because there's a huge network of tunnels in the mountain walls of this valley. Mills got authorization to dig more, using some machine he called the excavator, but the location of the entrance is a closely guarded secret. I figured out only yesterday where it was—in his quarters. I followed it to a series of apartments, a cafeteria, and a tunnel that led all the way through the mountain to the other side. He's been communicating with people out there, Vance. Maybe even letting them in and out. I know you have reason to be mad at me, but this is bigger than us. We are *all* in danger."

I processed that for a moment. "What are you going to do?"

"I don't know."

Voices outside told me someone had arrived. The door opened, and four guards walked in. "Pardon us, Mrs. Hawking, but we have to cut your good-bye short. Another prisoner is being brought in."

My mother flinched as if someone had stabbed her. "Can I embrace my son one last time?"

The guard hesitated, then nodded. The others leaped in as he unlocked the cage and opened the door. They were rough as they grabbed my arms, slapping the metal quickly on as if they expected me to fight. When everything was secure, they led me to my mother.

I hadn't touched her in over two years. I'd been taller than her by age thirteen, but now there was a good six-inch difference. She was about the same size as Treena, and they had the same color eyes—brown with golden flecks sprinkled in.

Why did that blasted girl keep slipping into my thoughts? I was being executed soon, and this was my last chance to say good-bye to my mother. Treena had no place in my mind right now or ever.

Mom dropped the blanket and threw herself at me, sobbing and wailing and acting more emotional than I'd ever seen her. She held me so tightly my sore rib ached, and her tears instantly wet my shirt. The guards turned away slightly, uncomfortable at the display.

It was then that I felt something cool and smooth slide into my pocket.

———●●●———

They hadn't needed to rush our good-bye because it was nearly an hour before the new prisoner arrived. Finally the door swung open and two guards practically carried a skinny figure in. They guided the prisoner into the cell next to mine, then removed the blindfold.

If they'd brought in my father's ghost, I wouldn't have been more surprised. I stared at the prisoner in shock. "Treena?"

A grin spread across her face as her eyes focused on me. "Vance!" She tore away from the guards and made her way to the bars that separated us. One of the men grabbed her arms again and unlocked them, then backed slowly away. She seemed too focused on me to notice. Her skin pulled tightly against her cheekbones and dirt smudged her delicate nose. But life danced in those large eyes, life and excitement and something far deeper stirring within their depths.

My careful composure slipped as that *something* pulled at my insides, removing all the layers I'd placed there and exposing a long-ignored ache. With a single smile, Treena had left me completely undone.

Right then, this girl was the most beautiful thing I'd ever seen.

46

TREENA

So this is where you've been hiding," I said. "No offense, but I think you need a decorator."

"You're here," Vance said dumbly. His hair was messy and his chin full of stubble. It made my heart leap. "How are you here?" he asked.

"I got your message," I said with a chuckle. "I mean, I know it wasn't exactly a message. But I knew what it meant when you gave my stone back. And when Dresden took the throne, I had no reason to stay, so I escaped. And then the underground settlers and I found the soldiers in the city, and everything blew up, and the settlers kicked me out, so I headed for the mountains to meet you, but I guess you guys decided to come here instead." I stopped for a breath.

The guards gaped at me, and Vance's expression wasn't far off. "Uh, you say Bike Boy stole the throne?"

"Yeah. He's the emperor. My stepfather gave up my rights while I was passed out."

His face darkened and his hands formed fists. "Gave up your *rights*? You won the throne, Treena. At great cost and sacrifice. We didn't go through all that so Bike Boy could take over."

I took a deep breath to calm myself. Vance had no idea that those innocent people haunted me night after night. I knew the sacrifices that had been made even better than he did. "I'm not happy about it either, if you couldn't tell. I was lucky to get out at all." I looked around the jail again. "Speaking of uh, what was supposed to happen, I thought you were the leader of your settlement now. What did you do to end up in a mosquito-infested jail?"

Vance flinched as if I'd thrown a knife into his chest. The guards' shuffling quieted. One of them cleared his throat. A dark, heavy feeling settled upon me. Something wasn't right.

"Tell me," I said.

"Treena," Vance began carefully. "Remember that deal I made with Rutner?"

"With two conditions," I said. "Yes."

"One of the conditions was that I'd turn myself in for my crimes against the clan." He paused. "They're going to execute me tomorrow."

The mountain lurched underfoot, and I swayed, processing his words. The word stabbed at my ears, over and over. *Execute.* A polite, sanitized word for what it really was. All the while I watched Vance's face. Sad, but definitely serious.

He wasn't joking.

So far. I'd come so far for him. We were supposed to be together now. The snakebite, the underground settlers, the attack, the explosion—it couldn't have been for nothing. Vance was the one person who could help me figure it all out.

This was wrong. He'd helped get his clan freed, and now they wanted to murder him? What was wrong with these people?

Horror turned to an icy anger. "They have no right."

"Actually they do," he said, his voice flat. "You shouldn't have come. I don't know what they'll do with you when I'm gone. It's not safe for you here."

"Shouldn't have come?" I snapped, taking an angry step forward. "You don't get to pull out of this. You invited me, and I'm here. Now we deal with it."

"I didn't actually think you'd come," he shot back. "You were supposed to stay there, safe in your palace with your lover boy."

I recoiled at his words, then the rage took over. After the weeks I'd spent outside clinging to thoughts of Vance as my body wasted away, his words stung.

"You're right. I shouldn't have come. I even recruited several hundred settlers who lost their homes to NORA. They'll be here tomorrow."

Vance cursed. "This isn't the best time for more settlers to come."

"You'll want to get some rest tonight, young lady," one of the guards said as they left. "Mills will be eager to speak to you tomorrow." The door closed behind them.

Mills? As in the man who had betrayed us? I gave Vance a questioning look, but he just watched me, his expression unreadable. It was not the expression of a guy who cared for me. We were only a meter apart, but it felt like entire planets lay between us.

"I told those settlers there was a man here," I said quietly, "someone who would help them find a peaceful and happy life." A man who hurt deeply and loved even deeper and saw life for what it was. A man I'd fallen for, hard and fast—and I'd done nothing more than open myself up for heartbreak. The pain was too much. I tightly shoved it into a box in my mind and filed it away, raising my chin. "Sounds like that guy doesn't exist anymore."

47

TREENA

Morning came.

I lay still on my cot, faking sleep. There was no sound from the corner where Vance had spent the night sitting up, and I wondered if he was finally asleep. He'd said my name twice in the night, but I hadn't responded. All I could think about were four words.

You shouldn't have come.

Voices at the door jerked me fully awake, and then two guards brought in a tub of soapy water. They unlocked his cell door, set it down, and then backed out as if offering food to a tiger. "Bathe," the first one ordered.

I snuck a peek at Vance's face. He still sat there, wide awake, his posture casual and uncaring. He didn't even acknowledge the guard's order. They locked his door again, dropped a pile of clothing through the bars, and then left.

"Waste of water," Vance muttered.

I lay with my face turned away as he washed. Soon he was shivering from the chill, his teeth chattering. Then a sliding sound told me he'd shoved the soapy water tub closer to me. "In case you want to get clean," he said. "They didn't let me take a bath for days."

"Thanks," I said, my cheeks warming at the thought of using the same water he'd used.

There was the muffled sound of cloth, and then a zipper as he pulled his trousers on. Then he grunted.

I rolled over to see his arm hanging uselessly while he struggled to put on a brown, collared shirt. Tiny black stitches held together a wound in his shoulder, and his entire side was covered in brown-and-yellow bruises. Something inside of me ached. Whatever his attitude toward me, Vance had been through a lot here. If only he would tell me what.

I took a deep breath. These were our last moments together. He obviously didn't have feelings for me anymore, but sitting here and ignoring him while he needed help was like looking away from the sunlight as I froze to death. I hesitated, then stood and motioned to his shoulder. "You should bandage that first."

He snickered. "Doesn't matter now."

"Here, let me help you with that shirt."

"I'm fine." But he stepped closer to the bars.

I reached through and helped ease his arm into the sleeve. There was a sharp intake of breath, but he let me help. When my fingers met his skin, he closed his eyes. I couldn't speak as I slid the shirt over his shoulder and fumbled with the top button.

"I thought I'd lost you," he whispered.

My breath shuddered. Without permission, my hands abandoned the button and slid into his open shirt, brushing against his bare chest. My brain was screaming now, shouting at me to stop this before someone got hurt. But I knew it was far, far too late for that.

"I didn't know I was so close to losing you," I murmured. "If I had come a day later—"

"Don't think about that." He reached around my waist, bringing me right up against the bars. Our foreheads drew together, and I could see deep into his eyes. Dark brown, the same color as his shirt. "This is all I have left. I'm glad I could spend it with you."

The bars were just wide enough to accommodate us. At least the fates had given us that much. I tilted my head back and leaned in close. His breath caught. I leaned in further, questioning, and gently brushed my lips on his. When he didn't respond, I began to pull away.

He grabbed my head and pulled me in for a deep, desperate kiss. His mouth moved with mine, his lips so familiar, so well fitted to mine. And then we couldn't get close enough. I clung to him desperately, and he held me against him like I was life itself. His fingers tangled in my hair. I felt every inch of his body against mine—his chest, his legs. The bars seemed to melt away.

Our last few moments together were spent like that, wishing we were in the same cell but also relieved that we weren't. He'd be gone soon, but I had to stay. I didn't need my heart torn into smaller pieces than it already was.

The jail door opened too soon. Guards streamed in, far more than was necessary. Probably a dozen.

I drew in a shuddering breath as they unlocked his door. "No. It can't be time already."

They entered his cell and grabbed his sore shoulder, tearing him out of my arms. Vance caught my hand as he was pulled away. They yanked it back and locked his hands in front of him.

All the while, he didn't take his eyes off me. His expression, so raw and vulnerable, stabbed me in the gut. "Will you do me one last favor?" he asked.

I choked back a sob. "Anything."

"If they bring you out to watch, look away. I don't want you to see it."

I clenched my jaw. "I've seen plenty of death." My wide-eyed self with a freshly opened uniform and high hopes was very different from who I was now, with my wild hair and phantoms chasing me into sleep. "But if it makes you feel better, I won't."

Dying isn't the worst thing that can happen to someone.

Vance's own words as they had echoed in a dark stairwell weeks ago. I had mourned the death of my friend. It was also the first time Vance had kissed me.

I wondered if he was remembering that moment too. He let out a deep, shuttering breath. "I'm sorry to cause you pain."

The guards pushed him out toward the exit, but I moved to the other side of my cell. "Wait."

Vance paused, and for once the guards allowed it. I hesitantly lifted a hand toward his face. He leaned in to my touch.

I smoothed his hair, then rested my hand against his cheek. "Don't let them see you as anything but Vance Hawking," I whispered.

He swallowed hard, his voice wavering. "I won't."

"It's time," the guard said and tore him out of my arms once again.

48

TREENA

It was two agonizing minutes before someone else entered. His Asian features were immediately apparent, but his head and face were strangely absent of any hair, not even eyebrows, which made his narrow black eyes all the more menacing. His gaze settled on me as he gently closed the door behind him. I fought the urge to shiver despite the muggy heat.

"The rightful heir to NORA," he said. "What a treasure you are."

"Are you here to escort me to the—" I couldn't say it. "The event?"

"No," he said. "I heard what a sweet display your good-bye was. I am sure that's exactly how Vance wants you to remember him. Although I must say, I am curious as to the origins of your relationship."

"That's none of your business."

"I see. Well, I hope you'll be more cooperative with my next line of questioning, as it's far more important. Resistance will only cause you pain. Forgive my presence here, but Mills is rather busy at the moment. I see you still wear the numbers of NORA."

I fingered my implant. "Not for long. Now that I'm here, I'll get them taken out as soon as I can."

"On the contrary. It announces to the world who you are, making you more useful to us."

I felt a stab of panic. "I'm not doing anything for you. I want to go to the execution, right now."

"I'm afraid that's not possible. You see, we have information we need immediately. What is a criminal boy when you have an entire nation to engineer?"

"Who are you?" I asked. "Tell me where you're from."

"Your boyfriend had similar questions, but he soon learned to keep them to himself. I am Ju-Long. Mills and I work together, but I will not tell you from whence I come." His hands closed around the bars, and I found myself backing away. "Now tell me about the settlers who are on their way. Who are they, and where have they been hiding all this time?"

"Why don't you ask them when they get here?"

"We lack time, and I'm asking you."

"I told you, I'm not doing this right now." My voice broke, but I hardened it. "Let me go to the execution, and I'll do anything you want. Just let me go."

With a look of forced patience, the man retrieved something from his sleeve and swiped it against my cell door. The lock clicked. He swung open the door and stepped inside. "What kind of weapons and technology do they have? How many are there in total? What are their intentions here? Tell me now, *nu hai*, or you will lose your life before Vance does."

Nu hai? I couldn't tell what language that was. He spoke it liltingly, choppily, almost like the soldiers in the desert—

The realization hit just before the blow came. Ju-Long swung so fast I barely saw it coming. Pain exploded into the side of my face, and I flew across the cell and landed in a heap. Black stars flashed around me, and I struggled to keep a grasp on consciousness.

"Answer," he said simply. "Tell me of the people."

"They're peaceful," I gasped. "Don't hurt them. They come unarmed. NORA attacked them and bombed their homes."

"Yes, I know," he snapped. "Who is their leader?"

Ruby's face came to mind, and a determination filled my body along with the pain. I had destroyed so many lives. But I refused to hurt Ruby. She had already been through enough. "I am."

The blow came again, this time on the other side. I slammed into the concrete wall and fell to the floor, dazed.

"You lie," Ju-Long said.

"They sent me—" The room spun, and my head and mouth felt disconnected. Pain filled my head so that I could barely think. "They sent me ahead to negotiate for accommodations. Their leader was killed in the attack."

His arm rose again, and I scrambled backward against the wall, huddling sideways, one arm up to protect myself. Something small and hard pushed against my hip uncomfortably. The guards had removed all my belongings from my pockets. Had they left the stone? It wasn't much of a weapon, but it was all I had at the moment. As Ju-Long approached, I reached around and closed my fingers around something long and smooth. Definitely not my stone. I glanced behind me.

A pocketknife.

One of the clan members I had left NORA with had owned one. She'd demonstrated it to me. I had no idea how it had ended up in my pocket, but that didn't really matter at the moment. I stuck one dirty fingernail into the groove and flipped the knife open, still hiding it from view.

"What are you doing?" Ju-Long demanded, raising his arm even higher.

"So you've taken over this settlement," I said, thinking quickly, "and you've managed to do it without a fight. Vance got in the way, and you figured out how take him out of the equation. Let me guess—you also launched a missile recently."

His eyes narrowed even more. "We could defeat NORA in a matter of hours if we wanted to. Now stand." He looked relaxed, but I recognized his stance. The moment I stood up, he would hit me again.

I exaggerated my dizziness and stood as slowly as I could, hiding the pocketknife in my folded palm and resting it against the wall as if to steady myself. "If you're going to kill me, just do it."

"Not until you cease being useful." He stepped forward. "Now, tell me more about the settlers."

"No."

His hand moved to strike, but I'd anticipated it. I leaped as his arm moved and buried the knife in his chest. He stared at the knife in shock, then shoved me away, clutching at his chest. I'd aimed poorly, hitting the fleshy area just above his heart. I wasn't out of danger yet.

I sprinted out the cell door, then closed it behind me. The lock clicked into place.

He grunted at the sound, then headed for the door I'd just closed. With a start, I remembered he had the key. He reached up to release the lock again. "You have sealed your death, *nu hai.*"

I caught sight of the tub of water Vance had left behind, then ran into his cell and tried to pick it up. It was far too heavy. I pulled it over to the bars and then, with a mighty heave, swung the water at him. He dropped the unlocking device, sputtering, standing there just long enough for me to whack the sensor on the door with the hard corner of the nearly empty tub. One hit. Two. Three, four, five. He reached through the bars for me, but then the red light on the lock finally went out.

With an angry growl, Ju-Long flung his arms through the bars at me, but I jumped back just in time and ran for the door. He pounded on the lock, then began yelling something in his language as I burst through the door and outside.

Two surprised guards greeted me, but I shoved my way past them. A group of people were making their way slowly up a trail. Hoping they were headed where I needed to go, I sprinted toward the small road, the thundering footsteps of the guards propelling me forward.

They would never catch me. I knew it down to my toes. I would run forever, if that's what it took to get to Vance. And get to him I would—because I'd come too far to let that awful man in the jail win. He was positioned to take everyone I loved from me, and his plans had worked so far.

He would not succeed again.

49

VANCE

itizens of Blackfell," Mills said. The amplifier chopped up his voice and sent it hurling across the valley. "Vance Hawking stands before you, murderer and traitor, ready to receive punishment. It gives me great sorrow to carry this through, but as your governor, I will do what must be done."

The crowd, so familiar to me now, was relatively quiet today. Even the children sensed the somber mood, and they looked around with wide eyes. One boy near the front, about four or five, had brown hair and sharp eyes. His father held him on his shoulders, and the boy's eyes darted away when I looked at him. He leaned down to ask his father a question.

"Amazing how many lies you can fit into one sentence, Mills," I said loudly.

Eight men stood next to me, all holding some part of my arm or shoulder. Mills was taking no chances today. One of the guards behind me elbowed me in the back. I tensed and turned to see who it was, but they shoved my head forward again.

"The prisoner will not speak," Mills snapped. "Your opportunity to talk is over."

"I'd say I have a few minutes left."

"Shut up," a guard murmured beside me.

"Guards!" Mills shouted. "Line up."

Across the way, there was movement in the crowd. People moved aside as another ten guards took their positions, facing me in a straight line. They gave a sharp salute, weapons resting at their sides. They were all Chinese.

"He's not guilty!" someone in the crowd shouted, but they were quickly hushed. I nodded respectfully to the audience.

Mills smiled. "Vance, your guards will now step aside. If you move, you will only be shot a few seconds early. For your own sake, I suggest you not do anything stupid." Then he motioned for my captors to step aside. The pressure on my arms and shoulders lessened, and cooler air replaced the space where they'd been. I was now alone on the platform, facing a silent crowd. Apparently there would be no blindfold today.

Most of the adults in the crowd glanced away then, covering their children's eyes. A few people looked on, dread or sorrow in their expressions. The couple I'd pronounced the blessing upon stood near the back. The woman buried her face in her husband's shoulder.

One face drew my attention immediately, a sobbing woman who covered her mouth with her hands, a devastating realization in her eyes. My mother. She couldn't understand why I hadn't fought my way free when I had the chance. She didn't know that I'd given away her knife to someone it could actually help.

I stood straighter and raised my jaw defiantly at the shooters. My mother was about to lose a son, but I would keep our family pride until the end.

"You can't do this!" Selia shrieked from the crowd. "It wasn't Vance. Mills is the murderer!"

"The audience will please be silent," Mills droned. "Guards, take aim."

The line of shooters raised their weapons, aiming at my chest. A series of soft clicks sounded as the safeties on the rifles were removed.

"You've silenced everyone who knows the truth," I said to Mills. "But someday they'll figure out who their true enemy is, and then you'll lose everything."

"He hasn't silenced everyone," a feminine voice called out.

Hundreds of heads turned at the sound of the voice. Even the shooters faltered for a moment, glancing over their shoulders. I followed their line of sight to a figure that had just arrived over the crest, breathing hard. Two guards sprinted up behind her.

Treena.

"I know the truth, Mills," Treena shouted. "Aren't you going to kill me, too?"

Mills stood to the side of the platform, but I could see his bright red face from here. "Guards, bring her to me."

"No need." Treena pushed through the crowd and climbed the platform to stand next to me. "If you want me to shut up, you'd better shoot me, too. Has anyone else figured it out? Let's have a party up here."

The guards who had brought me here stood on the ground, looking at her with uncertainty. Mills wanted her subdued, but the guards had no desire to be standing next to me when Mills gave the order to fire— which he would do any second.

"Is this some kind of noble suicide attempt?" I whispered to her. A dark bruise had begun to form on her cheek, but she seemed fine otherwise. Had she fought her way free from the guards?

Treena ignored my comment and addressed the crowd. "I think you should know that your settlement has been taken over right under your noses. Mills tried to take out the entire NORA government, but he had help from his Asian friends."

Trembling with anger, she turned to stare Mills down.

"You took everything from me," she told him. "And now I'm going to take everything from you. They know the truth. They'll never let you lie to them again."

I felt my eyes widen at her words, realizing that she was exactly right. The audience murmured. Mills's face had turned purple. He struggled for control, then pointed at the shooters still lined up in the crowd. "Fire!" he shouted. "Shoot them both."

The shooters, who had lowered their weapons in the confusion, raised them again.

"No!" the head of the assembly snapped. She stood at the back of the audience, and the crowd parted so she could make her way to the front. When the woman reached the platform, she turned to face the crowd. "Guards, disregard that order. The assembly requires a stay in this matter. Mills, come forward, please."

Mills stared at the woman, expressionless, and then nodded to the shooters.

I leaped for Treena. She stiffened in surprise. The shots echoed across the valley like a clap of thunder, but not a single bullet entered my back.

The audience gasped, and someone screamed. I turned just in time to see the elderly woman slump to the ground, her face twisted in shock, blood blossoming across her peach-colored blouse in several places.

Mills turned to Ju-Long, who had just trotted up. The Chinese man's gray uniform was darker than usual in the front. With a start, I realized he was wet. And injured, by the blood on the front of his shoulder. He scanned the crowd and pulled something out of his pocket. He brought it to his lips, then blew. A whistle.

Suddenly, hundreds of men and women who had casually surrounded the crowd before now closed in with weapons at the ready. But these weren't rifles—they looked more like stunners, shaped differently from NORA's, and probably much more powerful. I had no doubt they were deadly.

I quickly scanned the new arrivals. Most wore the same plain clothing as the settlers. Undercover soldiers. Mills and Ju-Long had hidden their numbers well.

My mom was right. I would have guessed that there were a few dozen of them here, but from what I could tell, there were hundreds, all armed.

Ju-Long whistled again, three long blasts. The soldiers on the perimeter began pushing the crowd together, even more tightly than they already were. A few people tried to escape. They fell to the silent weapons and thrashed about on the ground, then went still. Treena wrapped her arms around me, her eyes wide in horror.

Mills glared at Ju-Long, eyeing the whistle. "What are you doing?" he hissed. "This was not part of the agreement."

"You've lost control," Ju-Long said, still watching the soldiers herd the audience.

Mills gave a low growl, then climbed onto the platform and pulled a pistol out of his belt. "We tried to do this the easy way," he shouted to the crowd as they were herded into a tight circle. "You've trusted me to keep you safe. Sometimes that involves alliances you may not understand. Believe me when I say that I've kept your best interests in mind in everything I've done. Vance, face me."

Treena let out a sob when we broke apart. I turned slowly toward the man. A cold barrel was shoved in my face, just inches away from my eyes. Mills was determined not to miss.

"That's why you took Rutner out," I said. "He wouldn't have allowed the Chinese to take over. You've betrayed everyone."

"In aligning with the ECA, I've only saved their blasted lives," Mills snapped. "They wanted to kill us all. I talked them into letting us be a part of what they're doing. You've done nothing but get in the way." He shoved the pistol even closer to my nose.

My father was no fool. He'd taught me defensive techniques when I was five years old. Mills's paranoid fear had brought his weapon close enough for me to reach, even with my wrists locked.

I brought my hands up on either side of the pistol, flicking the weapon to the side just as it discharged. The shot was deafening, and for a moment I thought the bullet had slammed into me after all, but it went wide behind me as the weapon flew from his hand and clattered to the dirt. My would-be executioner growled again and stepped to retrieve it.

I leaped at Mills and threw him to the ground, wishing my arms were free to pummel him like I'd wanted to do for weeks. Instead, I tightened my hands around his throat. He grabbed at my arms and bucked me to the side, forcing me to pull my hands away to catch my fall.

A dark shadow fell across the crowd, and the audience began screaming and shoving past each other. I looked up to see two dozen shiny choppers descending overhead. I knew exactly what those choppers were. I'd spent endless hours inside them, looking down upon the world below. Still, it was an ominous sight.

NORA had arrived.

50

TREENA

The choppers came down like a cloud of reflective metal, one after the other. I lost count at twenty-three. It must have been every chopper NORA owned, and I was willing to bet they'd packed them full of soldiers.

"Come on," Vance said as he pulled me toward the edge of the platform and eased himself down. I leaped after him, scanning the clearing for some kind of shelter. Nothing. We were completely exposed, and NORA probably knew it.

Some of the Chinese soldiers aimed their weapons upward and began to shoot. The metal choppers hummed and crackled with electricity, but they didn't stop descending. In seconds the doors opened and soldiers in silver NORA uniforms streamed out, jumping with parachutes, shooting as they floated to the ground. Their weapons made no sound, but the Asian soldiers began to fall. Ju-Long yelled a command, and then every weapon in the crowd was turned toward the oncoming soldiers.

The first line of NORA soldiers went down in seconds, some even before they landed, and began thrashing on the ground. With the Asian soldiers' attention drawn elsewhere, the crowd's frenzy rose to another level as people screamed and ran. Some of the settlers got caught in the crossfire. They jerked and then fell. Some thrashed before they died; others simply stopped moving.

"Vance!" a voice called out.

I focused on a woman fighting her way to the front. Vance opened his arms to her, and they embraced. She had the same strong jaw and coloring he did, but her eyes were hard. She pulled away and turned to his cuffs, swiping something over the lock. The cuffs fell away. Vance immediately rubbed his wrists.

"The Chinese will call in reinforcements," she said. "We have to close the tunnel quickly."

"Tell me where it is."

She nodded. "I'll take you there."

"No, Mom. It'll be dangerous."

His mother looked him right in the eye. "I'm not letting you out of my sight."

Vance looked as if he wanted to argue, but instead he clamped his mouth shut. He bent down and retrieved a rifle from a downed settler's hand and then turned to face me. "Will you be all right, Treena?"

"I'll come and help."

"I'm not sure why NORA's here," Vance said, "but I'd guess it has something to do with you. Maybe you can stop them from hurting the settlers. I'll be back as soon as I can."

"Be careful," I said.

He pulled me in close and kissed me. "You too." Then he walked away with his mother.

"Is she the one you went back for a few weeks ago?" she asked him as they left.

I strained but couldn't hear his answer. I turned back to the horrible scene before me, wondering what Vance expected me to do. Asians and NORA soldiers alike aimed and shot at each other as the lines clashed, then began grappling. There were far more NORA soldiers on the ground than Asians, and far too many settlers. Definitely not a good start to this battle.

I headed toward a downed NORA soldier, intending to take her stunner. But the moment I stepped around the platform, I stumbled over someone's leg. Mills sat there, huddled over his pistol, putting in a new cartridge.

He glared at me. "Should've put a bullet in you first."

"That's almost exactly what the empress said," I replied and kicked at his hand. The cartridge flew across the ground and skidded under the platform.

Mills leaped to his feet, threw the pistol aside, and came at me, hands extended like he wanted to strangle me. The kindness of that first conversation with him, when he'd asked me to help lead the resistance, was completely gone now.

I ducked out of his way and threw a punch to his solar plexus. Unable to dodge it, he doubled over with a groan. His hate-filled eyes bored into me. I backed away, fists up.

"Jasper said you have a questionable past," I said, wondering what had become of my biological father. If only I'd thought to ask about Mills when I had the chance. "If you've been out here all this time, how does Jasper even know you?"

He straightened, holding his stomach. "After NORA integrated me, I worked for the empress as an assassin. Took down her competitors one by one with poisoned pills. I failed to cover my tracks one time, just one, and a few people found out. Jasper was one of them. Instead of admitting her part in it, Vallorah tossed me outside the wall, just like that. No supplies, nothing. I couldn't go back to my people after so long, not after all the things I'd done. So I came here and challenged the governor."

"You couldn't face the fact that you were a murderer, so you tried to murder more people instead?" I snickered. "Yeah, that makes total sense."

He growled and lunged at me. I stepped aside easily and met him with an elbow to the temple. As he recoiled, I put him in a headlock. He thrashed, trying to get free, and I tightened my arms around his throat. He froze.

"Well, congratulations," I told him. "You've officially failed to protect your own people."

"I'd let go if I were you," Ju-Long said from above us on the platform. He held one of their stunners, a long, slender plastic device. I released Mills and took a step back, arms up.

But instead of shooting me, Ju-Long aimed it at Mills. "Our location has been compromised. It seems all this was a waste of time and resources. Consider our agreement invalidated."

Mills's eyes widened, and he started to speak, but it was too late. There was no blast, just a faint buzz, and Mills began to flail around on the ground, his body spasming uncontrollably. A few seconds later the buzzing stopped, and he lay on his back, one arm bent unnaturally underneath him, facing the sky full of NORA choppers. He let out a long, silent breath and then was still.

The weapon turned on me.

I took off running, ducking behind NORA soldiers and settlers. Ju-Long cursed, but if he shot at me, I didn't feel anything. I pushed through the thinning crowd and hid behind a building, then peered out. Ju-Long turned toward the side of the mountain and looked upward, studying it for a moment. Then he strode up the trail in the direction Vance and his mother had gone.

51

TREENA

Fates. There was no way to warn Vance and his mother Ju-Long was on his way, and I had no weapon. Maybe if I followed him quietly enough . . .

A woman passed him on the trail, headed downward, and then hesitated when she saw the fighting. A man pulled up behind her, and then several other people, some holding children.

The underground settlers had arrived—and they were walking right into a bloodbath.

I caught a glimpse of Mandie through the crowd, still carrying her violin case. She stared in horror at the scene, then tripped and fell, rolling several feet toward the action. Her violin case slid even farther.

I sprinted toward her. "Mandie!"

The settlers saw me and stared in surprise but didn't notice the girl at their feet. When I reached her, she looked dazed. I pulled her aside and set her back onto her feet. "Mandie," I gasped. "Are you okay?"

"What's going on?" she asked, her face white. A woman stiffened just behind her and crumpled to the ground. It sent the settlers into a panic. They began running back up the trail, yelling and screaming.

"We have to get you away from the fighting," I told Mandie over the noise. She scrambled to grab her violin case. I grabbed her elbow and began dragging her back up the trail.

"What's going on?" one of the underground settlers demanded. It was the elder who had thrown me out days before. "Those are NORA helicopters!"

"This isn't your fight," I told him. "They don't even know you're here. Duck into buildings and hide wherever you can. If you see any stunners on the way, grab them. You'll need weapons if we're going to get your group out of here."

The settlers had quieted a bit, but now they just looked at each other.

"What?" I asked.

Coltrane pushed his way to the front, his face grim. "We won't be stealing weapons, Amy. We refuse to compromise the pact. But don't assume that being without weapons means we're defenseless." He locked eyes with a few of the men, and they nodded.

"You take our families up," the elder man said to me. "We'll cover your backs."

I felt sick. "Fair enough. Those with defenses can stay. The rest of you—we'll move as a group, the children on the inside." I paused and looked around. "Where's Ruby?"

"She's sick," Mandie said beside me, still clutching her violin case. "Ruby is still at the landing pad near the rim, resting. Maxim and my mom stayed with her until we could come back with a stretcher. But then all those helicopters came down."

"Fine." There was no time to get her now, but she was probably safer up there anyway. "Hurry, Mandie. Can you run?"

She nodded, then took a quick look behind us as we rounded the first switchback. The inventors below had already leaped into action, pulling out their projects and setting them up. Coltrane knelt on the ground, rummaging through his pack. There were only a few dozen defenders, unarmed yet determined to keep the soldiers from following us. I hoped it wasn't necessary.

The trip up the trail seemed to last days. I strode quickly, scanning the buildings above for the most protection. Looking at the families panting behind me, I couldn't help but remember that awful night in NORA. I had led people then, too, and it hadn't ended well. They had trusted me to make their lives better. Instead they'd lost their lives altogether. And then I'd left their families and friends to pick up the pieces alone.

These settlers had no homes, no weapons, and no future. They had blindly followed me here for the promise of a better life, and this was their reward. If they hadn't hated me before this, they definitely had cause to hate me now.

But, no. That wasn't true. Coltrane and his comrades had delivered their families to me, trusting that I could protect them. I steeled my resolve. The best thing—the *only* thing—I could do for them was take care of their loved ones. If I was all that stood between them and NORA, so be it.

This time, I decided with all the determination my body could hold, *I will not fail.*

52

VANCE

I expected my mom to head for some kind of tunnel, but instead she pulled me into a house. It looked like all the others—a wooden structure that jutted out from the rocky mountain wall. The front room was full of colorful NORA furniture, too soft and oversized to be practical for a mountain settlement. Mom lifted her finger to her lips and motioned for us to turn the corner. I lifted my rifle in front of me, knowing full well that it would be practically useless if we ran into Chinese soldiers.

"The opening is right around there," Mom said, pointing to the corner. I put a finger to my lips and stuck the rifle out first, then peered around. The room was empty.

Mom strode out and motioned to the far wall. I still didn't see anything. I followed, looking for a crack or a doorknob or anything to suggest that this was a door. I placed my palm against the rock. It was smooth like wax. A dusty residue coated my fingers.

"It goes all the way through the mountain," she said. "We have to block it before their reinforcements come."

"Maybe they already have. There are hundreds of Asian soldiers down there."

"Those are the ones he's been hiding for weeks. There are thousands of them out there, Vance. When the rest of them come, we'll be decimated."

Thousands of Chinese soldiers. The sheer magnitude of it—the amount of food they'd need, how much space they would require—was unbelievable. And Mills had hidden them inside the mountain, accessed through a hole in his dining room. "So the door swings open or something?"

"The door is fake. It's not real rock. Can't you tell the difference?"

I was about to speak when a thump sounded on the other side of the wall.

Mom stiffened. "We're too late," she whispered.

"No, we're not," I said, darting around the corner. I grabbed the expensive couch and dragged it over. It was heavier than it looked. My mom darted over to help, then we positioned it in front of the wall. No matter how I placed it, there was a small gap between the couch and the rock. With a little leverage, they'd be able to get it open in minutes. I glanced around the corner for something else, but this was the heaviest object by far.

"You go warn the others," I told my mother, who wrung her hands together in worry. "I'll hold them off as long as I can." I picked up my rifle.

"No, you won't," Ju-Long said from behind us. I turned.

His weapon was trained on me.

53

VANCE

My mother's face twisted in rage. "How dare you lie to these people and then betray them. We came here for peace. It wouldn't hurt you to leave us alone."

"Our honored president has plans for this wreck of a nation," Ju-Long said simply. "You destroyed yourselves long ago. We are just finishing the job." He started to pull the trigger.

Just as his finger moved, my mother leaped. I realized what she was doing and tried to throw her aside, but it was too late. There was a faint buzz, and then my mother arched her back and screamed.

Lightning shot down my body where we touched. I instinctively jerked away from her as she sank to the floor, and my pain instantly ceased. But my mother still writhed on the ground, her eyes wide in horror, body contorted. Her hands clawed at the air.

"Mom!" I grabbed her shoulder, but lightning shot up my arm, and I recoiled again with a growl.

Her eyes met mine, desperate and horrified, as her body convulsed one final time. Then she sank to the ground with a sigh.

My mother—widow, mother of three, and the strongest woman I knew—stared at the ceiling, never to see again.

I wrapped my arms around her again as if trying to hold her together, to take the pain into myself so she could be whole again. But whatever current had passed through her was gone, and her life with it.

Ju-Long aimed his weapon at me again, but the thumping behind me intensified. Ju-Long frowned and glanced at the wall. With a curse in Chinese, he ran to move the sofa.

I lunged. Ju-Long turned right as I reached him and tried to sidestep, but I was ready this time. I sent a punch to his face, forcing him to block it. It was exactly what I wanted him to do. The stunner in his hand clattered to the ground. I kicked it behind me, noting where it landed.

Another curse. Ju-Long leaped back and sent a kick to my ribs, the still-healing side. I moved to block it, but he redirected it at my solar plexus. I doubled over from the force of it, the breath knocked out of me. Idiot. I'd learned from a young age to regulate my breathing during a fight.

"My soldiers and I have trained since age two," he said. "This is not a wise course of action for you, Hawking."

I met his words with a fist to his mouth. He rocked backward, a trickle of blood escaping his lips, and then smiled.

He attacked then, the pounding and shouting of his comrades accompanying us like a strange orchestra. He moved forward, a whirlwind of motion. I blocked and countered and parried, feeling my body settle into a rhythm. I'd fought like this with my father while my mom looked on.

My mom. For a second I glanced at her twisted body lying there on the floor. Anguish exploded in my stomach, and I growled and attacked harder. Ju-Long's eyes widened a bit, then narrowed in determination. His attack grew more intense, more focused. I barely blocked a series of disorienting shots to the face when he swept my leg from under me and sent me to the floor.

Ju-Long's foot on my injured shoulder stopped me from rolling away. I filled my lungs with air and held my breath, refusing to scream, not letting myself acknowledge the pain.

A scraping sound drew my eye. The soldiers had managed to get enough leverage to move the couch. It wouldn't be long before they succeeded. I had to take out Ju-Long *now*.

"You have a strange determination," Ju-Long said, applying more pressure. "Even when sentenced to die, you still fought off my assassin. Such stubbornness is not the way of your people."

"I think you'll find that it is," I said breathlessly. My hurt shoulder sent blinding pain through my body. If only I could reach Ju-Long's weapon—but it had landed too far away.

"Ready," a voice whispered from behind me. I could barely hear it, but I knew it instantly.

I forced my mind to focus. Anton was there, hiding in the shadows near where the weapon had disappeared.

Our trigger sequence.

"Set," I gasped.

"Go," the voice hissed, and the weapon slid across the floor. I caught it in my hand. Ju-Long's eyes widened in surprise as I swung the weapon up and aimed it at his chest.

"This is the part where you beg for mercy," I said.

"Not today," Ju-Long said. He leaped to the side, executed a perfect roll, and rose at a run, headed for the tunnel entrance, where the couch had been pushed forward several inches.

I slid my thumb onto the button, and an invisible current buzzed through the weapon and caught him before he'd made it two steps.

It slammed him backward several feet and sent him writhing to the floor.

He flopped around like my mother had done, the electricity setting his body afire. Each second was an eternity. Then he arched his back and sank into the ground.

I didn't realize I was still aiming the weapon until a hand gripped my shoulder.

"He's gone," Anton said. "He won't be hurting anyone again."

I tore my gaze away and rushed to my mother's side, feeling her pulse. Nothing. Her skin was cool and soft.

"I'm sorry about your mom," Anton said softly, and I turned to look at him. "She was a good woman."

Was. She only existed in the past now.

Anton folded his arms. "I still think you're a traitor, but it seems we're on the same side at the moment."

I forced a grim smile, feeling numb. "We were always on the same side. I just got distracted for a while."

The scraping sound got louder, and then the sofa tipped over.

Anton dove behind a chair, and I took a position across the room where I had a clear view. The first soldier appeared. I aimed Ju-Long's weapon and shot. One, then two, then five. It only took a second of exposure and each man was on the ground, gasping and moaning.

After the twelfth soldier, the sounds coming from the corner stopped. If they came out *en masse*, Anton and I were toast. Time to get out.

With one last, wistful look at my mother, I sprinted outside and started down the trail, Anton following closely behind.

"Try to get our clan together, away from the fighting," I called to him. "Actually, help all the settlers find shelter, our clan or not. I'm going to take down as many of these guys as I can."

"You got it." Anton sprinted away.

I looked downward at the clearing where I'd stood trial. The battle continued. Bodies with silver NORA uniforms littered the ground. Only occasionally did I see a fallen Chinese soldier.

But the sight that stopped me was the group near the bottom of the trail. Their clothes were just a little different, and none of them looked familiar. Treena's new settlers, probably. They had barricaded the trail, preventing NORA and Chinese soldiers alike from going up. The strange thing was that they held no weapons. One lifted a box and yelled something. Those with him ducked and covered their faces. The group of

Chinese soldiers in front of them aimed their weapons at the settlers.

A white light exploded from the box. Pain slammed into my head. I wrenched my eyes away, blinking quickly. When my vision cleared, I looked down at the settlers again. The group of Asian soldiers were rubbing their eyes. They spoke to each other, reached for their weapons again, and looked angrily at the settler blockade.

I searched the area for Treena. She wasn't near the platform anymore. Hopefully she was safe, along with my little sisters. I'd have to find the twins soon and tell them what had happened to Mom. The image of my mother on the floor, staring at nothing, returned unbidden.

The sound of pounding footsteps on the trail above sent dread through my body. The Chinese reinforcements had broken through. They'd come upon me any second. I started down the trail, looking for a boulder, anything to cover me. I didn't know whether Ju-Long's weapon could run out of juice, but until it did, I'd put it to good use.

As one, the soldiers at the bottom of the trail leaped over the barricade of rocks and packs to surround the new group of settlers. Slowly the cornered men raised their arms to the sky.

With a curse, I ran down the trail, aiming Ju-Long's weapon at the group. It was time to see how far this thing could shoot. I pulled the trigger. A man fell to the ground and started to shake. I aimed again. One more, then two at once.

Their comrades jumped into action, running up the trail toward me. A few turned in my direction and aimed. I swore and looked around. If my weapon could cross that distance, so could theirs.

I dove behind a rock just in time. The shot slammed into the side of the rock, and my weapon slipped out of my hand, skidding across the ground. I cursed again. There were no other rocks or potential blockades for another several meters. If I left this spot to retrieve the weapon, they had plenty of time to take me out.

"Why didn't I bring the rifle?" I muttered, keeping my head down. Footsteps crunched in the gravel, coming toward me. Probably about a dozen.

The group from above was approaching as well. There were too many footsteps to count. They descended in all their might, yelling to each other in Chinese as they jogged down the trail. Once they reached the battle, it would be over. NORA simply hadn't brought enough soldiers.

And then they would turn on the settlers again.

The dozen soldiers arrived first, their footsteps slowing as they got nearer. There was no doubt they knew exactly where I was. The group probably intended to separate, to circle me on both sides. It was a maneuver I'd used often when we cornered smugglers. Now I knew exactly how the smugglers felt.

The front line of reinforcements came just then. A woman spoke, and another soldier whispered back. I could imagine what they were saying. "There's one hidden behind the rock. We'll surround him and take him out all at once." I looked around, but there was nothing but gravel. Not even a large stone. I would be dead in seconds.

A dark shadow passed over the sun.

I looked up to see a huge black hovercraft with four rotors slide over us, completely soundless, and then slow to a stop.

I blinked, but it was still there. The NORA choppers below it were like kittens beneath a grizzly. I'd worked in the NORA military for two years, and I'd never seen that monstrosity before. It had to be Chinese.

The foreign soldiers shouted as one and sprinted down the trail.

I waited a moment, then peered over the boulder. Chinese soldiers streamed down the trail, not even pausing when they saw me watching. They rushed downward, looking almost concerned.

Then it was quiet. The entire valley was tense, watching the hovercraft, unsure what it planned to do. I climbed out from behind the rock and saw what was left of the NORA soldiers positioning themselves along the valley walls, readying for the wave of Chinese soldiers they expected to descend. It was the most logical thing to expect.

They were wrong.

In a heartbeat the black aircraft sent a ball of fire at the nearest NORA chopper. Its reflective surface instantly exploded in flames. Its rotors whipped around, sending what was left of the chopper sideways and plunging into the lake. Another massive shot and a second chopper bit the waves.

This battle would be over in less than a minute. No wonder the Chinese were gathering.

The sight of NORA's choppers being shot down one by one sent the valley into a frenzy again. Settlers screamed and ran away, realizing that NORA was falling. I caught sight of Anton gathering some kids into a building. He turned back to watch another NORA chopper burst into flame and plunge downward.

There was nothing I could do. It was a horrible realization. There wasn't a thing in the world that could take the black monster down. NORA's technology was ridiculously behind when it came to fighting other countries. They'd just recovered from battling themselves decades before.

It was over.

54

TREENA

Were those really NORA helicopters?" Mandie asked, looking out the window. "Are they killing everyone?"

"Get down," I told her, but I couldn't resist the urge to peek out myself. "They're out there, but they're fighting on our side this time." I couldn't believe it. How had they known?

"Ours is the only unarmed group still out there," a woman said, covering her young son's eyes with both hands as she peered through another window. Her voice rose in pitch. "A group just came down the trail toward them. Oh, stars—they're going to shoot!"

"Somebody has to stop them!" another woman said.

"They're on their own," I said. My stomach lurched as a huge company of Asian soldiers surrounded our little group of defenders. I could make out Coltrane down there near the edge of the group, still fiddling with something in his hands.

I gasped as the soldiers raised their weapons. The settlers slowly lifted their arms skyward.

At my gasp, Mandie jumped up again to see, but I pulled her into my shoulder instead. "Don't look."

And then something happened.

All went quiet, and a single shout went up. I turned back to the window just in time to see an incredibly bright light flash across the entire mountain, like an exploding star. The sound hit next, a whoosh that sent my hair flying. The families in the home with me shrieked in surprise, and then it was over.

The valley was silent now, as if the light had pulled everyone away with it.

I rose and looked out. The scene was similar to what we'd seen earlier, only the settlers had lowered their arms. They stood there, looking at each other in amazement.

I gaped. The Asian soldiers writhed on the ground, their bodies convulsing and flopping around soundlessly. Every. Single. One. Only the settlers and NORA soldiers dotting the valley floor remained on their feet.

And in the center of everything stood Coltrane. He held something small and rectangular in his hand and lifted it triumphantly.

"It works!" he yelled.

55

VANCE

A deep groaning from the sky tore my eyes away from the source of the flash. The black hovercraft slowly tilted to one side, then tipped the other way. One rotor failed, then a second, and it was completely sideways. Then it began to fall. On its way down, it hit several NORA choppers, setting them instantly aflame.

I scanned the ground around the lake quickly for people, but it seemed the settlers were smarter than that. Seconds later, the huge black aircraft smashed into the choppy water, sending up a gigantic splash. It must have sprayed the ground for half a mile. Soon, pieces of fiery metal carnage floated across the water. The edge of a rotor sat just above the surface, still rotating as if in a final death rattle.

That wasn't even the strangest part. Bodies in dark gray uniforms blanketed the entire valley. Whatever had taken down the aircraft had also overpowered the Asian soldiers' weapons. They'd essentially electrocuted themselves.

My clan was safe. We had won.

I fell back against the boulder and slid to the ground, absently running a hand through my hair. No. *They* had won. I had lost—undeniably, irrevocably.

Hot tears came unbidden, and for the first time in years, I allowed myself to mourn what should have been.

56

TREENA

Two hours later, after Coltrane's community was settled in, I began the search for Vance. I found him sitting at the edge of the platform where we'd separated, staring at the ground. His eyes were bloodshot and his shoulders hunched. By the dried blood on his shoulder, his wound had torn open.

But the pain in his expression seemed unrelated to his wounds. He looked as if he'd just visited the darkest depths of existence. I hesitated, unsure whether to join him. But then he looked up, and a tired smile spread across his face.

Warmth settled in my chest. "And to think you almost had this party without me."

He chuckled, and the darkness in his expression fled. "Wouldn't dream of it." He opened his arms for an embrace. I gave him a coy look and grabbed the back of his head, pulling him down for a long kiss. He nearly slid right off the platform in his surprise, then he grinned against my lips and pulled me in closer.

We were so lost in each other that I barely heard the chopper approaching. We pulled apart as the shiny aircraft, one of the larger ones, emerged from above the rim and descended carefully, setting down gently on the ground in front of us. The settlers who had begun cleanup watched it warily.

Vance put a protective arm in front of me, but I shook my head. "It's just Denoux," I called out over the noise of the blades. He had probably circled the mountain, watching and waiting for NORA to win the battle before swooping in. Even if the chopper was packed with soldiers bent on destroying the settlers, we were armed and ready. I patted the NORA stunner in my pocket. Several settlers headed our direction, pulling out their own weapons.

The helicopter's motor cut out, and its rotors slowly came to a stop. The door slid open. But instead of the troops Vance had expected, a lone soldier jumped down and headed toward us. I felt my eyes widen. Major Murphy, Commander Denoux's assistant. He'd been the one to introduce me to Vance when I was commissioned into the empress's task force. Had it really only been a few weeks since then?

He didn't react at all when he saw Vance and me embracing. Instead, he said, "We want to talk with your settlement leader. I'm assuming you two know who that might be."

"That would be Vance," a blonde girl said, stepping out of the shadows. She shot Vance a bright smile, but he didn't return it. Instead, he watched another woman approach, a dark-haired woman with two boys at her heels.

"Indeed," the woman said, stopping to face Vance. "That is the general consensus among the survivors. Hawking, we would be honored if you would represent us in these negotiations."

Vance swallowed hard and nodded, pulling me more tightly against him.

Coltrane walked up, still clasping his device in both hands. I had a feeling he wouldn't let go of the thing for a very long time. He noted Vance's arm around my waist and looked at the ground. "Um, Amy, I think you should go as our representative. Ruby is resting. I think you know exactly what we need."

"Why not you?" I asked, and he looked away. It was then I realized how red his eyes were. "Oh, no. What happened?"

"I found my dad." He gave a weak smile. "His body, at least. He's the one who caused all this."

My hand flew to my mouth. "Fates. You mean Mills, don't you." It wasn't a question. It all made sense now—Mills's integration, his reluctance to return to his family after killing for a living. It was tragic, but to a degree I could see his reasoning. "Oh, Coltrane. I'm so, so sorry."

Coltrane shrugged and released a sigh. "It's okay. I barely remember him. It's just—it's just ironic that both my parents died within days of each other. My mom never got the chance to find out what happened to him, you know? And I never got to—say good-bye."

I pulled away from Vance to give Coltrane a hug. "Your parents are gone, but you still have a family here. Your settlement loves you."

"I know." He sniffed and waved at the chopper. "Enough of this. You have a job to do. Don't let them push you around." He grinned as if to say, *We both know that isn't possible.*

Vance turned to me. "Sounds like we have an appointment with the Demander. You ready for this?"

I nodded. "Absolutely."

57

TREENA

Vance held out an arm, which I took gladly, and we headed for the chopper. Major Murphy led the way and slid the door open for us. It was dark inside. Rather than being lined with benches and equipment like the military chopper I'd ridden in while serving in EPIC, it was cushioned and furnished with ridiculously soft-looking chairs and a desk, which were bolted to the floor. Typical NORA.

A figure leaned against the desk, his back turned to me. His strong shoulders and long torso revealed that this was definitely not the commander. The man wore a generic silver military uniform. I paused in the doorway, ready to bolt.

"I should have known you'd be here," the voice said softly, "in the center of chaos." He turned around.

Dresden.

I tried to hide my shock. "What do you mean, *should* have known?" I'd led them here. Accidentally, maybe, but it was my fault all the same. Except this time, it hadn't cost lives—it had saved them.

Dresden eyed Vance, then bored his gaze into me. "Denoux said you were dead. Buried under thirty feet of desert sand and rocks. And yet, here you are, with your so-called trainer."

I felt Vance's grip around my waist tighten. "But then," I began, "how did you know these people were under attack?"

He let out a long breath and walked around the table. "I didn't." He sat down in a chair and put his legs on the table. "Honestly, if I'd known the ECA had chosen today to make their move, we would have come tomorrow. Less mess."

"Stop acting mysterious and answer the question," I snapped. "Tell me why you're here."

Dresden's eyebrows rose in surprise. "You're not the same Treena I knew in NORA, that's for sure."

"Running for your life changes a person," Vance muttered dryly. "What do you want this time? Being emperor of one group of people isn't enough for you?"

"Watch it, trainer," Dresden shot back. "We just saved your settlers from a mass execution. You should be scraping the floor about now."

"You're not exactly in the habit of saving lives, Dres," I said. "You ordered the extermination of an entire settlement. We're talking peaceful, unarmed people hiding underground. Doesn't exactly make me want to kiss your feet."

Dresden's face reddened. "Everything I've done was to save lives, despite what you think. We've been monitoring some recent developments outside the borders. We intercepted communications that indicated an impending attack, but we couldn't lock them down to a precise location. When we tracked you to that underground settlement, Denoux thought that might be the enemy's hidden base."

I felt my eyes widen. So Denoux's insistence on leaving no survivors wasn't because of their location. He'd genuinely thought they were spies. "And instead of gathering evidence to confirm that, he decided to just kill everyone," I said. "And you didn't see anything wrong with that."

Dresden removed his legs from the desk and stood, towering over me. Had he always been that tall? "We're at war with the outlands, Treena, or have you forgotten? Everything that has threatened our peace has come from outside the border. Besides, you have no idea what trouble you've caused."

I blinked. "By crossing the desert?"

"By *leaving*. Did it occur to you that your departure looked suspicious? You're the rightful successor, then you disappear and I take your place, and you're never seen again." His eyes flashed, but there was something more than anger. He looked genuinely hurt. "Why would you do that to me? Don't I have enough to worry about right now?"

"Forgive the lack of sympathy," Vance grumbled. "Must be rough living in a palace and having people wait on you all day."

"The war with the outlanders was just the beginning," Dresden shot back. "A lot has happened in the last few weeks."

"So I keep hearing," I muttered.

Dresden helplessly threw his hands up. "Then why didn't you just come back? I don't get why you left in the first place."

I just glared back, and he sighed again, letting his shoulders slump. How many times had I leaned my head against that chest, letting him stroke my hair? The old Treena would have rushed to his side the moment he frowned.

That Treena was gone. I rested my head on Vance's uninjured shoulder, feeling warm and secure against his body. The simple closeness of his hand resting on my shoulder, the electricity his touch sent down my spine, filled something inside me I didn't know was empty. A moment with Vance was better than a hundred years with Dresden. A thousand years.

"Look," Dresden said, stepping closer and lowering his voice. "I know why the empress declared stricter laws. It wasn't just because of the smugglers, Treena. There's a huge renewal of interest in Old America and their ways. The empress was right to be worried. That, combined with your speeches about the Rating system being flawed and corrupted, has got people talking. And then you disappeared. People are crying foul all over the place."

"Doesn't sound like such a bad thing," I said.

"Yeah, well, that's just the beginning. The communications we intercepted, planning an attack? They were in Bendihua, a form of Pinghua, which is a rural dialect of Mandarin Chinese. They call themselves the ECA. They've been setting up bases in abandoned towns all around us, right under our noses. NORA is surrounded on all sides."

"But they attacked us, not you," I said. "What was the point of that?"

"The communications we intercepted said they were going to use this settlement as a base of operations. I think they intended to use the settlers as slaves to build their weapons. I wanted to hit them hard and fast, before they'd fully set up here." He paused.

"Denoux didn't think we were ready. I probably should have listened to him. Preliminary reports say we lost half our choppers today, and almost 60 percent of our manpower."

"Fates, Dresden," I said. "These are people. Don't call them *manpower*."

"It makes no sense," Vance said thoughtfully, missing the exchange. "If the Chinese are trying to take over, why not just bomb us all and get it over with? Why spend so much time positioning troops and setting up bases? It wouldn't be all that hard to take NORA out."

"Ju-Long told me that, actually," I said, trying to remember our conversation in the jail cell. "He said they could conquer NORA within hours if they wanted. But that makes no sense. They obviously want to, right?"

"I don't know." Dresden sighed and plopped down into his chair again.

I left Vance's side and approached the table. "Dresden, war or not, the settlers are not your enemy. Make an alliance with them. We have to pull together if we're going to get through this."

"Your Majesty," Murphy's muffled voice came from outside. "We've found their commander."

"Enter," Dresden said.

The door opened, and a stretcher was brought in. The man's face was swollen and bloody, but I recognized Ju-Long instantly. His arms and legs were tethered, but the guy looked like he struggled to breathe, let alone plan an escape. His gaze flicked to each of us in turn, but he didn't speak.

"He's alive," Vance said, his voice tight.

"Barely," Murphy muttered as he stepped back from the stretcher. "We found him at the tunnel entrance. We sealed it with explosives, but it won't stop them from coming by air again if they decide to."

"Should've held the trigger longer," Vance muttered.

I gave him a questioning look. "I saw him go after you. I'm glad you were okay."

"I'm fine," he said tersely, then looked away. His voice was husky. "My mother is not."

My breath caught. "No."

He waved his hand. "I didn't intend for Ju-Long to live after that, but since he did, let's see what he has to say for himself."

58

TREENA

Dresden took a moment before questioning Ju-Long. He drew himself together, lifting his shoulders and forcing his usual confidence back into his demeanor. I wondered how much of that was an act and how much was real. The last few months, the two had been synonymous.

"Explain why you've come," he finally said to the figure on the stretcher.

Ju-Long didn't move, but his eyes flicked to Dresden's face.

"Tell me," Dresden demanded. "Do you intend to kill us all?"

A smile graced the corner of Ju-Long's lips. "You should have . . . surrendered."

"What is it you want?" I asked. "Why the attack?"

"The sleeping dragon has awakened," he said.

I got right in his face. "Don't be cryptic. What did you come for? Tell me *now*."

"China is superior in every way," Ju-Long snapped, his eyes focusing on me for the first time. "Old America's economy would have fallen 150 years ago if not for us." He closed his eyes and took a deep, shuddering breath. "We have given billions of American dollars to your fathers, money that was never returned. We did not complain, for we had a larger plan in mind. A wise bank considers all assets, not simply those which are immediately apparent."

"You want our land," Dresden said.

"Your land is worthless. The resources are profitable, perhaps, but it is your location that is ideal. The European powers resist us, but when we surround them on two sides, they will be far more willing to listen."

"If you want control of what was once Old America," Vance said, "why not just take it? You could have bombed NORA to pieces."

Ju-Long's voice had become a whisper. "Unfortunately, there are politics involved. The Nations for Peace convention takes place in a few months, and the eyes of the world are upon us. We must allow them to see what they wish. Simply going in and bombing a weaker nation brings the whole world up in arms. But careful positioning, even if it has the same result, is overlooked."

"Why are you even telling us this?" Dresden burst out.

Ju-Long's face twisted in disgust, and his voice seemed to gather strength. "You dare call yourself emperor when you are little more than an impertinent child. I tell you this because you should be afraid. We will conquer your wretched country, and when we do, we will be well positioned for the next step in the president's plan. At that point, Russia will finally be persuaded to unite with us. The Eastern Continental Alliance will cover the globe. Great nations have bowed to our president. There is nothing you pitiful savages can do to stop us."

Images of Old America—empty towns, buildings falling into disrepair, skeletons writhing under tables— flooded my mind. It was going to happen all over again. Except this time, it would be the people I loved.

Vance bent down and got right in Ju-Long's face. "Guess you'll be surprised, then." Without a word, he punched Ju-Long flat in the face.

The Chinese man went limp.

Dresden didn't object to the abrupt end in conversation. Instead, he simply looked at me, his eyes haunted. "You're right. We can't afford to waste time fighting the settlers any longer. We'll need everyone we can get."

"We?" Vance repeated.

"Treena," Dresden said, giving me a pleading look. "I know you just got here, but the citizens think of you as a hero, a nobody who fought her way to the crown and exposed injustices or whatever it is you did. When you disappeared, there were protests and even riots in the streets. We can't afford for our country to be any more divided than it already is. I need you to tell them they can trust me."

"You're asking her to go back with you?" Vance said incredulously.

"Look," Dresden said, ignoring Vance's comment. "I know I've made some mistakes. But I can't lead NORA to war if they unseat me. Come back. We'll drop the charges against you. Help me get the country back on its feet, and I'll give you anything you want."

"No offense, Dres, but you obviously don't know what I want."

Dresden's shoulders sagged. "Fine. Stay here and let our country destroy itself. I may not understand you anymore, but I think you're still a good person. You'd never let people suffer if you could do something about it. Or has that changed too?"

"Treena," Vance said in a warning tone. "He's trying to manipulate you. Think long and hard about this."

I didn't have to. Dresden's words sank deep into my soul. He was using words as weapons, but it didn't make the words any less true. Dresden wore the crown, but he was as limited as anyone else in which laws he could alter. As long as the council limited his power, nothing would ever change. What we needed was someone who was above the laws, someone they couldn't touch.

Ruby had said leadership was in my blood. I'd sworn that, since a Peak had established the Rating system, a Peak would take it down. *I* would. But instead, I had run away, just like my mother always did.

Ruby was right. I'd been on the wrong journey all along. But it hadn't been a complete waste. It had taken an entire settlement to teach me who I was much more than one thing. I could be both girl and warrior. Loving and fierce. Destroyer and defender.

"NORA is in danger," I finally said. "We need to fix what's broken on the inside before we can defend it from the outside. That's why you need me, Dresden. I'll come, but with three conditions."

Dresden nodded. "Name them."

"First, I come unrated. My implant gets removed permanently. No techband, either."

"But your Rating is high," Dresden said. "Why in the fates would you hide it? Besides, I need you to help me unite everyone, not divide them further. Things are precarious enough without undermining the one thing that makes our country strong."

"That's just the first condition," I said firmly. "Second, I want the freedom to come and go as I please. When I decide to leave NORA, nobody stops me. If I want to travel somewhere within the borders, I get a transport for my personal use."

Dresden stared at me, his expression unreadable. "You really have changed."

"Third, I want Denoux unseated." I paused. "No, actually he can keep his seat. I want a new position created for me: Councilwoman of Foreign Affairs."

Dresden's face turned red. I could see his fists clench, but he finally spoke through gritted teeth. "The council will throw a fit."

"Let them. You're emperor, remember?"

Vance watched me with a guarded look. "What exactly do you intend to do with that position, Treena?"

"Think about it. The only thing Ju-Long was afraid of was Nations for Peace. Send me to the convention, Dres. I'll convince them that China is using us to position for war. If I succeed, they'll fight for us. I know it. We just have to last that long."

I didn't voice the second part of my plan. I refused to come home with my head hung in defeat. If the other nations refused to join us, there was only one course left—I would confront the Chinese president, plead our cause, and convince him to leave us alone.

And if that didn't work, I'd kill him.

Dresden and Vance looked at each other, a silent exchange passing between them. I could tell Vance didn't like the idea, but this wasn't his decision to make.

"It's worth a try," Dresden finally said. "*If* we can hang on until then."

59

TREENA

The sun had nearly finished its descent as we stepped out of the chopper. I saw shadows, figures moving about with stretchers. It would take a long time to recover from this day.

"Where did that Nations for Peace idea come from?" Vance asked, threading his fingers through mine. "They don't talk about international news in NORA schools."

I grinned. "Would you believe I learned it from a young girl?"

Vance chuckled, then pulled away to face me. "Even if the NP agrees to help, we'll need to gather all the settlers together in one place for their own safety. They won't like the idea of siding with NORA to fight.

There are strong prejudices on both sides. It's not something that just goes away."

I sighed. "You've survived worse than a bunch of grumpy settlers. If anyone can handle all that, it's you."

Vance pulled me close against his chest. I breathed deeply. He smelled of pine trees and blood, an odd combination. Life and death. He rested his chin on my head and sighed. "I can't believe you just agreed to leave again."

"Me either," I moaned.

He leaned down, his lips found mine, and he kissed me deeply, slowly. It felt like a new beginning, not a good-bye. Heat bubbled up inside and then shot to my fingers and toes as I pushed up against him, feeling the warmth of his body against mine. I'd never met anyone like Vance, who could leave me both weak and powerful at his touch.

A few minutes later he pulled away. "I'm sending someone with you," he said, his voice a little hoarse. He cleared his throat. "She can keep an eye on things and report to me if Bike Boy goes back on his promises. We'll use Mills's old feed to communicate until you come back."

"Sounds good. Who do you have in mind?"

I saw his smile in the darkness. "Oh, just a childhood friend."

60

VANCE

ONE WEEK LATER

The morning light settled on the western rim, setting the brush ablaze in reds and oranges. I could see for a hundred miles from up here. The view hadn't changed much since I'd arrived in chains, but somehow everything else had.

The city below had just started to awaken and begin their morning work. Everyone had a job now. The higher citizens had taken in the lower ones, and the land near the lake was covered in busy construction. First the muddy, mosquito-infested areas would be drained and fresh water pumped in from an outside lake. Mills's narrow, dark tunnels weren't very usable for living space, but they were perfect for transporting water.

Once that was finished, wooden homes would be built. Structures with actual floors and furniture, and windows for ventilation.

Most of our crops had been trampled by soldiers and hiding settlers, but the scouts I'd sent out days before had good news. The soil in the mountain range around us was decent. Now that we weren't hiding anymore, we could expand and start a summer crop. Something told me we'd need it for the winter ahead.

The tip of the Asian aircraft was still visible in the shadowed lake below. Scientists, mostly from Treena's desert settlers, had already set to work testing the water for contaminants. Divers had extracted what they could from the aircraft, including weapons and several tons of worthless electronics. Coltrane's strange device had completely disabled all of it.

Mills's funeral had taken place privately five days earlier, attended only by me, Edyn, Coltrane, and the underground settlers' leader, an elderly woman named Ruby. She gave a brief eulogy and then embraced Coltrane. They stood there like that for a long time as the fire died down.

The rest of the bodies, including my mother's, had been burned the next day after an emotional memorial service. I had refused to combine Mills's service with theirs. The people had agreed on that count. I was still surprised by how easily they'd accepted me in Mills's place. I wanted more than anything for my mother to see it.

It had taken me twelve hours to locate my twin sisters. Mom had hidden them with a friend, a woman who'd lost her own son to the fire two years ago. She insisted that she didn't mind raising them, but I knew that wasn't what my parents would have wanted. The Hawking family was battered and torn, but as long as some part of it remained, we could never separate again.

I looked across the rim at the desert stretching before me. My clan had seen a terrible battle and survived, but war tended to take far more than lives. Now we had to pick up the pieces.

"Hawk to Wildflower," I said into the radio again. We'd never been able to get Mills's system to work, but this radio did on occasion, as long as I stood right here and used it at certain times of the day. My heart still hadn't accepted the fact that Treena had come and then left again.

The radio emitted nothing but static. I rubbed my bearded jaw and waited longer than I should have.

I was about to give up and try again later when the static stopped. "Hawk, huh? Nice touch."

"Yeah, I figured why not?"

"I don't know. If you're trying to hide your identity, it may not be very effective." I could hear the smile in her voice. "How is Ruby doing?"

"She's doing great, walking around again. Asked about you again last night."

"What did you tell her?"

"That you're out there saving the world."

She paused. "I like the sound of that." There was fumbling, then soft voices in the background. Then she came back. "Dresden wants to know what you did with all the Chinese soldiers."

I frowned. Of course Dresden was with her. They were living together in the palace. In separate rooms, she had assured me over and over, but it still bothered me. "We put them to work. They're excellent builders. If the ECA ever wants to negotiate, we have thirty-one surviving soldiers to trade."

We weren't sure how they had managed to survive the electrocution from their own stunners. Perhaps they hadn't had a good grip on their weapons. Ju-Long was survivor number thirty-two, although I suspected his recovery was because he had built up a little resistance to the weapons in training. It would take more volts to hurt him than it would his soldiers. Anyone else would have run tests to find out how much he could take. But I had simply tossed the man into my old jail cell. There had been enough death here.

"Sounds good." More fumbling, and then she spoke more quietly. "What about Coltrane?"

"He's heading up the new science lab. Last I checked, he was working on a larger model of his disabler. He says he can't wait to take on the entire Chinese army by himself."

She laughed softly.

"What about you?" I asked. "Did Bike Boy keep his promise, or did he slap a techband on you the moment you set foot in NORA?"

"He's kept to our agreement," she said, and I heard a smile in her voice. "My implant was removed the day I arrived, and nobody's tried to shove it back in since. I miss you."

"Miss you too. Let's conquer these guys so you can come home."

"So that's my home, is it?"

"Only if you want it to be," I said.

Dresden groaned dramatically in the background, and she chuckled. "I have to go. Hopefully I'll talk to you again soon. Keep them all safe, Vance."

"I will," I said. "I promise."

READ WHERE IT ALL BEGAN . . .

Visit
www.AuthorRebeccaRode.com
to find out more!

GET FREE STUFF
AND FIND OUT FIRST
ABOUT REBECCA'S NEW RELEASES!

Sign up at
smarturl.it/NGnews
Or visit the website
http://www.authorrebeccarode.com

If you enjoyed this story, please leave a review. It helps spread the word and make NUMBERS IGNITE *more visible to readers like you. Thanks!*

ACKNOWLEDGMENTS

There's only one name on the cover, but I wish I could throw a dozen others on there, because this book wouldn't exist without them. Thanks to Clarissa Yeo of Yocla Designs for her amazing cover design. She is incredibly talented and worth waiting months for. Thanks to Lindzee Armstrong for her beautiful formatting and endless patience (and the ability to whip this project up in a day!) and to the ever-talented Corey Egbert for his chapter images. I appreciate the help of my editors Michele Preisendorf with Eschler Editing and also Bryon Quertermous. This book would be very different without their golden touch.

A thousand thanks to my fabulous critique group members and writer friends, including Ruth Craddock, Karen Pellett, Roxy Haynie, Jen Greyson, Angela Brimhall, Darren Hansen, LaChelle Hansen, David Powers King, and Lindzee Armstrong for their very timely and helpful (and sometimes painful, but in a good way) advice. Special thanks to Adrienne Monson, who broke some kind of world record in the last-pass beta read. Thanks, Adrienne!

Also, I have to recognize my sister and live-in nanny, Kalimba Myler, without whom this book would have come out in 2057. (I'm exaggerating, but not by much.)

And worlds of appreciation to my husband, that guy I keep gushing about. There aren't many dads in the world who would spend their vacation time watching kids so their crazed wives can spend fifteen-hour days in the editing cave. He'll probably never read this, but that's fine—I want the entire world to know how amazing he is anyway.

To my readers—thank you. Your emails and notes and your incredible, amazing, wonderful reviews kept me writing and I love you for it.

ABOUT THE AUTHOR

REBECCA RODE is an award-winning and bestselling author and journalist. Her books include *Numbers Game* and *Numbers Ignite* as well as her inspirational nonfiction work for mothers, *How to Have Peace When You're Falling to Pieces*. She also writes for Deseret News, KSL.com, Family Share, and Provo Daily Herald. However, she thinks writing for teenagers is much more fun. She enjoys traveling, reading, and martial arts, and she has a ridiculous addiction to her husband's chocolate-banana shakes.

Learn more at http://AuthorRebeccaRode.com or join The Clan for a FREE STORY and updates on Rebecca's hot new releases: http://smarturl.it/NGnews

Made in the USA
San Bernardino, CA
09 March 2017